What Others Are Saying...

"The road to hell is paved with assumptions and silence in Brooker's novel, *A Gathering of Doves*. His quirky president processes heinous means to a supposed heavenly end. But the author reveals the cancerous process by which power and loyalty mutate into rarified political seduction, of how a small band of formerly moral men blindly perpetrate mass murder in the name of peace."

Mistryel Walker, author of *Inverse Origami - The Art of Unfolding*

"A fine piece of fiction, though perhaps more fact than fiction, *A Gathering of Doves* is a sympathetic look at an American president gone mad, and how that leads us all down a path that takes us to our worst nightmare."

Jackie Wildman, author of *Teachers with the Courage to Give*

"Gerard Brooker's novel places the reader somewhere between *Seven Days in May* and *Dr. Strangelove*, a most effective place for fiction that at once fills us with dread while amusing us with the quirky thinking of a street-smart president gone over the edge."

Suzy Lamson, author of *A Rose Between Her Teeth*

"If you ever wondered how an American president might circumvent all checks and balances on his power in order to do the unthinkable, read Gerard Brooker's *A Gathering of Doves*. You will say your prayers before going to sleep, and you will be afraid to hear the news when you wake up."

Lisa Starr, author of *This Place Here*

A Gathering of Doves

A Gathering of Doves

GERARD BROOKER

TATE PUBLISHING & *Enterprises*

 TATE PUBLISHING
& Enterprises

A Gathering of Doves
Copyright © 2006 by Gerard Brooker. All rights reserved.

No part of this publication may be reproduced, stored in a retrieval system or transmitted in any way by any means, electronic, mechanical, photocopy, recording or otherwise without the prior permission of the author except as provided by USA copyright law.

This novel is a work of fiction. Names, descriptions, entities and incidents included in the story are products of the author's imagination. Any resemblance to actual persons, events and entities is entirely coincidental.

Book design copyright © 2006 by Tate Publishing, LLC.
All rights reserved.
Cover design by Elizabeth Mason
Interior design by Kristen Polson

Published in the United States of America

ISBN: 1-5988672-1-0
06.11.20

To all the doves
who have gathered together
in the name of peace.
May your numbers increase.

Acknowledgements

To Cheryl de la Gueronniere, David Remington, and John Del Vecchio for their invaluable advice about the story line and characters; to Lauren Baratz-Logsted for her encouragement; to Amy Gaal for her extraordinary technical assistance; to the talented and generous staff at Tate Publishing—Thank you all!

And to my wife, Sheila, the exemplar for all doves who flock together in the name of peace.

Prologue

It is a beach so removed that animals bathe in its waters and crap on its shores, a crescent shape that cups the blue lagoon. Overlooks splay out into green hills where sheep graze while keeping their covenants with nature.

The vista from the hills is clear, yet double-edged, an immediacy of sunshine against distant rain that falls like a black bridal veil, as the bleating of lambs break silence.

Suddenly, a fox streaks out of the trees, sheen of its red fur caught by sunlight, snatches a lamb by the throat and, before the flock knows, escapes into the maw of woods nearby. Its mother, watching now, backs up a step or two before continuing to eat.

Nothing changes. Except doves begin to whirl in tightening circles, looking for a place to gather.

1

The great organic pie of America re-cooks itself periodically. Such was the case during the presidency of Fletcher A. Nimer who added a few ingredients never before tried by content or measure. So we begin his story, which, by the joining of one man's temperament with a peculiar turn of history, becomes ours.

Fletcher A. Nimer had been awake since five a.m., contemplating the use of a small-yield atomic bomb on a city that would be chosen by God or a lottery, when the presence of his White House body-servant distracted him.

"My good man, though the color of your skin is darker than mine, you are of no less worth," he said in an artificially formal way. "Though this is so, you must still earn a worth greater than that which you received at birth. You've got to earn it, my friend," he said in a voice pitched slightly high, always an indicator of his annoyance, this time because Richard placed a twice-used tie out for the president's noon press conference.

Nimer usually ran two miles every day, and lifted weights for fifteen minutes while listening to briefing reports on both domestic and foreign affairs. With the exception of Secretary of Defense Norman Jarvis, everyone seemed to accept the practice. What did seem unusual to everyone was that the president never asked any questions about the information he received. Jarvis confided to friends that he thought the president was without imagination.

Like a magnet sucking iron filings to itself, the president drew bits and pieces of information from the sycophants who discretely used secrets to enhance their own sense of themselves. The president was pleased that the Secretary thought of him dull. It was a good concealment for a man who saw himself as anointed by God to end all wars by dropping an atomic bomb on an unsuspecting nation. He could easily hide beneath the dullness while secretly arranging the parts of his diabolical plan. Inquisitiveness was a signpost of imagination, but only the most obvious one. And he never wanted to appear obvious, a trait he considered to mark a man as unsculpted in his ways. If he was unformed in the image he had of his presidency, he would hide that secret behind dispassionate communication and an impervious bearing he wanted others to think of as competency.

He was pleased that the shoes Richard gave him to wear in front of the network of microphones were highly polished, and made it a point to let him know. "I like completeness in a man, Richard. I like the way you polish my shoes, front, side and back. Even when I am walking away, I look all together, right down to the back of my shoes, no uneven colors between leather and heel. It's a fine way for a man to be."

Richard said nothing and continued to arrange the trappings of presidential appearance. Once, some years back, he had responded to one of Nimer's similar observations with a remark of his own, but quickly got the idea that it caused an irritation in the lining of the man's temperament.

The president always slipped on a white undershirt beneath whatever shirt, formal or informal, he wore. He seemed to enjoy his dexterity and the way the many working parts of his arms, hands, shoulders and chest came together in the brisk act of covering his upper skin with a fitting cotton cloth. He had a way of putting the front opening against his forehead above the eyelashes and pulling back the hole so it got wider, but not too wide, before he slipped it over his hair and down his back, sweeping out its length, front and back. He could do this without messing his hair and without wiping off the mascara he always carefully applied to his eyebrows right after taking a shower.

For several months after he took office, Nimer played an hour twice a week in the basketball games organized by some of the younger staff members seeking favor after they heard that the president liked to play the game. Without explanation, he stopped playing once he realized that his sweating and the physical give and take of the game wiped some of the mascara off, leaving his eyebrows almost gray. It was important, he thought, for a president to present a youthful and energetic appearance. Except for the new tie Richard brought to him, he was almost ready for the press conference. He took the tie and began the methodical process of tying it under his collar and around his neck. It had to be done exactly so that the bottom of the tie barely touched the upper end of his belt, but only after he tied the knot tight, never loose, never allowing any white to show between the top part of the knot and the buttoned down neck. Loose knots suggested incompleteness, and that would never do. If he did not get the length precisely as he wanted, he would undo the knot and start over again. Sometimes, the job would take him ten minutes before it looked the way he wanted, dignified.

Looking presidential was especially important to him at his press conferences. Although the presidency is not a natural fit for any man, it was less than that for Nimer, who only dreamed about it as a child, in the quick and passing way that boys think about being a fireman or a policeman. It took some amount of ego for a man to feel adequate in the office, and a lack of ego to make a man secure there. Our president knew that he had neither of these qualities, that his ego was neither strong nor secure. His strength, though, was that he was aware that this was so. This capacity for self-monitoring was, in him, both a source of strength and weakness.

"Thank you, Richard. I'm off to lead the nation. Once more into the breach!" Being in the breach was the way he liked to see himself. By repeating it, the phrase caught on, with the press and him. He was The Man, the one in the gap, the guy who held the dike together against the forces of man and the might of nature.

"Once more into the breach" became the code for an assortment of experiences for some of the White House male staff, such as a return trip to the bathroom, or a visit to Nimer's office. Before long, the phrase took on the usual sexual connotations of dynamic young men on their way up the career ladder who thought life was mostly about the penis. To insert it into a breach, any breach, seemed patriotic.

The trappings of power were ready and on high alert in the corridor outside of Nimer's bedroom. Three secret service agents, two on the left, one on the right, stood at a "relaxed attention." Trained to convey security, yet ready to fling their bodies to protect the president, their heads did not budge. Their eyes darted left and right inside the immobile sockets of their heads. Their hands crossed near the crotch, as if the useful were guarding the profane. It was their way of folding their suit jackets together as if buttoned, a way of hiding their weapons, a way to guard against the pretense that the president was universally respected and well-liked.

"Ladies and gentlemen, the president of the United States."

It was 9 p.m. Sunday in Sydney, Australia, when Narelle Hailey began to settle in for the evening in her little apartment in the "Rocks" section of the city, the place where English convicts were first loosely imprisoned two hundred years ago.

The area was a bit noisy with tourists, but about this time the street traffic below began to slow down, as the restaurants began to fill up. It was the middle of summer in Sydney, and the soft buzz of patrons eating outdoors could be heard in the November air.

Normally, she would change into light pajamas, watch the Sunday movie on TV, then the news before going to bed. First period began at 7:30 in the morning, and she would have to be up early to get the bus to her school in the middle of the city. Teaching American literature to unruly adolescents was not easy.

Little mattered, though. She was in love with Ray Evans, a social studies teacher at the same school. They had known each other at the school for two years. Aside from eating in the same teachers' lunch room, they had little to do with each other, a regular way of doing business in a tightly departmentalized high school.

Then one day they talked briefly in the hallway about student behavior, a teacher favorite. Who knows what happens when two people really see each other for the first time, even if it is in the middle of a crowded hallway. Perhaps it was the way he looked at her, or how the sun shone on her blonde hair from the hall windows. Or how the light showed normally imperceptible fuzz beneath her ears.

Maybe that morning she didn't have enough time to take a shower so that her underarm odor, normally held tight by deodorant, seemed like an aphrodisiac to him.

Whatever it was, they quickly became an item. Even the students knew because of the way the two sparked together at school functions.

She was happy and relaxed on this Sunday night, even though tomorrow she would begin "The Great Gatsby" with her students. Normally, teaching the book would be a chore for Narelle. There was no way for Australian teenagers to identify with snooty upper class Americans of the 1920's. They simply did not have that kind of history.

Their hearty, self-deprecating jokes were not on the same page as Fitzgerald whose characters were too self-centered to catch the satirical nature of the Aussie, and filled with too much self-imposed dignity to allow them to laugh at the frequent ribaldry in the culture.

She usually would start a difficult lesson at 7:30 on a Monday by letting her students know she thought it against the Australian constitution to begin classes at that hour. This would usually draw a laugh from the students, a good way to begin a bad book for them.

Tomorrow would be different, she thought. She was in love and he would be in the same building. Her heart would be light, and so the characters would come to life, no matter the resistance. She discovered early in life that if she was "up" for the day then she had the Midas touch. Everything she touched would turn to gold. So it would be for tomorrow's lesson.

This Sunday night, too, would be different, she decided. Instead of watching the nine o'clock movie, she would read a little Australian history, maybe to impress Ray tomorrow, and go to bed early. She would change the Monday "drearies" into the Monday "sunnies."

She tried for awhile, then grew bored reading about how the early history of her country impacted the attitudes of today. How the rugged settlers from England were a rowdy, beer-drinking, fighting lot who eventually swept across the land, much like their American brethren, co-opting everything in their way, whether it was the land or the Aboriginal peoples.

There was a saying Australians seemed to love repeating as much as they loved singing "Waltzing Matilda." It had become a matter of pride to say, "If it moves, shoot it. If it doesn't, chop it down." No wonder American tourists learned to fly hours on end across oceans to visit this land and these people. Except for the accent, they might have thought they were home again.

If Narelle had stayed up to hear the presidential broadcast that came across the radio at 9 p.m. in Sydney, she would have gone to bed dreaming dreams different from the ones she did.

She dreamt about her lover, Ray Evans, about how they might get married and have children. About how they loved teaching and would have a career of double enjoyment while watching their own and other peoples' children grow. And how they would live out their lives in the peaceful country they loved, and grow old together as grandparents who would zip into their children's homes, bring gifts, spoil the grandchildren, and then leave before their own knew what had happened. They would do this over and over again.

In the history book she read that night, there was a section on the Aborigine custom of what would become known as "The Walkabout." It was a way to describe how the original families picked up their stakes in the Outback in order to move on to a new place where they would find new food for sustenance, new wood for the fire, new surroundings for their souls.

In time, the term had come to mean the act of simply leaving where you were in order to go somewhere else, most especially to find yourself and to make your mark on life.

She had read, too, about "Dreamtime," which was the way the Aborigines of Australia thought their world had been created by their ancestral spirits. These spirits had come out of the earth and walked the land performing miracles of creation. First they created the land and animals, trees, plants and water. Then, the first human beings, the Aborigines, came and with them the laws that would govern their behavior, as well as the songs and dances that would give them joy.

They believed that these spiritual ancestors lived on in nature, that people like Narelle, Ray and their children could call upon them for the continuation of what was needed to live a good and decent life.

If Narelle knew that night what might be in store for her and the city of Sydney, she might have asked for a different dream, one that could take them all away from there in their own "Walkabout," one where they might have been rescued by Dreamtime spirits who would give them food, drink and shelter, who would in their own tradition, scream against the wind, scream against the sky.

Once the president began with his usual, "Good morning, ladies and gentlemen," it was evident that he was in a spirited mood. There was an extra hop in his voice, even a certain joy that came through, a happy-to-be-alive kind of sound that is heard from those who have been in a fog that suddenly lifted.

"I would like to make a few remarks before taking your questions. Our recent incursion into Tehran was a direct attempt to stop Iran from further developing its nuclear capacity. I know you in the media like to call it another preemptive attack by the United States, but I assure you, that has not been our intention."

Old Charles Feery of the *New York Times* sensed a different tone here and was getting this down. In a deliberate attempt to fold the takeover of Tehran into a more normal set of daily negative news, Nimer continued, "And thirty two more Iranians died in two more explosions set by their own people. People killing other people for money is blood money. Blood money is the worst kind of money because it stains human kind. And this administration will not tolerate it any more. There will be peace on earth and we will see to that."

There was a feeling in the room now that something big might be coming. A reporter from a mid-western daily couldn't wait any longer, and blurted out, "Mr. President, what are you going to do about the increased violence in Iran?"

Were it not for the graciousness of the president, who smiled and said, "Wait just a moment more," the reporter might have lost his standing at the White House, as blurting out in the middle of a president's prepared remarks was not good protocol, and was, in fact, rude, something one did not do to the president in public without having consequences.

"I'm glad you asked that question, so I can move on right away to the most important matter at hand," he said, switching gears.

The spring in the step of his voice grew perceptibly quicker, the tone more excited. He put down his notes, a sign to everyone that he was now moving into an area he was passionate about. Like others, Nimer had three, maybe four, emotional levers that, when pressed, moved him to speak forcefully and with inner conviction. It was not that he would speak eloquently at these times, as he mistrusted eloquence. He thought it lacked sincerity, and wasn't from the heart. A man must believe what he says, right down to the backs of his impeccable shoes. If a man was straightforward and honest in his beliefs, he would have a hold on the truth. As long as he remained without deceit in matters of right and wrong, good and evil, he would be on the right road. He was willing to slip the knot of integrity in more practical matters, as long as these concerns were means in the pursuit of right and good.

"You all know that I and this administration have done everything in our power to make the world a safer place, a place free from tyranny and terrorism. If you go back far enough into history . . ."

Even the younger and less experienced reporters began to squirm, the way they would in college when a professor began a lecture that way. Nimer liked the broad stroke, they knew, but it could go anywhere.

" . . . you will find that mankind rarely stands with its feet firm to confront evil. Even modern America did not confront evil soon enough. Sometimes, yes, it did, as when," he paused to assert his sincerity, "with all due respect to our friends from Japan, it dropped the atomic bomb twice."

There was a shuffling of feet, a few nervous coughs. "But mostly it didn't. We should have, for example, gone right up through the 38th Parallel in 1952 and dealt with the menace that China was at the time."

Nimer knew that putting the menace of China in the past tense was presidential diplomacy at work. The polls showed that Americans liked his straightforward approach. Even during these times when foreign policy crises, as with an intractable Iran, were going badly, they wanted a leader who was bold and principled, a man of action.

"If we go back in time, we can see that we didn't act to save the Jews from Hitler. People in high places knew what was happening. Even the Pope knew what was going on."

He paused again and looked down on the crowd of reporters with a stern and challenging look on his face, Nimer's way of saying to the reporters that what he was about to say was worthy of their taking note.

"We could have finished off Communism for good in Vietnam by going all out to win, instead of pussyfooting around with napalm bombs and Agent Orange.

"I could go on." Another pause for the intended effect to excite curiosity, both in the room and in the world that he knew listened when he spoke.

"But I won't. Except to say that this evil must stop, even if it takes a more compelling action of ours to do that."

He loved the word "compelling" as it seemed to flow naturally with his breathing, with some force he felt in his body but could not explain.

"I think it's time now to answer a few questions."

Most of the questions were direct requests to have the president interpret what he meant by a "compelling action," or what he liked to call the "military move" on Iran that had occurred within the past three weeks. He managed to fend them off, almost in a clumsy way, until Marian Foster, duenna of the White House press corps, with the cunning cultivated by experience in presidential press conferences, would not be denied. She stood up and spoke out ever so loudly until she was acknowledged before a scene might take place. She was ready to retire and had nothing to lose. She was tired of presidential obfuscation, and would take no more.

Her question was designed to lead the president into the particulars of the "military move," hoping that Nimer, inspired by his own enthusiasm, might press one of the levers and spontaneously reveal his intentions about Iran.

"Mr. President, we know that you have explained the invasion of Iran," she started in a deliberate attempt to anger him, "as an expeditious military move to prevent the Iranian government from further enhancing their nuclear capacity. You have convinced the American people that Iran is an imminent danger to our interests in the Middle East. And you have also told the American people the actions of our military in Tehran are not a war or an invasion, but simply an attempt to stop, shall we say, an eligible member of the Axis of Evil from doing . . . well, evil. We would like to know what your intentions are regarding Iran, specifically about our stay in Tehran."

It was a most difficult question to answer. Things were changing from day to day in Tehran. Nimer knew, of course, that the back-door channels for negotiating the nuclear issue were not going well, yet he could not say that, or even reveal their existence.

"Marian, that's a good question. A hard question to answer with specifics. First, let me say that we are not at war with Iran. I know there is some legalistic talk that we have invaded Iran. I don't see it that way. We are there under the general rubric of fighting terrorism.

"It has become more and more apparent to intelligence that the Iranians have been making strong efforts in recent months to bolster their nuclear program. They say for the record that their nuclear upgrades are intended to generate electricity. Yet, our people tell us differently, that it is geared up towards making weapons.

"About our intentions regarding Tehran, let me say only for now that we will stay there as long as we must to clear out opposition to our presence. When that has been settled, we will insist on allowing our forces to make a full inspection of their nuclear facilities to see if they are being used for peaceful or destructive purposes. Until that bridge is crossed, I have nothing more to say about the specifics of the situation."

Nimer was quick to call on one of his favorites, Charles Dennison of the *Washington Post*.

"Mr. President, the American public would like to know more about our troop movement into Iran. We have been told that there are approximately twenty-one thousand American soldiers in and around Tehran, and that most of them have been pulled from our forces in Iraq. My question to you, sir, is . . ." He hesitated before asking the question, "How has this weakened our efforts to sustain the peace in Iraq, and are you satisfied with the peace-keeping efforts of the new Iraqi army and police?"

"As you know, Charles, the Iraqization of the war there has been going on for some time now. Order has nearly been established in the streets, terrorist attacks are few, sovereignty under a democratic government duly elected by its people is theirs, the oil fields are working full-time, the infrastructure is being re-established at an excellent rate. I am confident that the new all Iraqi army and police force will do its job."

A few more questions about the Iran situation were asked and the press conference ended. The president knew from the start of the conference how much he wanted to say, and would say no more. If he was to succeed in his plan to torture the world for several days before dropping the bomb, he needed secrecy.

2

Nimer wanted to be alone in the oval office each morning, at least for a few minutes, before the day's activities began. Richard would have a cup of very hot coffee, sugared and milked, ready for him as soon as he entered. The president would inquire perfunctorily about Richard's health, and Richard usually would say, "Fine, Mr. President," and leave, on standby if a second cup was ordered.

The coffee was placed meticulously on a circular corked ceramic tile with the presidential seal on top. Nimer would sit at the desk for a few minutes, sip his coffee, and pray.

His God was a standard one, not necessarily sitting on a throne somewhere "up there," but everywhere in the spirit of good men, though he did not show up in evil men. Ironically, Nimer's God was a kind of masculine judge of sorts who would keep track every day of how each person in the world was doing in the domain of right and wrong. He was a sort of supercomputer who kept the books on every man, and some women, but only some, as they didn't get as many opportunities to do evil.

God was a force for the president. He was the standard against which Nimer measured his every action and decision. So he thought. Really, he didn't think much about the matter. Somewhere along the line of his own unique fights, small and large, to establish his own identity, he equated his ego with being right. Literally with being right. Not as a kind of metaphor, but as an identity with his ego, with himself. That he must be right in order to survive, and that if he wasn't right he would die and be buried. Literally buried six feet under. Being right became a matter of life or death. By the time he reached his thirties, and later when he entered politics, it was necessary for him to be right in order to stay alive.

To do that was not easy, especially when his cleverness at intuiting what others expected of him was so vivid. Although he could sometimes verbally bully those of inferior social status, it was an entirely different matter when it came to those equal in position, education, or aggressiveness. Although being president leveled the playing field now in these respects, it wasn't always so.

He had struggled in the beginning of his political life to convey his ideas as well as he wanted. He slowly developed an accretion of skills that would serve him in his fast climb to the presidency. These ranged from a low-end, sometimes humiliating, shutting his mouth until the time came, and it would come, to filing positions in his mind—this came easily—so that later he could articulate his points. In time, he became adept at these skills. This took patience, which he was naturally good at.

As president, he had few problems with asserting that he was right. It became easy to remind, in no uncertain terms, those who insisted on the rightness of their opinions about their subordinate status.

Perhaps the most extraordinary opposition to Nimer's need to be right came from his wife, Priscilla. The fact that she was fifteen years younger than him gave balance in some ways to their relationship. She was more in touch with the popular culture of the day; he, by temperament, office and age, with the weightier matters of the day. In the subtle ways that a married partner can hold control over a spouse, he reminded her over the years, for example, that it was far more significant that America was on the side of England in the war over the Falklands in the early '80's than who the latest Boy Band was; and how important it was for us to stay out of it militarily "in a geo-political sense," as he liked to say. In time, more from boredom, she began to nod in the ways that suggested her agreement.

Given these kinds of victories of the intellect over Priscilla, Nimer established, so he thought, his dominance in the household. Even his son, John, and his daughter, Casandra, teenagers now, kept up the façade when he was around, which wasn't often. In the almost animal-like way that the young have, they would stay clear of him as much as they could because he related to them like a moral instructor, always distinguishing for them right from wrong, good from bad. He was a busy man, so what they wanted from him he could only give in small amounts.

Priscilla, on the other hand, was warm, and hardly ever didactic. They could actually see, first-hand and not on television, they way she led her life, and they knew her goodness.

Casandra had once shared her feelings about her father with a favorite and trusted teacher. She told Mr. Sullivan, her Latin teacher, that whenever she tried to talk with her father, he would quickly begin to tell her the answer to what sometimes was not even a problem. And when it was a real problem, all she wanted was for someone to listen to her so she could hear herself and by doing that get some perspective.

Although his professional job was to teach Latin history and grammar to his students, Sullivan knew that in the fast-moving world of the community that employed him, he needed to be more than an expert about the ways and means of Rome.

"Mr. Sullivan, what can I do to make him my father?" she asked in the blunt and exaggerated way of teenagers.

"Casandra, I really don't know the answer to that question. I know that your father is a very important man, and that he probably is very busy and often preoccupied with important matters.

"What I mean to say is that although he loves you more than you might know, he is forced by the circumstances of his life to take on a wider group of people, sometimes around the world, that he has to pay attention to.

"I don't know how to tell you, Casandra, how to get him to listen. But I do know how to help you to let him know how much you love him." This was the understanding and creative quality about how Mr. Sullivan related to students that made him a favorite. Here she was wanting him to tell her how she could get her father "to be a father," and Sullivan was letting her know how *she* could win over the president of the United States.

"Just go up behind him some evening when he is reading the newspaper in his favorite chair, and simply kiss him on the back of his head, and leave. He might not say anything at the moment, but I guarantee you that you will see a noticeable change in his attitude towards you. You see, all he wants, like everyone else, is to know that he is loved, especially by the ones he loves the most. That, my dear student, includes you."

With this, Casandra smiled the big smile of someone who has just heard a way to change her life, to fill an emptiness. She thanked Mr. Sullivan and left. Sad to say, Casandra, kind as her mother, did not have the heart to tell her teacher the results of her experiment. She did as he told her. Her father continued to read his paper, still on course with the Sullivan prediction of outcomes. Yet, in the aftermath, his attitude never changed. He remained as aloof as ever towards her.

The same quality that print journalists liked to refer to as a "cold demeanor" or a "distancing personality," was, in the ways that some people manifest their personalities, just the controlling part taking over for now in circumstances that, in Nimer's case, needed control.

He had known for some time that if he was ever to become the president, he would handle the power differently from his predecessors. His plans were bigger than the circumstantial and historical tolerances allowed by the office.

Nimer wanted to bring peace to the world, and he was ready to shock that world. In order to complete his agenda, he needed to be manipulative and controlling, especially over the media. If the slightest information about the complex details of his plan to drop an A-bomb on an unsuspecting nation got out, the plan would have to be aborted. Carrying the secret details of a blueprint for peace was a burden that demanded an order of control over everything and everyone, even his own words, which must not, for now, let slip the plan. He was naturally good at self-monitoring. Monitoring the media would call for a self-control that made him seem rigid.

Even his relationship with Priscilla took on more of an undertone of control, the work that never seemed to end for Nimer. Just when he thought at some mutually understood level that he was in control, a problem would pop us again with her.

Once, when she was excited about changing the colors of a few rooms in the White House, she worked for several weeks with consultants to match colors with furniture, drapes, and wood in the room.

Before giving the go signal, she ran her scheme by Nimer to share her selections, and to let him know that she was taking an interest in the legendary building. He fought her choices with a lot of attitude about hot and cold colors matching the function of the rooms, so that a reading room, intended for contemplation, had to have a warm color, and another room, built for presentations and the exchange of ideas, had to have cold colors.

She thought his rationale was odd in some ways, and began to challenge him. He was the president, though. It was his house more than hers, she thought. And in the end she deferred, but only because she didn't want to preoccupy him with matters of relative insignificance. The consultants came back in for another week, the work was done as Nimer wanted, and he never said another word about it again.

His court was, of course, easier to dominate than his house. That was why he directed George Bender, his chief of staff, to meet with him this morning. The president sensed in the past few weeks that there was some strain between the defense secretary and the commander of the joint chiefs at the Pentagon, General Jeffrey Arena, three stars.

"Good morning, George. How's Marjorie?"

"Fine, sir. Thank you for asking."

"George, let's get right down to business. I get a feeling that there's something going on between Norman Jarvis and Jeff Arena. It's just a feeling thing, you know, but I've noticed that they don't seem to be friendly towards each other lately. When they were in here last week they didn't even shake hands, just kind of nodded to each other. And at the meeting, they seemed to address their remarks directly to me, whereas in the past they made a damn good effort to include each other, to bring each other 'in,' so to speak. I can't afford these two guys not getting along, the country can't afford it, especially now with this Iran thing going on."

After a deep breath, he said, "Do you know what's going on here?"

"Well, sir, I don't know the details, but several of my sources tell me that they are having a disagreement about how to handle the 'Iran thing,' as you put it." Bender hated when the president, or anyone else for that matter, referred to political realities in a short-hand vernacular, yet he knew that Nimer appreciated it when his subordinates picked up on his jargon and then actually used it. He figured Nimer liked the intellectual simpatico. It showed that another could think of a situation the same way that he did, in this case, that Iran was just another "thing" to be handled like other "things."

Bender continued. "Apparently Arena wants to beef up the number of troops we are employing there. He says that we're 'pussyfooting around' there when we should be showing greater forcefulness in dealing with it, I mean the . . ." He was suddenly aware that he didn't know what to call the war with Iran. Was it an incursion, or an invasion? Or a war?

"What I mean to say, sir, is that Arena wants us to show the Iranians and the world how tough we can be in this kind of situation, that if we just put down any sign of insurrection or unrest, those people will know what it means and get back into line. That these people, like so many others in the Mid-East, have been psychologically trained to know what force and power is and how they better respond to that approach."

"Well," the president said, "it is difficult to know who the good guys and the bad guys are there. When I look at TV and watch them shooting guns into the air, it's hard for a man to tell them apart."

Bender didn't know what to make of this response, but he figured there must be something useful in it for the president.

"Mr. President, Jarvis, on the other hand, has begun to talk again about streamlining the military. That is, fewer men with a more high-tech component in their work."

The secretary of defense referred to war and peace-keeping efforts as "work," which reflected his own personality that looked at life as a series of jobs to be performed each day. Completeness on the job was the way Jarvis signed his signature. Whether it was his relationship with his wife, son, friends or colleagues, or even, as he would say, "the man in the street," doing what is expected and doing it right and efficiently was the most important thing. If you said you were the breadwinner, by God, be the breadwinner. And be it as productively as you can. He rarely spent more than ten hours a day on the job, including Saturdays. When he accepted invitations, he attended perfunctorily, engaged in the necessary conversations with friends and sycophants, and left when he calculated that enough time had gone by to have established an expected, and sometimes necessary, presence.

The productivity principle also informed the relationship he had with his wife and son. On arriving home in the late evening, he would have a martini, then sit with his wife to ask her how her day had gone. As soon as he sensed that she was complete, usually quickly, as she wasn't up to much that counted with him, he would ask how his teenage son, Norm, Jr., was that day, and did he stay out of trouble. Once she had given him the answer to that question, the obligatory time as husband and father was done. If he sensed that Joan was beginning to unravel some story about Junior's day, and that she might lean on activating his fatherhood in more than the usual way, he would ask her to get to the point. If the story implied talking to the boy, he said he would do that as soon as he had time. If it warranted a father's presence at school, for example, he would beg off, letting Joan know as precisely as he could how busy he was, how much the country needed him right now, and please go do it yourself, as you are very good at these things. Then he would change into comfortable clothes, eat with Joan, as quickly as possible, before going to his study to read books and magazines of a personal choice, his way, he told a few, to keep a well-rounded personality.

He had read somewhere that one of the indicators of a good marriage is a satisfactory sex life. From that point, he had Joan agree to a regular Sunday afternoon "tryst," as he liked to think of it, to have sex. Usually, before he left for two hours of work in the office, he would ask her if two o'clock was a good time for her. She would say yes, important to him, because he could then time his lunch to digest before dropping a 10 mg pill that would take about a half hour to work. If he timed his moves correctly, he would be ready to have sex at the appointed hour, 2:00 p.m. sharp. It took Joan twice being late for the appointed time 'til she realized the importance of keeping it.

After the second lateness, Jarvis explained to her that if he was to maximize the effects of the pill, which took a half hour to work, she must be on time. If he felt particularly aroused, a feeling that he noted over time was, ironically, directly proportionate to the degree of stress he felt on the job, he would get into it and try to arouse her.

If he had had a relatively easy week, he would try to arouse himself by thinking about his first love at Harvard whom he would meet on weekends at one of the cheap motels outside Boston where she would arouse his overworked body like no one before or since had.

It was hard for Jarvis to feel much about Joan. He respected her, in a sort of pro-forma way, as his wife, yet there wasn't much else in the relationship except for the Sunday couplings. His incapacity for intimacy was matched by hers, as is the case in marriages born out of need.

Bender continued to fill in the president about what he knew about the suspected Jarvis-Arena feud.

"I've heard that Jarvis keeps on reminding Arena about the Vietnam War, about how we lost over 50,000 men in a losing effort."

What Bender didn't know was why this explanation and warning about the use of power made Arena furious, an anger he rarely expressed to superiors, equals or subordinates. The war machine that he had at his disposal was the Big Stick he needed to express himself.

Arena was a student of war and war tactics. He believed that the United States never lost a war, not even the Vietnam War. He even taught this in his stint as a U.S. Military History instructor at West Point in the early years of his career. He concluded that we did not lose the war, that we lost the debate. How could anyone believe that we lost in a military sense. From the Tet Offensive to the battle at Kham Duc, in the rice paddies and little villages, and during the long years of slogging through deltas and in highlands, all you had to do was count the dead, about 3,000,000 Vietnamese, and you know we won the war. By a 50:1 ratio. If it wasn't for the damned politicians pulling their punches, we'd be sitting in Saigon today. Those little gook bastards would be polishing our shoes.

That Jarvis kept on bringing up the Vietnam War as a stop to his plans was another thing, an irritant in Arena's pimple-thin sensitivities. Arena called it being "stuck in your story," a character symptom that he despised. He had first come up with the idea about how people get stuck in their stories a long time ago when he was an idealist about life and its possibilities.

He started to notice during conversations with homeless people at the soup kitchens around Newburgh that the ones who were particularly lost were the ones who would talk almost endlessly about something that had happened to them deep in the past. Even when he would try to draw them back into the present, they were unwilling. Sometimes, he would intentionally invade their privacy in an attempt to get them angry or insulted, a kind of small shock that might bring them more into reality, as Arena liked to think about it.

Yet, when he would ask why they didn't have a job, they would invariably evade the question by going back to a bad experience that took place a long time ago. Perhaps a savage beating by their father, a threatened killing by a robber. Or, in the case of one woman, being raped by a man she had trusted.

Arena would grow weary, tired of this, and could not understand why a man couldn't get over a beating, or a robbery, or a woman over being raped. After all, he thought, the only way to live your life was to forget about the past and get on with it.

So he grew weary of Jarvis's talk about the past, how we lost the war in Vietnam and what we might learn by that. What we could learn by it, he thought, was to exercise greater force in any future war, to not let political considerations rule the battle plan. The guy who was beaten could learn to fight back, the man who was robbed pack a gun next time. And he felt like telling the raped woman that next time she ought to be careful how she dressed. Or when the perpetrator got hot, to cool him off by whatever means necessary.

Bender told the president what he saw and the little he knew about how Jarvis and Arena were not getting along. He knew, though, that the president trusted him.

"Mr. President, it might be a good idea if you talk with each one, first separately, then perhaps together. We know that their roles are pivotal to the protection of the nation."

Actually, Bender said this because he suddenly grasped the seriousness of the situation. The president was way ahead of him.

"I think you're right, George." Just then, a phrase rippled through Nimer's mind but, since his chief didn't have much of a sense of humor, he dared not soil the fabric of the conversation by expressing it. "By George, you're right" just seemed inappropriate.

"Set up a meeting for me with both of them together. I don't have time for this crap."

It was, though, as if Nimer inherited what the old Irish liked to speak about as the legacy for stepping in crap, luck. He would be meeting with two of the key players whose cooperation he needed to expedite his plan to blow up a city, to teach the world a lesson about peace.

3

Usually when two highly-ranked principals of his administration met with him in his office, the president tried to set a tone of cordiality. He knew that most wanted to please him, to let him know, almost lackey-like, what he needed to know in the most favorable light possible. His take was that, no matter his need for the straight truth, most would tend to sugar-coat it. Not because they were manipulative, but just because that is the way it was.

Today's meeting with Jarvis and Arena was extremely important to Nimer, and not just because he wanted to expose their differences. That was important, but it was more important for the president to size them up. And how they might fit into his plans to drop the atomic bomb.

He basically knew where they stood on defense and military strategy. What he didn't know was how much of their stand was rhetoric and how much real. He knew how to wheel and deal from his own experience as the chief executive officer of a middle-sized textile company, and then later as he climbed the political ladder from congressman in Arizona to senator to the presidency, all within twelve years. He knew that behind every question there was an answer that was leaning towards either the truth or a lie. It bothered him that he could not always say the truth. He knew, for example, that walking out on an onerous press-conference would not work, yet, as he confided to Priscilla one day at Camp David, at times he just felt like answering "Screw you" to an inquisitive reporter's question, and simply walking out. She said he ought to do it, that the American people would love it because each one of them probably had the same urge.

In order to put an edge on the meeting, Nimer decided to sit behind his desk, but just for a moment. Once the barrier of the desk had been established, he would get up, and move into his usual place, one of the comfortable seats that were placed in a tight arc just off the rug of The Great Seal of the United States.

Jarvis and Arena entered, Jarvis first, as usual. Arena thought that was fitting, though he was growing tired of it.

"Sit down, gentlemen," the president said briskly. "I asked you to come here today so we could discuss how we are going to win the peace in Iran. I know that we have cut through to Tehran like a hot knife through butter. General Arena, you know how grateful I am for the way you and your men are winning the wars, and, once again, you are to be congratulated. Two wins in four years."

Nimer knew that the military in the American way of governance was subservient to the wishes of a freely elected president, its commander in chief. He also knew the delicate edge to ideas like the Constitution, how easily an idea could be subverted by power. The traditions and principles of democracy had powerful cultural, chronological and historical currency, as well as an inter-locking network of institutional safeguards, yet democracy was only an idea. Somewhere deep inside the dark spaces of the president lurked another idea with equal collateral that a person could not always hang onto a principle, could not hold it in his hand. He could, though, hold a gun.

Arena barely acknowledged the praise. He was used to having his ass kissed.

"Thank you, Mr. President."

Nimer suddenly realized that he had smoothed the edginess he wanted on the meeting. In an attempt to re-establish it, he stayed seated behind his desk longer than he had planned.

"Norman, I am told that you and Jeff here are having some difficulties in how to deal with the peace we're trying to establish in Iran. I know that you are for streamlining our forces, and we have done some of that. By God, it showed in the quick race across Iraq to Baghdad. General Patton would have been proud of your leadership and executive ability."

The president turned his back on them, an intuitive move he made to increase the seriousness in the room.

He turned and rose from behind his desk

"Gentlemen, what in hell is going on?"

General Arena, as was his style, grabbed the lead. "Mr. President, I think that we should deal with the insurgency in Iran with an increased and forceful military presence. It is clear that ever since Mr. Jarvis made the decision to gather our fighting men into small clusters situated on the outskirts of cities in Iran they are safer, a bit more out of harm's way. But we are paying a price with the men. They are beginning to feel a bit like misfits, several have even used the word 'coward,' as if they are not doing the job they came to do. They are trained to fight, not to sit back and watch a country that so many of their comrades died to liberate go to hell in a basket."

Jarvis began to feel a bit uneasy because he knew that the president could be turned on by men like Arena, men who exuded a certain personality force, as well as a conviction in their voice. Certainty, whether based on good judgment or not, had a clarity that subtlety lacked. Jarvis was at a disadvantage in this sort of personal exchange of ideas in front of the president. His position required him to see everything that went on in the world from so many angles that often the net intellectual conclusion was ambiguous.

"Mr. President," Arena continued, "I think we ought not only beef up our contingent of troops in the Gulf, but also give their commanders' discretionary powers to search and destroy anywhere or any one in Tehran that they think is an enemy of the United States. At the moment, although our boys are a bit safer, as I've said, than before we began to corral them, they feel insecure and somewhat useless. Insecure, because apparently every gunslinger in the Muslim world has decided to head for Tehran to have a shot at Americans."

He was on a roll. "And they're sneaky, dirty bastards who don't come out in the open, but skulk around with satchels full of explosives set to kill American soldiers and anyone else who gets in the way. All they want is chaos and for us to get out. These people are goddamn . . ."

He stopped short.

"I'm sorry, sir, if I offended you by taking the name of the Lord in vain."

It was an almost biblical truth around the Pentagon that no one should ever do that within earshot of the president. It was also risky, though less, to use the Lord's name disrespectfully in print.

"As I was trying to say, Mr. President, these people are crazy, willing to blow themselves to kingdom come to get back at us. We must not allow that to happen."

The energy was gone from Arena's rant.

"That's enough for now, General. I get the point. And I'd like you to stay a few more minutes after we're done today. I have a few questions for you, but don't want to take up the defense secretary's time at this moment."

"Norman, is it possible for you to go along with the General, the part about beefing up the troops a bit?"

Before Jarvis had a chance to answer, the president said, more *at* Arena than *for* Jarvis, how important it is to have a fighting force "geared up" with the latest technology. He went on to talk about laser weapons as if they were an always accurate lethal fist that could strike an enemy target as if it were a mannequin rubber target, a "kill" waiting to happen. He spun a glib picture of the efficacy of these weapons, but Pentagon and Defense knew better about their inaccuracies. Both men blushed when Nimer continued to wax enthusiastically about weaponry that the mass media extolled, knowing that their underlings, in briefings, had given the president only the rosy picture.

How can it be said that a man who has deep access to reality thinks like a man who doesn't? Perhaps it is because he wants to hear what he already thinks. Or maybe his ego can accept no less, that the smallest chink in the armor of being right is the beginning of the end for him.

Whatever, it was sensed as quickly as an electronic impulse running through the inner circle that Nimer listened more to whoever reinforced his prejudices than he would to those who told him the whole truth.

Nimer often scoffed, too, at the opinion of the masses. What could they know, he thought. Once, in a moment of pique at the peace rallies being held around the world to protest the impending war against Iraq, he sneered at their voice, calling them "irrelevant."

"Mr. President," Jarvis answered, "with all due respect." This was a way of speaking that Nimer both enjoyed and detested. "I can't in good conscience agree with that request." He added the word "totally," as it was in his practiced nature to do so.

"We could, of course, whenever you want, build up our forces. A directive to the National Guard would do that. What I am trying to prevent from happening is for us to go through the insurgency movement like crap through a duck and leave lots of our guys dead at the other end."

Arena thought it amusing that whenever Jarvis tried to be persuasive he used metaphors that he thought were clever, yet they only half worked and did not make sense. Nimer, though, got the point, and that was the only thing that mattered.

"We must hold down the sting of the body bag," Jarvis said, hoping that his earnestness would move Nimer towards favoring a lean fighting machine.

What he didn't know was that Nimer, although seeing himself as enlightened, thought of "body bags," oddly, as an expression of a number. If the number got too large, his popularity went down. If it remained steady and on the small side, say a soldier a week, public backing would remain constant, as most Americans knew that small wars required a small price. Nimer figured one a week was acceptable, even perfect for the rhetoric he used whenever Americans would falter or begin to back off in their support of his wars. Support for the race into Iran was unfailing in the first few days. Americans could be counted on for that. What was difficult to sustain was a national moral subsidy for keeping at it. So, whenever he felt it necessary, he would take a quick trip to a small setting, usually a school, and make a little speech about heroism and patriotism, about sticking together in times of crisis. This was an especially effective way to keep Americans in touch with reminders about how they were all in danger from terrorists.

It was his ability to wrap patriotism in the Stars and Stripes that enabled Nimer to talk the Congress and the American people into supporting the foray into Iran after it happened. This was no mean feat, as the country was coming off a problematical war in Iraq. At one point during the Iraqi war, it even appeared that he would lose the election to his Democratic opponent. As it was, his opponent's platform, built on his war record in Vietnam, turned out to be made of cardboard that collapsed under the weight of his lies about that record.

It was not too long after his re-election that Iran began to rattle its own sabers more loudly about belonging to the "nuclear club," as their Foreign Minister Kamal Kharrazi put it. When Nimer realized the implications for the Mid-East of Iran's refusal to allow U.N. restrictions on its nuclear program, he began over time to ratchet up the rhetoric needed for a new war. Once the peace was being established in Iraq and sovereignty being secured, it was easy enough for Nimer to send surplus American troops across the border in a rush to Tehran.

He knew, too, and sometimes it bothered him, that the sorrow he might express for the dead cut down at an early age was more rhetorical than real. He liked to think that he was steeling himself against sorrow and possibly self-pity, and that was why he felt little. After all, a president must make major decisions in the name of his principles, and he could ill-afford to let the consequences bother him.

Didn't Eisenhower talk with the paratroopers he knew he was sending to their deaths over France in 1944? Didn't Churchill urge on his fellow citizens to fight the Nazi on the beaches of England, though he knew thousands of them might die in doing that?

It was sometimes necessary for a man to measure himself, make a difficult decision and move on. Most notable in his mind was the decision made by Harry S. Truman to drop atomic bombs on Hiroshima and Nagasaki, even though he was certain that thousands of innocent people would die in flashes of bottled lightning. Truman would mention later that he never lost a minute of sleep over his decision to drop the bombs. Nimer wanted to be like that.

"I understand your concerns, Norman," the president said. "And I agree with them. What I want most here is for you and General Arena to talk some more. Go into a room, tell your aides to bring you coffee and stay there until you can come together on this. I'll get Richard to send over a few Havanas.

"What I'd like to see most is for us to beef up the troops a bit with, of course, the most technology possible. At the same time, I want some kind of a new plan for our troops on the ground over there. We can't have them holed up in tents like squirrels in trees afraid to come down to find their nuts, because when they decide to come down they might find they don't have any nuts left." Nimer thought this immensely clever, though no one laughed. He shrugged it off as a sign of over-seriousness on their parts.

"So, we are on the verge of wrapping up our mission in Afghanistan. Kabul is free, the schools are open there, women don't have to wear burkas anymore, and they are on their way to a freely representative government. We have done all that we can for now. The plan for withdrawal that you have drawn together tells me that you are a team, that when you sit down and come to grips, you are first-rate people, and leaders of the American people. I want you to finalize our withdrawal plan." He hardly took a breath before continuing.

"Every Afghan man who has watched our men knows what we can do. Although we are leaving, I want the spirit of who we are to remain there. I want the world to know that we are strong there, and that we have not been there just to be strong. That democracy is everyone's right. We must leave a legacy that allows them to know what freedom is.

"I want to speak a little about where we're going together, I mean you and I and the people of America."

By now, Arena wanted a cup of hot licorice tea. Whenever he felt anxious, breathed on or bored, his choice was a cup of hot licorice tea.

"We've already talked about getting out of Iraq, and the time is soon. We have set an example for the rest of the world. We have kept our promise to bring democracy there."

What he would say next startled both Jarvis and Arena.

"Gentlemen, what I am going to say now is in the strictest confidence, and can never, as such, leave this room. What you do with this information, and how you process it must be done in disguise, even from your associates and closest confidants. Do you understand?"

They both nodded, pleased for now that they were to be privy to the most concealed thinking of the president of the United States.

Eirik Narsaq was 64 years old. He rented a small apartment in Ilulissat, Greenland, about four hundred miles north of the Arctic Circle. He lived alone now whereas he once lived with his son, Lief, on the island of Uummannaq, about 200 miles north.

Lief's mother had died in childbirth. Eirik was an Inuit Indian who was once old-fashioned about his fishing. He would go out in a small motorized boat he bought after many years of fishing for others in their craft or in his own rowboat. Eventually, though, he bought a shotgun for fishing. When he got lucky and caught a seal by gun or line, he would stay home for a period of time so he could be with his son.

Eventually, though, when the waters of the Arctic began to be polluted from sources thousands of miles away, he was out for more extended periods of time trying to catch what he needed for his family.

He tried his best to be a good father, even saving money to buy a television set for Leif. He figured watching the TV after coming home from the small village school would keep him pre-occupied for the hours between the end of school and his own arrival home, which, in winter, was almost always about the time it got dark.

Their little village with its brightly painted wooden houses might appear to anyone not familiar with the brutal conditions of winter that far north to be a good place to raise children.

It was not. The winters were long, very cold, and filled with snowfall. Even the stone Inukshuk placed on high ground to guide man and beast home to the village were not enough to keep lost children from a lingering and bitter death in the snow.

Sometimes in the springtime their bodies would be found, little skeletons eaten by the crows of winter. Many times, they were less than 300 feet away from the village.

Eirik was the son of an Inuit who also was a fisherman, though with less sophisticated tools than his son's fishing line and boat. He would wander with his family and perhaps a few others from place to place where they might ice fish for their catch of the day. Every item of clothing as well as each tool they used was made from one or another of the animals they hunted for food.

Now and then, the men would pack up in search of a polar bear. Sometimes they got lucky and killed one. There was great rejoicing in the little groups of families when that would happen, as they knew the bear would provide ample food and clothing for awhile, and the men could take a rest from the daily grind of hunting.

At least Eirik got to stay in one place, an improvement over the necessary wandering ways of his father. Mother Denmark was a good and bountiful mother who paved the way more than half a century ago for the scattered Inuits to gather into bigger groups by the sea by building them wooden houses where they could have some of the amenities not offered by igloos.

Eirik's son, though, was more than occupied by the television set his dad bought for him. It set him free of the bored, indifferent life he was leading, stuck somewhere between not having to fish and hunt for his daily bread and the Danish dole that allowed him to idle away his days.

People in the village speculated after Leif blew his head off with his father's shotgun that unfulfilled freedom was no freedom at all, but a burden that could lead to desperation. Sitting in a little wooden house watching the comforts and joys of the folks back in Denmark with their beautiful blond women was calculated to make a seventeen year old one generation removed from the igloo feel incomplete.

If he even had a chance of someday having a few of the luxuries he saw on foreign movies, maybe he would not have killed himself. His father had once talked with him about the possibilities of going to school in Denmark, paid for by the Danish people. Perhaps he could learn to be an electrician and come home to Nuuk farther south and filled with homes laden with electrical appliances. Or he could learn to cook in the Motherland before coming home to the good life at one of the restaurants in Ilulissat.

Sometimes ambition cannot be nurtured in the Arctic, and Leif chose, like so many of his male contemporaries, to end his life before it had gotten started.

There was nothing left in Uummannaq for Eirik after the tragedy, so he moved to Ilulissat. He didn't have many skills that a city of over 8000 people might find useful. But he had a small pension. And this he supplemented by delivering the newspaper to over a hundred homes a day.

It was not really difficult work for him. He was used to getting up early, as well as using his old body for labor. Some of his customers lived in new condos not far from the waters of the Davis Strait where they were packed in closely enough for him to deliver many of the newspapers in one continuous route.

His customers were mainly the nouveau riche of the city who made most of their money on the tourist industry. As small as the city was, it was considered big and cosmopolitan by its people who were a mixture of Inuit and Danish blood, beautiful for the eye to behold. There was very little royalty in the little city, and not much of a class structure that anyone used to make social distinctions, except practical and useful ones. It was as if the old ways of Eirik's father had been transposed onto a modern society. No one too high or too low to be seen with others. No barriers standing in the way of friendships or marriages. In many ways, a backward place ahead of its time.

Ilulissat was situated in a good spot, surrounded by icebergs and not far from the Jakobshavn Glacier, the fastest moving glacier in the world. Even its port was in an large alcove of sorts that allowed ships of every kind to pull into its safety. There was lots of pack ice on the fringes of the city, as well as large icebergs not far out to sea. Most of them broke off from the Jacobshavn and some floated towards the east coast of America before melting into the Atlantic Ocean.

↘

"Now that we're pulling out of Afghanistan, and will be getting out of Iraq soon enough, I want the both of you to begin thinking about where we can establish our military presence in the world. I am not talking about the kind of thing we are doing in Tehran now."

Jarvis and Arena stole a quick look at each other, startled.

"It's probably a good thing for us, now that we're at it, to clean up the world a little bit more, rid it of a little more evil. Now, we don't want to start anything big, nothing we can't handle. We don't want to bring in the Chinese, or the Russians, for example. Or anyone who has the ability to weaken our international stature."

They were both aware of the code words. "Weaken our international stature" meant defeating us in a hot war.

"I'd like you to both go back with your people and do some work on this. Take a look at who the trouble-makers are, what trouble they are causing. I'd like Frank Daniels at the State Department to take a look at your reports and see what he thinks of them, how feasible he thinks they are, how acceptable to the American people. I'd like you also to prepare rationales for us to attack."

Jarvis was the first to speak. Arena seemed numb. "Mr. President, this is a most unusual request. Attack who?"

The gears of Jarvis's mind that sugar-coated his words were well-oiled . He would have to use them now.

"Except for the invasion of Iraq, for which we had clear justification, I have no experience in preparing for a war of the sort you are talking about. It's not that I don't know where the trouble-makers are, or who they are."

For the sake of keeping on the right side of Nimer here, he added, "The list is long, practically endless."

Jarvis continued the thought, "We've got North Korea, maybe a full war in Iran. Or Libya, Syria, insurgents in the Philippines, rebels here and there fighting democracies. I could go on and on," he said, although he knew he couldn't right now. He added, without knowing why, "We could even get Vietnam back into our grip, and finish some old business there."

Nimer could tell that Jarvis was flustered, and he was pleased at the effect.

"Mr. President, the request is most unusual. I can get you what you want, although the justification part might be difficult, and the selling part will take time. But, we've done it before and we can do it again," he said, feeling a bit timid, as he always did in the face of power. Perhaps it was no fluke that he was secretary of defense.

"I have just one small request of you, Mr. President."

"What is that, Norman?"

"Mr. President, would you kindly direct me to do that in writing?"

Jarvis knew that the times were tumultuous, the kind that historians liked to pick over endlessly and for years to come. He needed protection against his craven nature.

"Jarvis," the president nearly shouted. "Didn't I just tell you that what I just told you was to be held in absolute confidence? How can we do that together if I put it in writing?" he asked, and then answered his own question by saying, "We can't!"

The secretary of defense was stunned and reeled a bit before composing himself.

"I know how strong you feel about this, Mr. President, but it's not unusual for a man in my position to ask for reassurances."

"Neither is it unusual for a president to have his orders carried out without excessive excuses. Think about it, Norman, and before you leave here let me know your answer."

He knew what that meant. In the face of the consequences, his answer was predictable.

By this time, Jeff Arena had already rehearsed his own response, one driven more by temperament than a desire to please.

He paused first so the tension in the room could abate a little before he asserted himself.

"Mr. President, if I may, I think your idea is excellent. We are in the middle of great times. For once, an American leader has pre-empted the enemy. We got Saddam," he said, adding "Hussein" as an afterthought. "For once we took the initiative before getting hurt first. For once . . ." he trailed on, as the room nearly shook from the spirit of Nimer breathing, *Yes, yes, yes!*

Arena was his, and Nimer knew it at once. He wasn't surprised, though, because the signs of his convictions were always there. Arena made sure that his fighting machine was oiled, his men trained and taken care of. He tried to get them every logistical advantage, whether it was food, gear, or technology. He fought for tactical advantage, often sparring with Jarvis about the details of the end game. He was the first military man to declare that he was "in" when Nimer began to talk about invading Iraq, and the one who immediately stepped forward when Nimer first inquired about raiding Tehran. Arena was about offense, Jarvis about defense.

"Jeff," the president said, "I'm glad I can count on you."

Arena felt a bond here, perhaps a fleeting nostalgia for the way he felt about his brothers in the jungles of Vietnam, the guys who kept him going, the real reason, maybe the only reason then, that he wanted to stay alive in the midst of so much death. He would do anything for his brothers then. Today, he would do anything for his president.

There was an almost awkward moment of silence, the time for a man of action to return from an odd side trip to the heart.

"Jarvis, are you in?"

"Yes, sir." It was the only way for him.

"Then let's get going. You'll get together to report to me in writing about how we can accelerate getting out of Iraq while giving them the democracy we promised. And I want a report from each of you about our next target, justification, etc."

As Nimer liked to think of himself as a leader and a teacher, this was a nice, neat wrap up, like a re-cap at the end of a class.

"One more thing," he said. "The reports should be given a title that's ambiguous, and it must not have on or in it any reference to today's meeting, or that the report is a response to any directive of mine."

A pause, then "Are we clear?"

Together, they responded "Yes, sir." Jarvis shook Nimer's hand and exited, still a little dazed at what had just occurred and his role in it.

4

"Jeff, thanks for staying a few extra minutes. I know how busy you are, and I won't take but a few minutes."

"My pleasure, Mr. President."

"You know that I have a real problem with any open search and destroy tactics that you have used in the past and might want to use again. I know it helps to get right at the enemy, and I know it helps the morale of your men. We both know that they are trained to fight, not to be policemen. Policemen are trained to fire back when fired upon. Our men, yours and mine, are trained to bring superior fire power upon targets. But, as much as I'd like to give you the 'go' on that in Tehran, I can't. I just can't."

He knew that Arena understood why he just couldn't do that, yet it was somehow necessary to say it so they could have a mutual agreement on it, no matter how repulsive that might be to both of them.

"Most nations and their peoples will see such actions as being too aggressive. They will call us aggressors and occupiers. The Iranian people and their insurgents will say the same. We're caught in a tight bind. If we're too pushy, we get called names. If we're too soft, we look like we don't stand for anything. Especially to the ordinary people of Iran. And we've got to get to the ordinary people because they really rule what goes on there. We've got to win them over, so that when they fire their guns into the air, they'll be firing with us and not against us.

"I'm asking you, then, as much as it hurts you and me, to instruct your leaders to have the men out there and seen, but not seen too much. And when they have to shoot to kill to protect themselves and other innocent people, try to have them do it discreetly. Whatever you can, try to keep the bad stuff out of the news."

"Of course, sir. I'll do my best to pull in the rope and to let it out, in the spirit that you are suggesting."

Nimer felt good about Arena's response. He could always trust him to do the right thing.

The president asked him if he wanted something to drink, perhaps a shot of brandy, or a cup of coffee.

"Thank you, sir. I'll have a cup of licorice tea, if that's available."

He could have used the brandy, but everyone knew that the president did not drink, and he did not want to drink alone. Besides, there was an important meeting later at the Pentagon, and Arena wanted to be fully present to himself and the judgment calls he might have to make about several important issues regarding requisitions.

Nimer pressed the inter-office button and asked for two teas, which arrived several minutes later, tiny sugar cakes on the side.

Sipping his drink, the president said, "By jove, Jeff," he said, trying to be cute, "this is good stuff. I'll have Priscilla get me some."

And then, without missing a beat of his breath, he disclosed his reasons for asking the chairman to stay behind.

"General, I think that you must be as sick and tired of it all as I am. What I mean is the way the world is. People killing people everywhere. Evil men stalking innocent children, men raping women without any reason. Heads of state jailing, torturing, maiming and killing their own people.

"I think sometimes about Priscilla, Casandra and John, how these things could happen to them. And I shudder to think of it.

"Jeff, I've met your wife, Jennifer, but I don't know if you have any children."

"I do, sir. One daughter named Teresa. Everyone calls her Terry. She's nineteen and goes to Georgetown."

"So I guess you must shiver, too, when you think about the things they could do to them. Why, I guess you know about the horrible things Hussein's boys did to innocent people. Torturing athletes because they didn't win. Picking out newly wedded brides to rape, and cutting up their bodies to mail back to the newly wedded spouses when they complained. I can't think of anything more horrible, and it's got to stop, Jeff. It's just got to stop."

"I agree with you, sir."

"You take the Japanese, and the horrible things they did to our prisoners. Cutting out cuticles, cutting off penises, and breasts of Chinese and Korean women. And the Nazis killing all the Jews in gas chambers like they did. Poor little children dying before they could live. Stalin killing his own people in Ukraine so he could get his way with a new farm program. Pol Pot in Cambodia torturing and killing his own.

"I even read once that if a Cambodian man's hands were smooth, or there were eyeglass marks, you know, reading glasses, around his nose, he would be suspect of being educated and well-read, and a threat to the state.

So he would have them kneel down and tie their hands behind their backs with wire and have them shot in the back of the head.

"General, there's a lot of evil men out there, and we've got to stop them. This stuff we're up to in Iran is just peanuts compared to what we've got to do. We catch a few today, they spring a few new ones at us tomorrow. It's never ending. I think it's going to wind up like Israel and the Palestinians. Tit for tat, an eye for an eye, a never ending fight of these forces."

Arena listened carefully and, although he agreed in principle with Nimer about the world, he thought his point of view to be a bit simplistic. Yet, all the while, he kept nodding his head in agreement, not as vigorously as a bobble-head doll, but resembling one.

Perhaps it was this very act of constant affirmation of the president's riff that drew Arena into Nimer's confidence.

He looked at the general as if he were looking into some deep place inside him, a place that Arena knew existed only when he, too, was frustrated with the ways things were going.

There was a difference, though. In Arena's case, the wellsprings of his frustration were light, round, and smooth like the slightly turbulent surface waters that a destroyer created when it went in circles looking for a prey below. For Nimer, frustration had arced to a deep, white-hot fire with everything to consume.

He had rid the world of Saddam Hussein and his crazy sons, as well as many of the top echelon of al Qaida. Iran was being taught a lesson about American power. To keep the fire from consuming himself, he needed new material to burn.

"General Arena, suppose I told you that I had a plan to stop all the killing, a plan so remarkable in its scope and vision as to turn the tide of history?"

The general squirmed in his seat, wondering if this was more of Nimer's overblown rhetoric, or his need to let off steam. The former would become a good cocktail party story; the latter a flattering display of confidence.

The itch in the squirm for Arena, though, was prompted by the possibility that the president was about to tell him very privileged information. The itch was about to be rubbed.

"I must tell you, Arena, that what you are about to hear from me now never came from me, and I want you, for now, to tell no one. Not even your wife in a moment of intimate weakness."

The general nodded again, this time the kind of nod that was ironically nuanced so that the lowering of the head implied assent.

"If I were to tell you that this plan is so different from anything else anyone has ever tried, literally in the history of man, would you be interested in participating?"

"Mr. President, you know I would."

"Suppose, though, I told you that there was a chance in pulling off this plan for many people to die.

"I didn't say that right. Let me try again. That if we pull off this plan the way I see it, lots of people might die."

"Tell me what you mean, Mr. President. I don't understand."

"I've got to back up a bit first and explain. If lots of people die . . ." He paused, then said, "Well, probably lots of people *will* die."

He seemed deep in thought for a moment as Arena watched him seriously, by now both intrigued and confused.

"It's important for me to tell you that because lots of people might die, probably will die, that lots of people who might otherwise have died will then live. Lots of good will come of their deaths.

"That God is on our side in our endeavor to make the world a safe place. The execution of the plan will be our legacy to the future."

This kind of talk made a tiny spasm of fear run through the general's stomach, the kind of fear he hadn't felt since getting caught in a jungle trap once a along time ago in Vietnam.

Nimer continued, yet almost haltingly, as if he was conceiving the embryo of his plan right at that moment, in that instant.

"I want to explain that a bit, as it might sound odd. My thinking has to do with means and ends.

"You and I, both good Christians, have always been told that the end must justify the means. It's my feeling that this kind of thinking has put us at a historical disadvantage."

Nimer liked to think of himself as a figure in the stream of history. His plan might very well place him in the middle of that stream, so central to its workings that it would ebb and flow forever more in certain ways because of what he had been planning, up to this point only in his mind.

"General, you probably have guessed that you are the first and only person I have told this to, and I need to know your thinking about means and ends."

It was the kind of philosophical and ethical question that was much discussed in the military, and Arena had his own ideas about it, though he mostly was prompted by circumstances of his position to answer conservatively. Today was different.

"I agree with you, Mr. President. That is, that we have been put at a disadvantage by this thinking."

At this, Nimer perked up by settling down in a sort of foot-over-knee position he fell back on whenever he wanted to suggest easiness under pressure.

Arena continued, "I remember once in a required military ethics class when we were asked a question about whether or not it would have been ethical to assassinate Adolf Hitler at the beginning of his dictatorship in order to prevent the deaths of millions of people later at his hands. Many of the guys thought it would have been okay to kill him. Others thought it was not only okay, but that we had an obligation to kill him. A few had reservations about killing anybody in cold blood."

"What was your opinion?" the president asked.

"Well, sir, I thought, and still do, that if any man is so cruel as to deliberately kill others the way Hitler did, well, that he should die as soon as possible."

"I'm glad that you think that way, General. As you know, I signed a directive several years ago that authorized the killing of Hussein. No man has the right to kill others the way he did."

He continued, but Arena was too deep in his own thoughts to hear. He was still uneasy with the scope of this conversation. His job was, mainly, to give advice about goals, and then to take orders, envision a plan and a strategy and, with the help of his subordinates, develop tactics to complete the goals of his civilian superiors.

He was also, almost subliminally, uncomfortable with what he was hearing about the magnitude of the president's "plan." Whatever exchange of ideas he had had about what might be called "murder" in certain courts of law was always in the context of killing a single person or groups of people.

The conversations, though, never included the deliberate deaths of lots of people, and the president said that "lots of people might die, probably will die."

He knew the exact words, as his memory was as sharp as his leadership style.

Trained in deference to the presidency, it was difficult for Arena to interrupt Nimer.

"Sir, would you please tell me more about your plan and how it probably will result in the deaths of many people."

"Not right now, General. All I'm trying to do here today is to see if I can reliably enlist you into such a plan, if you are interested enough to go along with me on this."

Nimer knew that the general was a man of exceptional integrity. If Arena knew the details of the president's plan and the implications sounded sadistic to him, there was chance he might withdraw. Without his cooperation, at least in providing the necessary strategic, technical, and atomic weapon support, Nimer could not complete what he felt was his destiny—to scare the world into peace by letting it know beforehand that the United States would drop an A-bomb on one out of four cities announced two days before it would happen, enough time for the world and its leaders to imagine the results which would scare them forever more into the peace he was seeking.

"I've already asked you today if you would draw me up a list of possible new targets for us to show our will and purposes to the rest of the world. When I get that report from you, I'll tell you more. For now, General, that will be all."

Arena stood up, stepped back at the sort of awkward "at attention" he always assumed before exiting a meeting with the president. Because he thought the importance of today's meeting warranted it, and perhaps as an added sign of his allegiance to Nimer, he saluted him.

Nimer, with fingers stiffly together, as he sometimes practiced it in front of the mirror after shaving, saluted him back.

Just as the general was about to leave, Nimer said, "General, in an unrelated matter, I've been told that a major in your communications or tactics wing at the office is married to a Japanese woman whose mother was in Hiroshima when the atomic bomb was dropped. That she lives with them here in D.C."

"That would be Major Overstreet, Sherman Overstreet, who is married to Noriyo Nagaoka. He works for PT and C, that is, Planning, Tactics and Communication, and, yes, I've heard him say that a relative was there."

"I was wondering, Jeff, if it's not too much to ask, or if you don't think she'd be uncomfortable with this, or her husband, if you could ask her to call my personal secretary and arrange a meeting here with me in the White House, perhaps lunch. I'd like to ask her a few questions about the bombing. You might have heard that I'm a fan of World War II, and I'd be curious to know a few things about the bombing. I know some of your guys have briefed me in detail about our atomic weapons, tactical and such, but I'd like to know a bit more from a personal account about the human aspect. I hope you don't mind."

Though he thought the request was a bit odd, Arena said "Not at all, sir. I'll speak to the major. If that will be all."

"Yes, thank you, General."

Arena left the office he had entered an hour ago, feeling elated at the president's confidence in him, yet he was also troubled by a feeling that his life was about to change. That perhaps Nimer was planning to pick a new target to wage war against, but maybe this time with tactical nuclear weapons. It was dreadful to even contemplate these thoughts, although the general's mind raced through the assignments he had been given, even quickly picking the nation he thought could use a good lesson. Rationales came a dime a dozen to him, so quick was his ability to justify any action he ever took.

Even the planning and tactics came fast, first in great generalities, then in tight specifics. He had an extraordinary ability to envision the end game before the game was defined, or its boundaries outlined. Given these, he could adjust his larger thinking to fit the details, even the other way around. War was like a game for him where he played the pattern of objectives recursively. He could do this so quickly that often he asked his coterie of advisers to meet with him only as a professional courtesy.

By the time he was getting into a staff car in the White House reserved parking area, he knew the name of the country he was going to recommend in his report, the possible presidential objectives, as well as the rough planning and tactics for each objective.

It had taken him a long time to accept his lightning-like mind. After seeing it work its wonders, after finding his projections so right so many times, he finally surrendered to the gift. Maybe today was the day, he thought, in the flighty and fantasizing way he sometimes had of thinking, when he would have the chance to use it for the benefit of mankind.

If later he could have reflected back on this day, he might have regretted having the gift. The truth about this day was that President Nimer, while trying to assess Arena's ideas and the fierceness of his loyalty to these ideas, had played him for the fool. There wasn't to be a new conflict or a renewed demonstration of our superior military strength.

The president had something much bigger in his plans, a presidential lottery that would include four possible targets for an atomic bomb drop.

5

Major Overstreet's wife was deeply trained in Japanese traditions. She chose to be in her husband's shadow, like a branch that grows from the trunk of the tree which was her husband, Sherman.

Noriyo Overstreet, although well-educated at Sophia University in Tokyo with a degree in business, was, unlike some of her contemporaries, steeped in the culture of her ancestors, as well as loving of their ways. Her desire in life was to keep intact the traditional Japanese household.

She was up every morning at 6 a.m. in order to prepare the family breakfast at the kitchen table where they would gather each morning at seven. The major always sat at the head of the table in a chair that was slightly more ornate and a little higher than the others. Grandma Satoko, as she was called by her grandsons, Nobu and Aki, always sat at the other end, the boys on either side of her. Noriyo, while making sure that everyone had what they wanted, would periodically sit and grab a bite to eat. That was good, too, a way to keep her thirty-seven year old body trim and beautiful for the slightly younger Sherman.

Noriyo Overstreet scheduled each day as if it were a contest to beat time. After the children left for school and the major for work, she would see that Satoko, slightly crippled from the effects of the A-bomb, was settled into the Buddhist temple room adjacent to the kitchen where she would spend most mornings talking with the spirit of her first husband, as well as Noriyo's father, Yoshito, who had died of leukemia in 1976.

There were pictures of him on the wall, as well as certain kinds of sugar cookies Yoshito once liked, on a small offerings table. Noriyo would sometimes buy these from Miyajima Island to place beneath the picture of her father. Usually, after a week, Grandma would bring the cookies to dinner and place them gently on the table, beseeching the grandchildren to eat them because "your grandfather wants you to."

After Satoko was settled in, Noriyo would spend time cleaning the dirty dishes, rice steam pot and heating pans. After putting these away, she would tidy up the rest of the kitchen, sweep the counters with a wet rag, and make sure the garbage was neat.

She would then gather up each person's dirty laundry, run it through the washing machine and dryer before ironing and folding each piece. Then she would lay the clean clothes neatly in piles at the foot of each bed. Sherm received special consideration. Each pair of his jockey shorts was also folded into the same neat configuration as they had been in plastic sitting on shelves in the mall before being purchased. He loved this special sign of care and affection, kidding her about how his buddies could just "eat their hearts out."

Early afternoons always began by eating a light lunch with her mother at the kitchen table. They usually would talk about the children and Sherm, sometimes about Yoshito, stopping always for loving inquires about her health. The routine always included specific questions about her breathing, chest pains, legs and back. She had had a mild heart attack three years ago, and her back, hurt in the blast, was a constant source of concern for the family.

Satoko would take a long nap after lunch. During this time, Noriyo would lay out in her mind the food for the evening's meal, and then either read for a few hours or take an hour or so in the deep hot tub.

She loved reading, not just for its own sake, but in the traditions of being a knowledgeable, well-informed woman. It was important, too, for her to know what was going on in the world, as it allowed her a certain measure of comfort at cocktail parties. She knew with a kind of instinct how to chatter at these functions, yet that alone was not dignified enough for her. She never aspired to greatness at parties; she only wanted the kind of adequacy that drew forth respect. Books, magazines and a few dailies would provide the necessary material.

As much as she liked reading, it played second fiddle to the hot tub. In the ways of old Japanese, she would first take a warm shower before soaking in the tub for the better part of an hour. On the days that she would soak, she would go through a ritual of sorts, perhaps one that many women reaching her age did.

She would stand in front of the full-length mirror with her long white silk bath robe on. Then she would slowly untangle the silk belt and let it slip to the floor, looking at herself in the mirror, satisfied that she was still in the fullness of her beauty, yet sad because she knew it would not last.

Naturally, on the day of her luncheon with the president she cared for neither a hot tub nor a fantasy, such was her nervousness at the thought of meeting him. Except for once shaking his hand on a reception line, she had no more access to him than any ordinary citizen.

Sherm knew that she was nervous about the meeting, so when he left work for an early lunch, he hurried home, more as a sign of his support for her and his excitement for her rather than as an expression of undue concern.

As he expected, she was doing fine. He knew that she always had her feelings under control, that they never had her, never took over. Within that framework, whether natural or cultivated, she could feel and express her emotions without them ever taking her over or preventing her from acting or saying what she wanted.

"How do I look, Sherman," she asked. The blue business suit she decided to wear was perfect, he thought.

"You look as pretty and beautiful as the day we met."

The thing with Major Overstreet was that he meant it. He was in love with her and she knew it. He had nothing to prove at home, nothing to battle Noriyo about. In every little thing, he let her have her way, not because doing that kept the peace, but because it helped to make her happy.

He knew, too, that she didn't need him to be this way, that she could handle whatever attitudes he could throw at her. Without explanation, it was simply accepted by the both of them that this is the way it was. And she never took advantage. He liked to be this way towards her, and she received it as such. It was a simple, yet essential, way they had to express their love for each other. They both realized, too, that it was a neat way to avoid the pitfalls of many marriages. The little decisions that sometimes can be fraught with power struggles became thousands of links that added strength to their relationship.

↘

The president took it upon himself to find out what Noriyo Overstreet might like for lunch and was proud to let her know. It would be a sign to her how personable and caring he could be.

"I took the liberty to have your husband called yesterday to ask him what you eat for lunch. He told us a salad, consisting of romaine lettuce, cherry tomatoes, fresh sliced cucumber, and balsamic vinegar dressing. He said that he would keep the 'call from the White House' confidential so that you would be surprised today."

"Thank you, Mr. President," she almost whispered. She had decided in the limo that as soon as she was introduced to the president she would unobtrusively pinch herself, perhaps at the back of her leg, as a reminder that she *was* having breakfast with him, that she *was* where she was, and get on with the business at hand.

She pinched herself just as she sat down, then took a deep breath in a quiet way, ready to go as she would ever be.

Lunch was served on an intimate table that was covered with white linen embossed with the presidential seal. Smaller tables for setting the hot foods were placed strategically on either side of them. There was an ample salad for Noriyo, and enough rolls for an army. A cheese omelet awaited the president, who personally poured tea for them both. He had noticed over the years of public service that the common touch could turn everyday things into gold.

"I notice that you touched the table linen. It's quite fine, isn't it?" he said.

The observation, simple as it seemed, touched some primal modesty in her, as if a small private part of her had been invaded by an intimacy not wanted.

More from politeness than desire, she said yes, that was so.

"If you like, I'll have it cleaned when we're done and sent over to you and the major as a keepsake. Heck, you might even want to use it sometime."

"I'd like that, Mr. President," she replied, again, from deference only.

Somewhere in her studies, she had heard a lecture about the nature of human interactions, why they seemed to be attracted to or repulsed by others. Studies showed that a conclusion was reached within three seconds, perhaps dictated by the subliminal smells exuded.

She realized that her conclusion about Nimer took longer, about two and a half minutes longer. She did not like him.

"Mrs. Overstreet, I have heard through the grapevine that your mother was in Hiroshima at the time of the atomic bombing in 1945, and I wonder if I might ask you a few questions about that day?"

Before she had a chance to respond, he continued.

"I hope you don't find it intrusive of me. I get briefings about our weapons along these lines, but I learn best when I hear stories by people who were there. Stories like that are very real, packed with the flesh and blood of reality."

He only wanted to use these phrases to let her know how real it could make the results of the bomb to him, yet he did not realize the implications to a Japanese woman, a descendent of a *hibakusha*.

"I understand, Mr. President, and I would like to be helpful, but my mother has told me only a few things about the bombing. So, I will tell you what I know. First I must know if it's all right for me to continue eating while I talk?"

Nimer thought the question "very Japanese," as he would tell his wife later that night.

"Yes, of course."

"Mr. President, do you know what an *hibakusha* is?"

"Yes, I am told that it is someone who has survived the A-bombs that were dropped."

"That is so," she said, slipping into the terse syntax Japanese people sometimes used when speaking English.

"Like other *hibakusha*, my mother is quiet about what happened to her. In Japan, victims were shunned by other Japanese because they were afraid of what was inside them. They did not understand radiation or what it does to the body. My mother does not want to be a victim. She is a proud and dignified woman who lost her first husband, Jiro, that day. His body was probably vaporized."

"I'm sorry to hear that.

"I hope I don't seem insensitive, but I wonder if you could tell me something about what your mother has told you."

"Yes, I'll do my best, Mr. President. If I don't seem to be eating my meal, it is because I am not hungry. I hope you understand."

"I do, Mrs. Overstreet."

"I would, though, like to continue sipping my tea."

"Please."

"I will go on. My mother's name is Satoko. She has the face of one who has suffered much. Most of the sparkle left her eyes a long time ago. It is only when she is with my children that she seems to have any of the excitement and aliveness that is everyone's birthright."

Noriyo quickly realized that she was beginning to lecture, and she must remember not to do that.

"My mother told me that she was at the railroad station in Hiroshima City that day, waiting to buy a ticket that would take her back to her older brother who was in a secure place on Kyushu island to the south.

"The bomb exploded at 8:15 in the morning. My mother says that the flash was so great that it cannot be compared to lightning. There was an enormous sound like thunder rolling over the rooftops.

"Flying glass was everywhere. Money was found as far away as forty miles from the wind that blew. It was even reported that a tornado developed from the air being sucked out of the streets and the surrounding mountains. My mother tried to help others, but she couldn't do much, she said. So many people were walking around dazed. Many had the skin from their arms and necks hanging off them, red and raw, so it seemed like you could pull skin from hands like it was a glove. She said that the hair on many people was standing straight up and burning. She was riddled with flying glass and bleeding."

At this, Nimer began to squint, a look he had effected to perfection as a way of making a show of his concern.

Noriyo continued. "Some were vomiting black blood, and others began to jump into the Moto River to try to stop the heat that was in their bodies. She tried to pour water on the heads of people who were burning.

"Soon after the bomb exploded, a great fire swept over the city. Black clouds and smoke were everywhere. Black raindrops began to fall on the city, and no one knew what they were. It was found out later that they were radioactive raindrops, called 'black rain.'"

She noticed that the president stopped eating his food.

"Would you like me to go on?"

"Yes, I would, if that is all right with you."

"I will go on. My mother knew that she would not be able to get out of the city to find her brother. She then tried to find a friend she knew in the city. It took her eight hours to find her friend, who had a child strapped to her back. But the child was dead. A wounded child was also clinging to her legs. My mother said that she did not know what to do, so she took the wounded child and began to walk towards the mountains.

"On the way she helped to dig a young woman out from under the debris of a banana stand where she had stopped to buy some. She could not walk. She told my mother that she remembered feeling the air spreading, then a great bang of fire and wind, she said, like lightning across the city. Just before she went unconscious, she saw a young girl on a bicycle evaporate. Simply disappear."

Noriyo began to sob. President Nimer picked up the phone and asked his secretary to come in, saying that Mrs. Overstreet was "indisposed."

Mrs. Joslin came in immediately, with several tissues and a back-up box of them. She gave a few to Noriyo, and placed a hand on her shoulder in the warm and understanding ways she had learned from years of experience.

"I am so sorry, Mr. President. I usually do not cry when I think of these things. But today, here. . . ."

"Think nothing of it. I understand. And if you'd like to stop, yes, please."

"No, I'm ready to tell you the rest."

Mrs. Joslin knew the cues and began to leave, but not before Noriyo said, "Thank you . . . please, what is your name?"

"Mrs. Joslin."

"Thank you, Mrs. Joslin, for your help."

Picking up on the sincerity of the moment, she replied, "You're very welcome," wanting to add, "My dear." But, she knew her place and left the room.

"I will go on. My mother helped to carry her to an elementary school. Every corridor was filled with people burned, many without arms or legs. In some cases, she remembers blood squirting out of broken arteries. One man was sitting on the floor, moving his head up and down without ceasing, and mumbling something about his daughter Yukiko.

"My mother learned that after the blast this man had gone to the streets to look for his daughter. He found her, totally dismembered, a torso breathing. He went to find a cart so he could take her out of that place. While he was looking for one, the authorities placed her on a pyre, one of many used that day to prevent disease. When he returned, he knelt down where she had been and said, 'I am sorry I was so late.'"

The president listened carefully, hunched over in his seat so he could hear every word that an increasingly somber Noriyo was saying. He seemed to be genuinely moved by her account.

"My mother continued her journey to the mountains. That night she could see the city below, still burning brightly against the black night.

"She suffered many cuts and her hair fell out, her gums bled. She has suffered from a relatively high white cell blood count. She bears no ill-will towards America."

"She must be a great lady," the president said.

"Yes."

Mrs. Overstreet felt drained. As was Nimer, whose purpose was now satisfied.

"Thank you for coming. I'll have one of my men take you home, or to wherever you'd like. And as soon as I have the table cloth cleaned, I'll have it sent to your home."

When she left the office, the president called his secretary to tell her that he wanted to be alone for at least fifteen minutes.

6

Major Overstreet left his office as soon as he could. He and Noriyo had agreed never, except for emergencies, to call each other when he was on the job. It had always bothered him when he overheard colleagues talking with their wives or sweethearts on the phone. He was old-fashioned, and his work ethic would not allow it.

He stopped off on the way home to get a dozen red roses for her as a way to let her know how proud he was that she had lunch with the president of the United States. How many other majors could say that about their wives?

As soon as he was home and entered the hallway, he yelled, "Is this where the woman who met the president today lives? Is this where the lady who lunched with the leader of the free world lives?"

With that, trying to reciprocate his playfulness, she came into the hallway and said, in the flirtatious and drawling ways of a Mae West, "Here I am, big guy. Why don't you come up and see me sometime."

So close were they in tune with each other that Sherm could tell when he hugged her that something was wrong.

"How did it go?" he asked.

"I cried, Sherm. I cried."

"That's okay, babe," he said, almost reflexively. He knew that she liked it when he called her babe.

"I had lunch with the president. I told him my mother's story about Hiroshima. He listened. Carefully, I think. And he is giving us the table linen, one that has the Seal of the United States on it."

They walked towards the kitchen so she could prepare a vase for the roses. While doing that, she said, "Sherman, I know it was a great day, yet I feel confused a bit. I don't know why he would invite someone like me when he could pick up the phone and have someone come over yesterday to tell him whatever he wants to know about Hiroshima and the A-bomb."

"I don't know either. But he did. And that's what counts," Sherm responded in a practical sort of military way.

"Please, Sherman, don't ever tell any of your buddies what I'm going to say, but I don't like him. There's something about him. Maybe it's the way he said to me, 'I noticed the way you touched the linen,' or something like that. I think it's kind of sordid to notice how anyone touches something."

She was quick to add, "Of course I don't mean you. I know how you've told me that you like it when I touch you on the face with my hand, how warm that makes you feel. I didn't mean you. You know that, don't you?

"Yes, my sweetest heart, I know that."

As she finished holding her finger under the tap water to measure a good temperature for her roses, she let enough water in the vase, opened the green tissue that covered the flowers, and parsed them out on the table before placing them just right into the ornate white crystal vase she had bought in Belgium years ago.

⌒

"I don't know why he wants to see you. Something about the conversation he had with your wife. He wants you to call for an appointment. My secretary has his secretary's number. I'll tell her to give it to you," Arena said. As an after thought, he said, "Just do it."

With this thinnest of a connection to the meeting, Major Overstreet arrived at a side office of the White House to meet with Nimer.

"Glad to see you, son," said the president, putting out his hand to meet the major's.

"It's my pleasure to meet you, sir, I mean, Mr. President."

"It's all right, Major. Sir or Mr. President will do," he replied, adding with a smirk he thought would lighten things up. "You can call me what you like, just make sure you call me."

Overstreet tried hard to laugh, but he wasn't built for pretension. You got from him what he was, nothing more, nothing less.

"I asked you to come over here so I could talk with you about the meeting I had with your wife last week.

"You know, some men are lucky. Through no fault of their own, they luck out in marriage." He stopped for a moment, realizing that he had just committed a faux pas that he now hoped Overstreet would take as another joke. Nimer realized more now than ever that he would sometimes get stuck in the rhythm of the words he chose, especially at the beginning of sentences. When, for example, he would start, as he just had, with the words "through no fault of their own," what he meant to say was the opposite, yet he was not spontaneous enough to think of what the opposite might be. As an intellectual fault, it was easy enough to do, yet he resented the way some of the media made fun of this. Whatever *could* be the opposite of "through no fault of their own"? Very few would know, he thought. Yet, it never occurred to him to allow his discourse to become flexible with the oil of openness. He could, like others, simply back up by acknowledging a false start before saying what he really meant. But it was hard for him to pull his foot out of his mouth.

He continued. "You and I are lucky. We have wives who are pretty, know how to talk and when to listen. We're mighty lucky to have them on our arms."

"Yes, sir, Mr. President."

At this, Nimer knew he would have to loosen up Overstreet if he was to get what he needed—help with the lottery. A frontal pitch was not going to work. It would take a little time to get the major's confidence.

"Major, I'm a little thirsty. I've just learned a little about the great taste of licorice tea, and I wonder if you'd enjoy a cup with me?"

"I would, Mr. President."

"And how about a little pastry? I always enjoy those ones with the soft cheese in the middle. How about you?"

"I do like those, Mr. President."

"Two cheese pastries coming up.

"And, by the way, Major, why don't you just go with your military training and use 'sir.' I'm kind of tired for a while of being called 'Mr. President.' It's a little imposing and doesn't let a feller relax."

"Yes, sir, I'll do that."

The licorice tea and cakes arrived and they began to eat and sip.

"Major, your wife gave me the most stirring account of the bombing of Hiroshima that I have ever heard. The descriptions of her mother's experiences were so vivid that I nearly cried when she was telling me about them.

He paused the "pause for effect" pause.

"The whole thing came to life for me. I've heard so many military briefings on atomic weaponry that I'm nearly exhausted with them. They don't ever really tell you about the human face of suffering that goes on, how your mother-in-law suffered and how your lovely wife suffers when she thinks about it. I could see it in her eyes as she spoke." The major was beginning to relax.

"Yes, sir, she does hurt when she talks about it." He was finally getting away from the tendency that military underlings have of responding in their quasi bi-polar ways. He was beginning to express what lay between yes and no.

"Son, I hope that I'm not being too pushy, and, if I am just say so and I'll back off. But, how does it make you feel when you see her sad about the killing of so many people so long ago?"

"Well, sir, it makes me feel bad. Sort of confused." Suddenly, he thought he had gone far enough.

"What do you mean confused?"

"Well," he started in his habit. He didn't really plan to use the word so much as he did, yet he found that when he did a new mood was created with his listener. The word seemed to give pause, to bring two people closer together, as if the user were going to speak with sincerity or authenticity. He noticed that when someone in a room cried while they spoke that others would listen intently, as if they were in the presence of the most real part of the one crying, that there could be no deception in crying, that it could not be an act. This is what he thought. He noticed, too, that whenever he started a reply, especially one in response to a question, with the word "Well," people listened more intently, as if it were some kind of signal word that he was now under a self-imposed oath to tell the truth.

"Well," he continued, "I am a member of the U.S. military and it was us who dropped the bomb on Hiroshima. I am loyal to my country, but I know that my country dropped the bomb that was responsible for the deaths of many people, including Noriyo's mother's first husband."

"I appreciate how you feel. I sometimes feel the same way. The only thing that gets me through sometimes is that I know I'm commander in chief, and, as such, must make decisions that sometimes will bring grief to others.

"The fact is that the bomb killed 100,000 people in one day. I know, some say 80,000, but what's the difference. A lot of people died that day, probably family friends, too. And it brought much suffering to her mother, what's her name?"

"We call her Grandma Satoko."

"She must have suffered terribly," the president responded.

"Noriyo tells me that she did. I get upset whenever I think about it."

Nimer sensed he might have an opening, and pounced on it.

"It's just another example of what has been going on since the history of man. Men killing other men. Raping, maiming, brutalizing. It's another example of how sometimes a country with good and honorable intentions, such as this great country of ours, is forced to take an action they don't want to, but must in order for the greater good.

"I'm sure that Truman did not want to inflict all that suffering, but he had to. I'm told that when his aides asked him if a third bomb was ready after Hiroshima and Nagasaki he said there would be no more A-bombs dropped. That he was, and I think I have his exact words here, 'tired of little children being killed.' Now, there was a humanitarian if I ever saw one."

He had warmed up the major.

"Sir, if you don't mind my saying it, I'm tired, too, of all the killing. I'm tired that Grandma Satoko is weary and hurt. I'm tired that my fellow soldiers are being killed almost every day in Iran. I'm tired of Israelis killing Palestinians, and Palestinians killing Israelis. I'm...."

He stopped, thinking he had gone too far. Here he was, a lowly major, telling the president what he thought about things.

"It's okay, son. Please go on."

This was encouragement enough. Perhaps it was the tea and cakes, maybe the president's politeness and considerations, his care and concern for Noriyo's feelings. Whatever, it was enough to draw the major's confidence.

"Mr. President, some days I wake up and I want to vomit when I look at the news, or get to work and see reports coming in about how things went during the night. It's hardly ever good news. It seems like in every nook and corner of the world, someone is killing somebody.

"It's getting more cruel by the day, more personal." He paused, deep in his own thoughts.

"I couldn't believe it the day I saw the photos of the dead Americans in Iraq being beaten by people with shoes. Their bodies were incinerated, and the people were so crazy that they still beat the burned bodies. And hanging them on bridges. Sir, did you see the pictures?"

Overstreet realized that the president must have seen the pictures and been told what happened, perhaps even awakened that night. Yet he was so worked up about the murders, so revolted by what had been done to the dead bodies, that he didn't care. The shock and horror he felt leveled the playing field between him and Nimer.

"To take burned and incinerated bodies, stringing them up like so many dead cattle, like strings of meat. There's no honor there, no respect. I even read that they pulled apart pieces of the burned flesh. We do that to barbecued chickens, and they did it to people."

He said, "I just don't get it," in a way that sounded like an abrupt end of a crescendo.

"Well, I get it, son. Let's face it, there's lots of cruel and uncaring people populating this earth, and they don't seem to care about anybody but themselves and their own cause. And when we get in their face, they don't want to talk, at least talk in good faith. You know, the kind of talk that men do, like we're doing here today."

The young major was listening intently, happy to have had his say, and feeling a bit inflated that he was here speaking to and being spoken to by the president.

Nimer knew he was sucking him in. It was time to see if he could be recruited.

"Young man, I want to take a minute here to talk with you about something very important to this country.

"But first I want to say this. There are times when a president, because of national security purposes, wants to tell someone something, yet he needs to do that in the strictest confidence. So that what he says cannot be told to anyone, not even a wife, or if it's the case, a lover. Not even their boss. That it's strictly between the two parties, one being the president.

"I want to know if you understand that. And, secondly, if you're willing to abide by it, more than just man to man, but, let's say, man to country." Whether from inexperience, naivety, or being in the throes of flattery, he answered that he understood and was willing.

"Excellent," the president said, pleased with winning over this young man who would be instrumental to his plans.

"Major Overstreet, what would you say if I told you that as president of the United States I have a plan that could end all killings, perhaps forever. A plan so clever, powerful and efficacious that it will put an end to wars and to the horrors you are speaking about?" He loved the word "efficacious," too, as it seemed to express so much of his own character, which was about getting things done. He liked it when plans were "efficacious."

"Before you answer, let me say a bit more. Your role in this plan would be an important one, a very important one, one that could some day make you as famous as Albert Einstein, or Mother Teresa. More famous than Neil Armstrong. And it will, too, make you a hero in the strictest sense of the word."

In a sort of breathless way, the major was taking it in. For a moment, he thought that this was a joke, that Noriyo and the kids would come barging through the door yelling "surprise, surprise." He knew, though, that presidents didn't use their time for surprise parties. Moreover, he couldn't think of anything anyone might want to surprise him with. His 32nd birthday was three months away.

"Do you know what a hero is?" the president asked, almost disdainful of the major's intelligence. It was the old-time teacher's way.

"It's not someone that little children look up to. It's someone that we, as mature people, find so extraordinary in their deeds that we are filled with a sort of exceptional awe at what they have done. Firefighters and policemen, for example. And the men and women who get the Medal of Honor. These people put their lives in danger for strangers and comrades. I think the Bible says that no man has any greater love than this.

"Some people need heroes because their lives are drab. Sometimes we create heroes for them, like we did with that little Jessica Lynch girl a few years ago. Athletes can be heroes, too, and that's a good thing. Keeps people occupied and not thinking too much.

"Yet, as much as we admire these people, they really don't get to what I'll call 'the nerve center' of our desire to be inspired in those places that call forth our best and sometimes demand the highest price, such as sacrifice and courage."

Nimer had these words memorized, and continued to use them periodically.

Continuing, he said to Major Overstreet, "It's not really the guys who play guitars or hit a ball or sing and act that we most admire. It's the guy who inspires our most noble instincts, like life, liberty and the pursuit of happiness, things we can not have if people keep on killing each other."

He took a breath before saying, "Do you want to know who my favorite hero is?"

"Yes, sir, I do."

"It's a guy called Arland Williams, Jr., a passenger on the plane that went down right here in the Potomac. I think it was in the winter of 1992. He was trapped in the river, caught in some of the plane wreckage floating in the ice. He gave his life vest to another person, and two times handed the lifeline given to him from a helicopter to another person before he drowned. He gave up his hopes and dreams, his loves and life's possibilities for others."

He seemed a bit touched by his own words.

"Now, that's a hero," he said.

"Really, Mr. President. A real hero."

"Now, I'm not saying that you'd have to give up your dreams, or your family, nothing like that. But, if you are willing, one hundred and ten percent to be in on this plan, you can be a hero greater in history than any of these others.

"When the others are forgotten, the people will remember Major Sherman Overstreet."

Flushed with a sense of his importance, he said "Mr. President, you can count on me. But, I would like to know some of the details about how I'd fit into all of this. Your plan, that is."

"For now, you must simply stay with your commitment to the plan, that you said yes to me, and when the time comes for you to be involved ... that might be soon, I will be in touch. But probably not directly from this point on.

"When it's time, you will know. Someone with the name 'Back Seat' will call from time to time to set up meetings. Whenever he calls, just say ... What is your middle name?"

"Justin, sir."

"Do you ever use it?"

"No, sir."

"Good. Then just say, 'This is Major Justin Overstreet speaking,' and he will know it's you."

"Mr. President, I don't know what to say. I'm overwhelmed by the information you have given me, and I can only say, well, yes, sir, you can count on me."

"Thank you, son. You won't regret the decision you have made here today. If you'll just tell me who will be calling you, you may leave."

"That would be 'Back Seat,' sir."

"Thank you, major. Remember, you are to tell no one about this."

Overstreet saluted, and left, with the weight of mountains on his shoulders. He felt as if he were in a dream. How could a major in the army, a father of two boys growing up, and husband of a woman who was all the world to him, be in this spot? He began to think the thoughts of someone suddenly overwhelmed by circumstances. Yet, it was greater than that. Was he really here, leaving the president's office? Could this be some kind of joke?

He was grounded enough to know that he *was*, indeed, leaving the president's office, and that he had heard what he had heard. Yet, what he heard left him numb.

Oh, sure, there were times in his life when what he thought the impossible suddenly became the possible. When he asked Noriyo if she would marry him, and she said yes; when he and his teammates thought the state basketball championship was only a dream, and they won it; when he was accepted into West Point. And he remembered the day when he prayed so hard for his ailing father, who was weak and rapidly losing weight to cancer, thinking that he would soon be dead. And then he recovered and lived for ten more years. It seemed more a miracle than a natural recovery.

So, he was familiar with dreams fulfilled and with the impossible. But this! This was different, and how could he ever withhold the information from his beloved Noriyo?

They had long ago made an agreement, more like a vow with moral implications that were never to be violated. What they wanted most in their relationship was to be intimate. They were smart enough to know from the beginning that the intimacy of their sexual life had limits, that flesh to flesh would probably grow less compelling as the years went on, and that something else would be needed to sustain them.

"You are my soul mate," he said to her one particular day after they had sex more tender than lusty. "And you mine," she whispered back.

Part of being a soul mate, they agreed, was to share everything with each other. There were to be no secrets. At least no secrets from the time they met each other. It was hard for them to draw the line at things, especially sexual, that might have transpired before they met each other. But, after sharing early on in their dating a few of their escapades from the past, they both realized that they didn't want to hear any more, he out of a gnawing jealousy he felt creeping into the exchange, and she from her sense of modesty.

Part of the agreement to be soul mates included even the secrets others, perhaps friends, told them. It was difficult, at first, when someone, after telling a secret, might enjoin them not to tell anyone, "not even Sherm," or "not even Noriyo." Eventually, though, they decided that the pact included everything. That there would be no secrets at all. It would be a part of working things through.

Instantly, a dilemma arose in the major's mind. Was his loyalty more to Noriyo or to the president? Although he and Noriyo had their covenant, he had made a pledge of loyalty to the army and to his country. Now he was, perhaps, at the center of a plan that could involve national security.

Besides, he thought, if he told Noriyo, it might endanger her. No, he immediately thought. He probably was over-interpreting what the president had told him; he probably would be just a minor cog in the big machinery of the plan. Just like always. Yet, some intuition told him that this was different. If he were only a minor part of a plan, the surely president would not have told him so many details.

For now, he decided to handle the dilemma by not saying anything to Noriyo. It would be a break in their agreement, yet these words came to him, a bit over-dramatic, like a character in a John Wayne movie: "sometimes a man's gotta do what a man's gotta do." Though silly, they summed up his predicament.

⌄

Sometimes a man really does have to do what he has to do, if only from habit. President Nimer, from the earliest days of his adolescence, had a habit, before going to bed, to review the day's events, what happened, where he had done well, where he had been less than the complete success that was always his goal. There was a mechanism in his spirit that would not allow it to rest, to be secure, unless he did his tasks perfectly. Not as perfectly as possible, but perfectly.

The last few weeks had been more important for him than any in his presidency so far. Even more important than the way he had handled the many crises that had plagued his term so far. This day was especially important. He could not, dare not, share what he was up to, his "plan," with anyone, not even Priscilla. He had to hold on to his conception until the last possible moment.

But that was okay with him, as he didn't need to share with anyone the way Sherman Overstreet needed to share with his wife. Nimer was a loner.

The advantage he had, though, was that he *knew* he was a loner, and he was good with himself that way. He knew that he got his energy from quiet pursuits like watching TV, or taking care of whatever land he might own, small at first, then larger as his wealth began to grow. The textile business had been good to him. The political business even better.

He liked to sit in the small White House theater and watch movies by himself, though his aides were under strict directives not to reveal the names of movies he watched. Nimer thought that his private life was no one's business. Besides, he didn't want anyone to use the prestige of his name to support commercial efforts.

Though he loved Priscilla, he slept in a bedroom by himself. Sometimes, he would get to bed late after a state function, or have late night meetings, though everyone knew they were off limits except in the case of an emergency.

He sometimes liked to read a few briefing reports in bed before going to sleep. That kind of self-image was very much in the way he liked to see himself as president, working 'til he dropped. If he dropped, he figured, it might as well be in bed.

It was thoughtful of him to use a separate bedroom, as in this way his habits wouldn't keep Priscilla awake. Whenever he needed a sexual liaison with her, he would let her know beforehand and politely ask if such and such time was good for her, knowing that she would always say yes.

Usually, he would choose around ten o'clock in the evening, the time it was his custom to retire. On these nights he would always cancel appointments or meetings, except emergencies, that were scheduled after 9 o'clock. After a while, the quips would go around the next day on private cell phones about Nimer's getting laid the night before, and little boys' jokes about how hard he was going to be on them that day, or if he would come at them more than usual. In the halls of preoccupation, a joke was a joke.

On this particular night, he went over "the plan" in his mind. He had made some good overtures to Arena, and had probably won Overstreet over. Meanwhile, he had Jarvis and Arena chasing a wild goose about the next small war and how to wage it, high tech streamlined or with overpowering brute force. He was pulling out of Iraq, and had Iran on a string.

So far, so good. But, he needed at least two more men on the inside, reliable people who had access to strategic communications in the capital as well as at the Greenbrier, West Virginia, the underground site where the government would be moved in case of an imminent attack. His best bet, he figured, was Overstreet.

Sometimes, the "largeness" of what he was up to came home fully to him. It came in contrasts, and usually at night after the hubbub of the day's events was over. How most people led quiet lives, going about their business of the day. There was a kind of little routine about most people. Going to and from work, being with their families in unspectacular ways, mostly just being around each other, hardly ever really *with* each other. Without ever having enough awareness about the matter, Nimer knew that he was never really *with* others. There was a certain emptiness in him, some central part of him that couldn't really connect with others.

Once, when he was about thirteen, another boy, bigger and tougher, pushed him down in front of his friends at school because he didn't like that Nimer had referred to the bully's baseball glove as "a trapper's mitt." He remembers looking up, resting on his elbows and doing nothing. The incident simmered in him like a hot coal sitting in a mound of straw. Until one day the bully tried it again, this time across the street from the first incident nearly two months before.

The results were different. Nimer's rage showed up as an incredible strength he didn't know he had. After grappling for a few minutes, he got the heavier boy's head and shoulders under his own legs and knees, and proceeded to grab his sweatshirt collar with one hand, pick up the boy's head by the neck, and raise his own right hand to pound the bully's head into the pavement. In his mind, he saw the boy's nose crushed and bleeding. He pounded the face and nose over and over in his mind until what had been a face was now a nosed crushed flat and spilling itself, its blood and bone, from cheek to cheek. But, again, only in his mind.

He couldn't bear the idea of doing this to another person, so he let go of the boy's collar, got up and ran, and ran, and ran until he was exhausted and could not run any farther. At this point, he hustled into the stairwell of an apartment building, sat on the stairs, crying heaving sobs of confusion, perhaps even despair. When he stopped crying, he vowed that no one would ever again gain access to him without his permission. He drew an imaginary box around his heart. This would be the wall to protect him. Priscilla, and she only for brief moments, was the only one he ever allowed in.

Nimer was aware that the incident might have had an effect on him. Yet he knew that one incident alone does not a loner make. Troubled when younger by the feelings of being cut off from others, he went to a counselor for a brief spell, but tired of the sessions, whether because of fatigue with the work of self-discovery or the plain busyness of his life, who could tell.

He always knew, though, that he did not want to lead the small and quiet life of most people. Yet, he did not grasp the essentials of the opposite lifestyle, the one he saw close up mainly in the business men and later the politicians and diplomats around him, as well in as the storied statesmen who went before him. Men like Ronald Reagan, even the later Richard Nixon. Men like Henry Kissinger, whom he saw as a latter day Albert Schweitzer, who preached respect for life, all life, except for the mosquito that was about to bite you. Then you had every right as a superior life form to crush it.

He saw these men as wise and honored. Sometimes reluctantly, but honored nevertheless. They had been through real and symbolic wars. They had made significant contributions to the world, had the wisdom of the elders, but now could reap the rewards of their struggles and experiences.

He was always impressed, even staggered, by men who lived their lives large. He had heard the stories before about how some presidents used the power of their office to advantage. How Kennedy would at state dinners slide his hand under the dresses of women bending over him to introduce themselves; how he would leave cabinet meetings to go into the next room for a "quickie" with a young secretary, buckling his belt as he came back so the boys would know what a stud he was. How LBJ would come into a young secretary's room in the middle of the night, looking for sexual favors, reminding her that "This is your president speaking." How they declared wars that would send hundreds of thousands, even millions, to their deaths.

The bills they signed that could make some rich and others poor. The leverage of their words. All of this dazzling. Even the way some of them died was larger than life. Shot in the back of the head from long range. Shot in the eye from medium range. Shot in the temple from close range. That these men were powerful enough to attract sick little men who wanted to live large was in itself beguiling. There was a magnificence in them that transcended the desperate lives of most people. He could not, though, make sense of his response to greatness.

He only grasped that every now and then someone would come along who had the chutzpah to break the boundaries of normal realities. He was about to crush those boundaries like no man before. Even the simple ways he was going about it by enlisting unwitting accomplices and using silly code names like "Back Seat" were so small in their magnificence as to attract little attention.

When Richard asked if there was anything more he needed before retiring, he realized that all he needed was a little luck to complete his plan, and the world would soon know that he, President Fletcher Nimer, had the biggest gunny-bags of them all.

7

In the several weeks after Nimer set the stage for springing his plan into action, the world had been behaving normally. The death toll of U.S. soldiers in Iran went over 100 with two bombings in Tehran. The Pakistani army, in a move to mollify the U.S., continued to hunt down and kill insurgents who were regularly crossing the border between itself and Afghanistan. Bombings of government buildings in Western Europe continued. More than ever, Taliban in the north of Afghanistan were being hunted down and killed, a reminder from Nimer's government that it had not forgotten this, the first of his wars. Sporadic killings were taking place in places like Uzbekistan where Wahhabi Islamists were striving to take power. And the Saudis continued to crack down on al Qaeda terrorists on the Arabian peninsula.

There were, though, bigger things on Nimer's mind. He was so fired up about the possibilities for ending killing forever that he was paying little attention to these events, sleep-walking through briefings, even those about the dance of payback killings between Israel and the Palestinians.

Those around him, including Priscilla, were noticing that he seemed preoccupied. Most often, though, they responded to their observations by lame inquiries, or by being overly sincere.

One night, after an attempt to have sex with Priscilla ended in frustration, she asked if he was okay. He said yes, that he had tried to enjoy himself, yet felt preoccupied with his responsibilities. He said that he was sorry he had failed her.

"It's good to see you, General Arena. I appreciate your bringing your report to me personally."

"Thank you, Mr. President. I think it best to tell you at the outset that Secretary of Defense Jarvis and I have reached an agreement about troop buildup and technology and how we can best complete an honorable and total exit from Iraq. The Secretary has authorized me to speak on his behalf today, although you certainly might want to speak with him. I understand he will report to you himself as soon as it is possible.

"He and I have also agreed that his report to you about other targets for a military action is his alone, and that we have done our, shall we say, 'homework,' independently."

"I understand, General. Now, please give me the first part of your, and the Secretary's, thinking about how best to compromise on your differences, and how to best to withdraw from Iraq without looking like we're backing off our commitment to bring democracy to that nation."

"About the first issue," Arena responded, " instead of increasing our readiness forces in the world by the 20,000 that I would like, we have decided to recommend to you an increase of 10,000. These 10,000, again this is our recommendation, would go into the field only after they have been equipped as a model force of the 21st century army."

"Tell me more, General."

"They will be quick-strike mobile units, with field vehicles equipped with laser signals on every side, including the back, that will project a signal up to 40 yards that will explode roadside bombs."

"Wonderful, General."

"There's more, Mr. President. The vehicles will be made of a composition stronger and more durable than any metal we're ever used before on vehicles, and without compromising their speed. Even the sight windows will be made of a new kind of organic compound that the polymerization process renders almost indestructible and able to resist launched grenade attacks.

"With these vehicles, we could get from point A to point B, for example, to interdict a possible attack on a localized area, with speed and safety."

"That's wonderful work, General Arena. The technology is coming along, the men are safer, we are streamlined. Norman Jarvis is satisfied?"

"Yes, sir."

"And you?"

"Yes, sir, I am."

"Now tell me how in hell we're going to get out of there without losing face."

"Mr. President, if I may back up a minute. I forgot to tell you that Defense will initiate, upon your approval, the contract bidding on these features. Preliminary estimates are that the work of development is already underway and can be completed in six months."

"I'm very pleased, General," Nimer replied, without enthusiasm. His plan for world peace through the A-bomb was far greater, far larger than the details of force and protection being enunciated for him by Arena.

"About getting out of there, Mr. President. I know that you have been reluctant for us to show force in such a manner that might result in the deaths of any more of our soldiers or Iraqi civilians.

"Therefore, the secretary of defense and I are urging you to undertake a UW, as we like to call it—an unconventional war, like the ones we have done in Guatemala and Honduras, or Nicaragua, southern Africa, even Indonesia.

"What we have in mind is a covert operation of massive proportions whereby we will train former Iraqi soldiers, some of them who used to be the bad guys, in the ways to eliminate anyone who gets in the way of what we are trying to do there, that is, bring democracy to the people.

"Our plan is to train them at a secret complex, modeled on the ones we've run in the south in the States, to do our work. We could get some of the boys from the Special Forces who operated in Vietnam. I'm sure they'd love to get back into the action, and they're not too old to do the supervising."

Nimer was intrigued by the foresight and details of the planning.

"This is good work, General."

"Yes, sir, I'm glad you like it. We can put it into effect pretty quickly if you give us the go signal. Soon enough, they'll all have to watch their asses, Sunnis, Shi'ites, Kurds, all of them.

"Another advantage to increasing our technology-enhanced force in the world is that we can, at the same time as we are preparing the UW in Iraq, release all the forces no longer needed there into Iran, if and when you say. At the same time, we will remain prepared for other eventualities."

He was on such a roll of enthusiasm that Nimer thought it was time to reveal his plan for world peace, the one he had been considering for over a year. It would be risky to share it, especially the details, now, but it probably was as good a time as ever.

Remembering that great men lived large, he took a deep breath before saying, "General Arena," feeling the bond that at this moment he felt pulling him to the core of Arena's enthusiasm, "I want to interrupt you for a minute to let you know, to tell you something that has been on my mind for a while now."

8

"Before I go any further, General, I want to let you know how much I admire the way you go about your business. When we needed you to plan the invasion of Iraq, you did it with precision and flair. Your plan was exceptional, and if it wasn't for those damned Turks, you'd of done it sooner, probably by a week or so. And the way you siphoned off combat units from Iraq to get us the necessary foothold in Tehran was an extraordinary piece of logistics.

"Every time we've given you an order, even though you might have disagreed with it, you spoke your mind, waited for an answer and then did what you were told. We never had to worry about you being a McArthur. You're a good military man who knows his mind, speaks his peace and gets on with it."

"Thank you, sir," he responded flatly, more interested in hearing what was on Nimer's mind.

"I've noticed, too," the president said, "that the things that are important to me are the same things that seem important to you."

If it wasn't that the president was speaking to him, Arena would have more than likely stopped this kind of conversation dead in its tracks. He was a man who lived to accomplish goals by executing plans, not a man who lived to be flattered or analyzed.

"I know that the weekly mortality reports on your men must have grieved you as much as me. But you never whined about this. You know why?" he asked rhetorically.

"I think you do, General. Yes, I think you do. Because you know that the preservation of these United States of ours is far more important than the life of any man. Even the lives of many men. Hell, without the country, what's the point? I think you know that it's our collective existence that's important, and not this man or that.

"I like that thinking in a man. I like, too, that you just served up a report to me that's filled with technological advancements. It shows that you know what real progress is about. Without these kinds of advancements, there'd be no progress. And I know, too, that our great science and industry will turn these military advancements into capital gain for the civilian population.

Arena was growing weary with what he felt was gratuitous flattery.

"There are so many people out there in so many places who would like to see us destroyed. Because we're smarter and more powerful. We know how to do things, and I think they are jealous. We know how to make money to buy the things we need, like good refrigerators and cars, washing machines...."

He stopped because he thought of a story.

"Once when I was in China a long time ago with a group of other young men and women interested in silk, I noticed that the people would gather on neighborhood street corners in the evening to watch TV. You could see a long extension cord going into a building for electricity. At one of the meetings, I asked how many Chinese families had washing machines and dryers. Some had old-fashioned machines with two rubber cylinders they'd run the clothes though by hand to dry them out. That was their dryer. Some families had small refrigerators, I was told, like the ones our children use in college dorms. But for the whole family.

"There's a lot of bikes there, too. You'd risk your life crossing a street. It was a terrible feeling to try to cross and get stuck in the middle of thousands and thousands of bicycles, each one ringing that little bell on the handlebars. It sounded like the circus coming to town about to run you down."

Nimer suddenly came out of his story and back into the room.

"What I'm saying is not new to you. You know there's lots of folks out there who would want to kill us. And we're mighty happy to have you on our side, General.

"Both you and I know, too, that if we're ever going to survive that we've got to get out front of it all. We've got to pre-empt them, hit them before they hit us. The world has become a kill or be killed kind of place and if we're going to survive we've got to kill them first.

"I read somewhere, General, that sheep in nature sit together in rows. They sit side by side with some of nature's magnetic lines, like they're being drawn together by them.

"Well, we've got to get them all together on the lines before they get us, and blow them all to kingdom come. You know these bleeding hearts animal lovers wouldn't like to hear this comparison, but it's true. We're in command here, and when the bad guys get in the way, we have no choice but to destroy them. And I think God would want us to. God's for the good," he explained, adding, "and not for the bad."

"I think I've said about enough of this for now, General. I just wanted to let you know how together I am with you on most matters."

"I think so, sir," Arena said.

The echoes of what had just been said filled the room before Nimer picked up where he had left off.

"General Arena, I want to tell you something. For a long time now I've been thinking about all the evil we see in the world, the killings. For centuries upon centuries. And it just goes on. Yes, we talk a good game about peace, but we never really *do* anything conclusive about it. I've gotten in the dumps even about this Iraq thing. In fact, it's the way things have been going lately that really got me thinking about how we can establish peace in the world."

For the first time, the president was about to reveal his plan to another. To get the maximum drama out of what he was about to say, he stepped to the window in the Oval Office and looked out at the lawn with his hands behind his back. Once he felt that he looked contemplative enough, he turned to Arena, and said, "It's not going to be with small wars like Iraq or even Iran. I'm in a little despair, especially about Iraq. As soon as we leave, even with your UW plan, there'll probably be a civil war. And then, who knows? Maybe a little democracy will come in and stick. I'll feel good about that, even if it saves a few lives, and allows a few more people to get to where they want. You know how they say every little bit helps.

"But, General, I'm tired of it all. I'm tired of the compromises, I'm tired of giving *this* to get *that*. I'm just flat-out tired of all the killing decade after decade, century after century. And no one does anything about it. Not really."

Arena was listening carefully to the president, who was on a roll.

"Well, I'm ready to do something about it," he said, forgetting to pause for effect. "And I need your cooperation to do it.

"I have a plan. Something I want to do that will make the world sit up and take note that someone for once is going to put an end to the killing."

Now the pause.

"Would you like to hear it? Before you answer, I want to know also if you would like to be a part of it. If you say yes, you'll be a most important person, the most important cog in the machine."

"Sir, it would be my greatest honor to be a part of bringing peace to the world," the general responded, as if his great patriotic chord had just been touched.

"Okay, then here it is . . . In 1945 we dropped a small atomic bomb on Hiroshima and then one on Nagasaki. It is my belief that if we didn't drop those bombs and have the knowledge of the destruction they did, that the world today probably would be a wasteland. As you know, these bombs were small compared to the weapons we and our enemies developed later. If one of these later type bombs had ever been dropped, especially, let's say, on the Soviets, it probably would have resulted in a retaliation. We would then drop other, bigger ones, probably lots of them. And them back at us. We had more of them, and better delivery systems, so, in the end, we most likely would have been the winners.

"But most of the world as we know it would have been a wasteland. We might have been all better off. At least there'd be a world without killing any more. Well, I've done some investigating about the, I think you guys call it the 'yield,' of the Hiroshima bomb. It was small, but it did the kind of damage I think would make the world pay attention. You know, look up, and take note. Take note that conditions must change, that at least one man will not tolerate it any more.

"You know that I had that remarkable young man of yours, Major Overstreet, over here a few weeks ago, to ask him a few questions about his interest in helping with a plan. Of course, I did not give him the details I'm about to give to you here today, but I think he's interested, and would be a major asset."

Nimer then spoke quickly and abruptly, like lungs full of air held onto too long being released in quick puffs.

"General, here is my plan. To drop an atomic bomb, the same size as the one dropped on Hiroshima, on a nation and city we think would do the trick of bringing the world to its senses."

The pent-up air continued to rush out, yet more like a splutter, as Nimer began to hear himself out loud about this for the first time. At times like this, when his most exaggerated fantasies about the presidency being "large" would begin to take real shape, he tended to become formal.

"We have all noted that after the bombings of Hiroshima and Nagasaki there has never been an atomic bomb dropped on mankind. . . ."

At this point, General Arena felt compelled to stop him, as he was in a kind of low-level shock.

"Mr. President, with all due respect to you, sir. I am somewhat overwhelmed by the gravity of what you are telling me. We've, I mean all of the collective wisdom of civilian and military men for over a half century has been on the alert to not allow the genie to come out of the bottle, and here we are talking about just that.

"Again, sir, with all due respect...."

With this, Nimer stopped him, saying, "General, let's stop the 'all due respect' crap. I want to talk with you here today man to man about this plan. I've got to know if you think it's a good plan, if you agree with my thinking, if it's feasible, and if you're willing to be a part of it. It's going to take a whole lot of planning, a whole lot of rationale that our citizens will buy. Though to tell you the truth, it doesn't really make a big difference if they do or not. I think it's a good plan. In time they'll see the wisdom of it all."

"Mr. President, what I'm saying is that I have this sense, this feeling, that dropping a bomb like that might be a very dangerous thing to do. I know that you have introduced a pre-emptive strike policy that I agree with.

"An atomic bomb is different. It's not like fifty or a hundred people dying in an air strike. In this case, it would mean thousands of people dying at once, and the wounded would be such a mess that the peoples of the world would come down on us hard. Isn't that what you are trying to avoid?"

"That's exactly the point. Don't you get it? That the world will see what an atomic bomb can do, and be so scared by the thought that they will never want to wage war again. They will know what we *could* do, if we wanted."

Arena couldn't believe what he was hearing.

"But, Mr. President, if a hundred thousand people die in one day, as the result of one bomb, wouldn't that attract a world-wide focus? It's just like when an airplane such as a 747 goes down and three-hundred and fifty people get killed, it's in all the papers. Yet on the same day, let's say it's a holiday, the same number will be killed in car accidents. Because it's in one's or two's or three's, no one pays any attention."

"General, that's exactly the idea. We *want* the world to pay attention. Don't you see?"

"Even if that was so, what would the world say if we just dropped an atomic bomb without warning and without a compelling reason, such as our own survival?"

"That's where you come in, General. When I see your list of nations you recommend for a first strike, I want to talk with you about how we might provoke them into doing something stupid, or doing something that might not happen, if you know what I mean. Like the Gulf of Tonkin. Were those enemy ships on the radar or weren't they? Who could take a chance? And then we had to do what was done. To this day, probably only a handful of men know what really happened that day and they aren't going to tell. They're patriots and won't tell because they know how that would make the parents and sweethearts of the men who died in 'Nam feel," said Nimer, thinking that using an "in" term like Nam would help.

"Once we have agreed on a target, General, we can begin to prepare our citizens for our attack. This will stop the bleeding hearts from bleeding all over the landscape. We'll withhold information until it's time to drop the bomb. Everyone will realize the good that will come of this when the stories and pictures begin to come out.

"We'll take the wraps off the press, no more imbedding for the time being. We'll let them take those horrible shots they like and put them in the dailies.

"There's nothing like a picture of a little girl in her tiny, torn dress wandering about looking for her dead mom to get the heartstrings vibrating with concern. There's nothing like the scared look of a father staring off to make us wonder what he's thinking about. Maybe the horrible and prolonged death of his wife or his own son. I remember reading a story about a man in Hiroshima who was looking at his son riding his little tricycle in the back yard when the bomb blew. He said that the boy just disappeared in the light. He buried the boy's bike in the yard because he thought that no one would believe him that the boy simply disappeared. Of course, the Japanese didn't know much about the bomb at the time."

When Nimer used the word "Japanese" instead of "Japs" like some of his poker associates would when talking about WWII, he thought of himself as a respectful person, well-aware of the world and how to speak in deferential ways. It was an inner way he had to ingratiate the careless parts of himself with the concerned.

"I hate to say this, General, but it's true. And for every photo of this sad girl, thousands of others little girls will live because everyone will see the destruction and grief that the bomb will bring."

It was time to stop and to hear Arena out, though he had to add, "I just know it will. I just know it."

"Mr. President, if I may respond. Mr. President, I don't really know how I want to answer. It's a big thing you're asking me to do. And I'd be out on a limb doing it. I've got to know who else is involved and what they are thinking."

"General, as of this moment, there is no one else involved except an overture from me, without details, to the major, Overstreet. A journey of a thousand miles must begin with a first step. Your answer will be the first step, or," he paused, "without you, no steps will be taken."

"Well, sir, in principle I am with you. But I need a little time to think about this. It would be a giant step for me. I just need to weigh the pros and cons before I answer you. I am aware, too, that, given the nature of the information that you have revealed to me today, you'd rather I didn't speak about this to any one. And I won't. I just need a little time to think about it."

"How much time do you need, General?"

"Could you give me five days?" He knew from experience that on important decisions that presented a dilemma to him he needed three days to clarify things for himself. On this one, clearly the biggest of the decisions he had ever been asked to make, he would need more.

"That'd be fine, General. I want to be honest with you now. There is a possibility, with the mid-term elections coming up soon, that whatever you . . . we . . . decide might be moved up or pushed back some. I'm trying to juggle a few things in my mind, and I've got to have a little room to maneuver. I know that sounds like a contradiction. I'm asking you to make up your mind in a matter of days, and then I turn around and say you might have to wait. It's just that events happen fast and I've got to pick the right time to do this so it has its maximum effect. And I've got to know if you're in or out. Just like the Truman administration picked the city of Hiroshima for measuring the effects of the A-bomb, I've got to pick the right place and time to maximize the effect of this one on the world.

"Not everyone knows this, but the city of Hiroshima was off-limits to the Air Force. The administration wanted the city to be 'clean,' free from any regular bombing so the effects of the big one could be measured. One pilot dropped his load on the north end of town about two weeks before the day, trying to get rid of them before going home. He didn't even know about the order not to bomb there. Fortunately for us, the results were negligible and didn't dirty up the study.

"Perhaps the best time will be the time when the most killing is going on in the world, when people are fed up with death and dying." Then he added, almost like an after-thought, "And then, just maybe, the best time is when things are quiet, when dropping the bomb would be most shocking.

Arena was anxious to speak. "I understand, Mr. President. But, *you've got to understand*. . . ." He wanted to pull back the words, as they implied the president might be deficient. Everyone knew he had his weaknesses, yet the game of deference had to be played.

"What I mean to say, sir, is that the longer a secret of this magnitude has to be kept a secret, the greater the possibility is for it to be leaked."

At this remark, Nimer jumped all over the general.

"General, what you've got to understand is that until I give you the 'go' signal you are not to tell anyone about what I've just told you. Anyone. I repeat, anyone!" Nimer shouted in a sharp tone and with a voice so loud it made Arena look around to see if there was anyone anywhere who might hear what was being said.

Arena wasn't used to being talked to this way, and took it as a personal attack on his intelligence. With a raised voice, he replied, "I do understand, *sir*," with an emphasis on the word "sir," but not in the stiff-as-a-mannequin style of a private or junior officer responding to a senior officer when "sir" meant deference and obedience. The tone of Arena's "sir" implied a sneer that said "Screw off with the up in my face stuff. I get the point."

Tempers were rising, so Arena thought it better to just drop the secrecy part for now.

But he still needed to know more about his role in the plan.

"I need to know, sir, what my part in this plan will be."

Nimer stared at the general for a length of time he knew from experience was intimidating to most subordinates. He replied, "I knew you'd ask me that question. I'll need you to get an A-bomb prepared for us that is the same size as the ones dropped on Japan. Same yield, same damage. You need to get me someone on the inside of the communications network we have set up so that when one of the nations we identify as the one we will strike, the one that makes the presumptive threat to us, I will go to the Greenbrier and set up there. Once our citizens are told that I am there, they will see that I was forced to 'hole up,' and will know how great the threat is."

He continued. "I will need someone in the Pentagon at Command Alert to get me through the code identifications to authorize the release of the bomb on the nation I choose. I will need someone at the Greenbrier who is thoroughly an expert in how the system works, who knows the codes, both for my personal identification as well as for my interactions with Command Alert at the Pentagon. You must authorize him to have access to the briefcase codes. He must be a man of impeccable character, one who is loyal without question to our nation and to its president. He must be intelligent, but loyal. We don't want anyone on the inside questioning what we're about to do at the end."

He stopped to ask Arena if he had any questions so far. The general simply opened his arms wide, palms up, as if to say that he did not.

"In a word, General, I need you to set up the bomb, and prepare a way for me to cut through all the communications crap so when I am ready to have the bomb dropped, it will be dropped on time, and on target."

"I can do those things, Mr. President," replied Arena, adding the critical words, "if I decide to be in."

"What about the Overstreet fellow I've recently met? Seems like the kind of man I'd want here," Nimer said.

"He is that kind of man, although it would be better if you asked him yourself. Your plan is somewhat outside our normal thinking at the Pentagon," he said, knowing that was an understatement intended to keep things courteous.

"I'll do that. I want to say, too, that if he decides he wants to be a part of this, I am going to instruct him not to say anything to you until I know your answer."

"I understand the need for that, sir. Is there anything else?"

"Why, yes, of course. Did you forget why you came here today?" Nimer said. He felt angry at Arena, believing the general did not have enough savvy or guts to give him a quick and decisive answer about the bomb.

"I want your best picks for targets of this opportunity, as well as the rationales we might use to convince the American public that we are justified."

"I have them here, Mr. President, in an unmarked report, as you instructed. I'll leave it with you."

"Yes, do that," Nimer said coldly, "but I want you to give me the report right now in your own words."

It reminded the general of the day he had gone for his doctoral orals at the University of Virginia, and one of the committee members had made him put down his notes written on 5x7 cards and directed him to answer the questions without reference to them. He remembered how angry he had been, how he had gone to the two previous defenses when note cards were used without question. And how he had picked up his note cards, slowly stacking them into a neat pile while he also ordered his anger before saying to them, "If that's the way you want it, that's the way it will be." His defense was flawless.

"I've chosen three targets of opportunity. First, North Korea. They have been spouting off about having atomic weapons that can reach the west coast of America. They are dangerous, and we can convince the American people of the legitimacy of our move by spreading a high level disclosure by a North Korean official that they have targeted Los Angeles for such an attack.

"Second, Red China. I know you said nothing too big, but they have been rattling sabers again about threatening Taiwan if it makes any official declaration of independence. We'll say they are imminent about such an attack, that a strike against Taiwanese democracy is a strike against all democracies. You can ratchet up our reaction to the threat by speaking directly to the American people about where this would go next, where it might leave them, etc., etc., something, Mr. President, you are very good at.

"Third, Syria. It has been leaking out to our people, in the context of the Iraqi war, that its government can be brutal, has been known to torture its dissidents, censors the press, etc. That, generally speaking, it has the kind of repressive ways that the American people would not openly tolerate. This, in itself, once we leak out the details, will be enough to win over the American people to such a war, although it will take time. If we rush to get out massive pieces of information too quickly, this might seem strange, especially to those who follow such things."

"Okay, General. Sounds good."

"I might as well tell you now," Arena said, in that way he had of going beyond tactics into strategy with quickness and speed, a gift that even he did not understand, "that I've chosen a few 'starter cities,' you might say. Please keep in mind, sir, that the cities I'm going to identify were chosen as targets of conventional bombing. Perhaps only hundreds would be killed in any one raid, not the thousands we've spoken about today, and not with the kinds of horrific fallout we know A-bombs can leave."

"I know that, General. Nevertheless, perhaps these cities will be as useful as any others we might choose. And remember, it's just one city we're talking about."

The weight of confusion was again pushing on the general's head, as he responded, "I'll begin with China. There's a medium-sized city in the northwest of China, near the Kunlun Mountains, called Hotan. It's mostly out of the way. Interestingly, although it was chosen because of its size and location, as I said, a good "starter place" for a war of choice, it does have the mountains, so a bomb there, coincidentally, might replicate the effects of the Hiroshima one."

"Good work, General."

"Let's turn to North Korea," the general quickly said. "There's a city in central North Korea, almost literally in its center from all points north, south, east and west, called Jilin. It's far enough away from Mongolia so as not to upset the Chinese, yet big enough to let the North Koreans know we mean business."

A nod of approval from the president indicated to Arena to go on.

"Syria has a tough choice of cities. As you know, Mr. President, it is small. But, there are some cities strung out in the north that would be perfect, especially now with what you have in mind," he said, referring to the plan as if it was becoming an unmentionable.

"There's a small city, if you want to call it that, called Al Bab. It's pronounced 'Al Babe.' On the plus side, at least I thought, it's kind of isolated and small. On the negative, it's part of the Mid-East situation, and thus could be volatile for us. A plus, too, is that it might teach some of the small countries in the area to cut out the crap."

"General Arena, I knew I could count on you," the president said. "This is a most remarkable report. Quick, incisive, to the point." Before Arena could respond, Nimer said, "Call me no later than five days from today, as I want to know where you stand. If you're with us, we will all be in your debt. However, if you should not be with us, please do not be against us."

Nimer thought there was power in the cliché. His confidence was growing. "Should you choose to opt out, be certain that this conversation never took place. Fact is, you would not want anyone to know it took place because after the victory is won and the details come out, you won't want anyone to know that you had a chance to be a part of history and turned it down."

"If that will be all, Mr. President," Arena said crisply.

"That will be all. Talk to me soon."

"Yes, sir, I will." He saluted and left, unaware that he was being set up, that he really knew only some of the details of Nimer's real plan for world peace, a plan that was diabolical in its conception and wicked in its execution, surely a double dose of evil. Arena did not know that Nimer would first torture the world before dropping the bomb.

↳

Things were starting to fall into place, thought the president. He had set up Arena, possibly, by catering to his abilities to size up the ways and means to execute a military plan, and by appealing to his ego that he did so much to hide. Nimer could tell that Arena liked being significant, and loved being a part of the big picture, the major goals of a nation's military posture.

Nimer was pleased. He was being persistent, setting up things, one thing at a time. He knew that soon enough, if he was patient, all things would fall into place. And if anything did not fall into place and the plan had to be aborted, no one would ever know that he tried to break the highest and most revered precept ever promulgated by God or man: Thou shalt not kill. Especially in cold blood. Especially the innocent. Especially without warning. Especially after torturing them.

The next step would be to get Jarvis' unwitting cooperation about how the details of the system for a first strike worked, as well as a recording of their meeting, knowing that some of what they would say would be needed to complete his vision.

9

Norman Jarvis' nature was not decisive enough for Nimer to include him fully. Yet, the president needed his piece to complete the puzzle. He asked his chief of staff, George Bender, to set up a meeting with Jarvis, ostensibly to hear his report on the countries he had chosen for a conventional attack.

However, Jarvis quickly found out that Arena had already met with Nimer. He called for a meeting, which was arranged for five days later, the same day that the general was to let the president know if he was in or out.

There was, then, much at stake on the day Nimer met with the secretary of defense. His impatience with this conservative man, reluctant to make decisions before he thoroughly thought them out, as well as his own nervousness about Arena's answer, made him irritable this morning.

"Good morning, Norman. I suppose you have your report ready for me. General Arena has told me that you and he agree on the final exit strategy for us regarding Iraq.

"It's a damn good one, Norman. You both have much to be proud of. I've already run it by Frank Daniels who also thinks it's good. The UW part is a bit risky, and requires a great deal of military complicity as well as secret funding. But, basically it's a sound plan.

"I want you to all get on it right away. Be ready to report on the broad aspects at the next principals committee meeting, which Daniels is heading. Meet with him first so you're both on the same page about how to talk about it, to keep the lid on any aspects of it that might be problematical. It's a great job, Norman. It's too bad that when the air clears and we're out of the hole you won't get much credit because of the nature of our exit strategy. Remember, though, who your friends are around here and how they appreciate what you are doing for your country."

"Thank you, Mr. President. Now if I may, I'd like to let you know about the countries I've chosen for the next incursion, if I may call it that." He spoke in a crisp sort of way that was his whenever he was trying to impress the president. He knew that Arena had gotten to him first, and probably had impressed him with the certainty of his response. At best, Jarvis could neutralize that certainty with an appearance of conviction.

"I've chosen three countries, one high risk, one medium, one small.

"First, North Korea. It has been regularly threatening our security for a half century, enough time for even the most uninformed American to perceive them as a threat. Like slow rain sinking in. On the downside is their proximity to China, as well as their boast, which intelligence says is more than just bragging, that they have nuclear warheads that can reach parts of America, probably with longer than mid-range missiles."

Nimer interrupted him with a quick question that he wanted to take back as premature as soon as it left his tongue. "What would you say, Norman, if I told you that I was thinking about dropping the big one on North Korea?"

There was a long pause as Jarvis tried to find the right fulcrum point between his shock and an appropriate response.

"I guess I'd have to know more, Mr. President. No doubt you've weighed the pros and cons of such a decision. My quick response, without having time to consider the pros and cons for myself, is that we would be taking a great historical risk of starting World War III. The results of that, as you know, could be cataclysmic for everyone because who knows who might get in on it. We're talking Red China here. They might not like the idea of our dropping a nuke so close to where they live. And they could see it as an excuse to invade Taiwan, something they've been wanting to do for a long time."

It was at that very moment that Nimer excluded the secretary of defense from his real plan. Jarvis was neither bold in his thinking nor decisive in his actions. He would not be useful.

"I was just kind of thinking out loud there, Norman. But, I wouldn't want it to get out of this room," he added, hoping in some ways that it did get out of the room. Knowledge of it might provide the cover he needed for the technical cooperation he needed for the lottery.

"May I resume, sir?"

"Please."

"My second pick is Iran. A full and complete military follow-up to our break-through into Tehran. Many Americans know, I wouldn't say a lot, but enough to give you a core, that the present Iranian government is repressive. It speaks some of the words of democracy, but when push comes to shove, it doesn't practice them. It's continuing work on nuclear facilities to develop the A-bomb is enough in itself to justify a full invasion. A little work on your part will convince the American people that the country is an obstacle to peace in the region and in the world. Though negatively speaking, it is in the Mid East and we might not want to stir up the pot in that region any more than it is now."

Jarvis felt as if he was giving a good presentation, a well-thought-out point of view. He took the president's lack of reaction as a sign of approval.

"My third choice is different. It's a full and powerful blow against the continuing bad conditions in Afghanistan. With all due respect, Mr. President, we know that the war there is not going well. We've only got 9,000 troops on the ground there now, and they are very spread out and they are being over-worked. Once we stopped our capital bombing campaign, we began to lose the regional warlords that control most of the population. Right now, it's only Kabul that is working reasonably well. The only way we keep peace with any warlords is by bribery and looking away from their poppy fields. This is not good, as the heroin is easy for our own troops to get. And the first signs of trouble in that regard are there, I am told.

"I know, Mr. President, that the country is a wasteland of oases pretending to be cities, but it's symbolic value to us is enormous. We can't abandon them again like we did after the Russians pulled out. If we do, it will become the home base once again for the al Qaida."

"Well, Norman, just what *do* you propose?" an irritated Nimer said.

"I propose that we go in there and bomb the hell out of them again, this time more than ever. That we take 75,000 streamlined, high-tech troops in there, a combination of what both Arena and I would like, and clear out the rot before it gets really bad and we lose them for us and for the democracy movement that the history books will credit to you.

"All you have to do is to ignite American feelings about terrorism again, this time even more strongly than ever by reminding us of the threats everywhere to our safety."

Jarvis thought that he would stop now, a good way for the report to end.

"Good work, Norman," the president said, holding his hand out as if to high-five the secretary, but pulling back into a handshake.

"I'd like to move on to something else before you go. I want a quick and updated briefing about the specifics of communications if we are ever on a serious and threatening war footing."

"What do you mean, sir?" he responded in an up-beat sort of way, feeling now pretty good about himself and his report, especially the last bit that acknowledged Nimer's wisdom.

"Let's say we hit North Korea with a massive bombing attack, calculated to let even the giants know that we mean business about evil in the world, and let's say we target their nuclear arsenal and are wrong, bad intelligence, that the hard stuff is somewhere else, and we know they are getting it ready for a nuclear strike on one of our cities. That I'm holed up in the Greenbrier in West Virginia, and I want to pre-empt them or, at worst, retaliate. How does that work?"

He continued, "I know there's the briefcase with specific instructions in it, and that someone is always handy with it and a key to open it. I've already been briefed about how this works generally, and I know my code name and password. But I don't want to get bogged down with some geeky guy's instructional manual while we're waiting for the North Koreans to drop an A-bomb on us."

Drawing Jarvis in, Nimer proceeded to say, "You know that my code name is *Snappy* and my password is *Oreo*," hoping that the revelations of his secret code and password names might open Jarvis to reveal his own.

What Jarvis didn't know was that the conversation was being taped on the most sophisticated taping technology ever devised, a system that could replicate a man's voice with such exactitude and clarity that whoever heard it would swear that that man was right alongside him.

"And I know that you have to second my authenticity, command and directive before anyone down the line can release an atomic weapon," Nimer said. "What I don't understand is what happens after I speak to the Command Alert with my own code name and password, plus the sequence of letters and numbers from the briefcase. How do you come in?"

"It's simple. After you I.D. yourself and give the sequence, you stand by 'til they get me on the special secure cell phone I always carry on my person. I have a back-up one, too. You are put through to me, identify yourself by name, code and password again, after I'm first told of your legitimacy as authenticated by the sequence. You must always speak first and I respond with these words, 'I am the secretary of defense, Norman Jarvis, code name *Cobra*, password *Data*. I am verifying and duplicating the specific command of the president of the United States.'

"It's as simple as that," he admitted, adding as an afterthought, "a simple action that takes but a few seconds that in less than an hour can leave the world in smoke and dust."

Norman Jarvis had just become a part of one of the most cruel plans ever devised. Ironically, the essential part he would play was just now completed. And he didn't even know it.

10

The time was 10:05 a.m., the date October 2, just one month before the mid-term elections. Al Qaida planned it well. In fact, it wasn't even difficult.

Its operatives, Muslim "sleepers" living in New York City, had watched the Queens-Midtown Tunnel for about a year. They noticed that small and large trucks entering the tunnel were assigned a separate entry with a two-part process: first a quick, yet thorough, inspection by man and dog, then payment at the toll booth.

They noticed, too, that big cars with big trunks were not stopped. After countless rides in and out of New York City via the tunnel, they concluded that a car with a large trunk could be packed with enough explosives, timed to go off at a specific place by a waspy looking person pulling the trigger, to blow out the side of the tunnel. It was easy enough to get the tunnel plans, via a bribe or the Internet, that revealed just how vulnerable the old tunnel was.

It had been constructed long ago, its side-wall and ceiling strength designed to withhold the pressure of accumulated water, not explosives. The plans also showed that at two points the tube's road was slightly curved. These two points formed a more concave shape whose surface area was naturally greater and bent outward than on the straight-ways. An ammonium nitrate bomb on the walls at either of the two spots would stand the greatest chance of breaking through.

Their calculations were correct. They chose a Monday morning because a day early on in the week would leave the rest of the work week disrupted with shock, grief, mourning and the beginning of cleanup. Besides, it would probably be crowded in the morning with late workers, shoppers and foreign tourists visiting the city. The terrorists had checked the airline schedule, and most international flights arrived between 6:45 and 9:00 a.m. at the three major airports in the area. The explosion would leave New Yorkers fatigued with déjà vu.

The roar of the explosion echoed down both the east and west length of the tunnel. The cars nearest to the impact point were mangled as if they had been caught in a the maw of a junkyard crusher. The percussion of the blast ran through the cylindrical shape of the tunnel like a tornado, pushing cars against each other in a tangled mess of steel and flesh. Some of the drivers near the entrances tried to reverse their cars once they recognized the catastrophe taking place in front of them, but they couldn't budge against the back-up behind them. Witnesses said later that they could hear the sounds of cars smacking into each other like bumper cars at an amusement park.

Many of the pedestrians who were walking near the tunnel said they first heard an incredibly loud explosion, then a swooshing noise followed by black smoke blowing out the exits of the tunnel. In a matter of minutes, some said, others seconds, they could hear a sucking sound when the regulated air in the tunnel began to explode out of the tunnel before the water from the river came in a rush.

One witness described it as the phenomenon that took place in a bathtub when one held a plastic quart cup, turned it upside down, and forced it into the water before tipping it upright again. First the air rushed out, then the water in, all very fast.

Bodies, metal, rubber, crushed cars and whole cars came rushing out, and then the flood was on. Part of it flowed in an almost naturally easy way south and on into the ocean. Another part ran over the streets and canyons of the east side.

More than a few caught near the exits and entrances to the tunnel were lucky and survived. But, as the tunnel was a transit point, the loss in lives was hard later to calculate. Bodies that were easily identifiable were the first to be counted on the rolls of the dead. Some were drowned in their cars, some floated in time onto the banks of the East River. Others were found by fishing boats at sea.

A central control number was broadcast to the public to phone in cases of loved ones not returning home at the end of the day. To make certain, the authorities asked each caller to phone again in three days if their family member continued not to show. In this way, they hoped to compile numbers.

This system was difficult to order, as many concerned people called the number to ask about the whereabouts of their loved ones, clogging the mechanism against its intended purpose.

Then there was the question of foreigners. Weeks, even months, went by before the inter-agency connections could be established with foreign governments to streamline a system for missing persons. People who thought their loved ones might have been in New York City began to call from all over the world to make inquiries or, in the cases of the more pessimistic, to declare their loved ones missing or dead on the probability that they were in New York City on that day, passing through the tunnel at that time.

In the end, the authorities from city and federal agencies simply extrapolated a ratio of probable visitors to confirmed deaths of foreigners, calculating a final number based on those figures. No one could ever know how many bodies were obliterated, floated away in their broken parts, or were eaten by fishes in the sea.

Nevertheless, to satisfy the insatiable appetite of Americans for numbers, 1,432 was the estimated number of those who had died that day, domestic and foreign together. In the ensuing weeks, as more bodies surfaced, newspapers kept score by domestic, foreign, and total number. Most foreign victims were from Western Europe, mainly French and German. There were also many Japanese. To kill Americans and foreigners together was a brilliant coup by al Qaeda.

The loss of property was incalculable. There was flooding on many blocks beyond the first floor. Water marks on the outside of buildings were evident in subsequent weeks, bearing witness to the height of the flooding. Restaurants were hit especially hard, as walls, rugs and furniture were ruined, meats and poultry rotted, kitchen ovens and assorted hardware soaked by water.

Computers in offices were soaked, as was the inventory of clothing in dress shops along the way of the flooding. Numerous cars were seen floating in the streets. There were also a few kayaks, commandeered from stores by those wanting to help, wandering aimlessly about, good bytes for the spontaneous TV coverage.

The time and the place for this terrorist attack, once again, were chosen brilliantly. There was no better place than New York City to get the word out to the world what had been done to the American giant. Television stations with mobile units sprang into action to let the citizens of the city, the country, and the world see what was happening. Newspaper reporters, experienced in emergency reporting, ran their stories more quickly than the raging waters of the river.

It seemed, too, that every person who had access to a video-recorder was in the streets, taping dramatic shots of people negotiating water, and interviewing anyone who could find dry ground for a few minutes. It was the chance of a lifetime for fifteen minutes of fame, or to make a few bucks. Perhaps both.

In a few days, after the initial shock was beginning to wear off, this time more quickly than with the 9/11 disaster, editorials urged the city fathers to build another tunnel as quickly as possible. It would be "our way," they said, to let the bad guys know that we were not defeated, our progress only delayed. A fleet of small boats began to ferry commuters from Queens to Manhattan and back, more to show the world that New Yorkers might say "ouch," but they never flinched. The Daily News called it "Operation Dunkirk," in honor of the British civilian boats that saved so many soldiers from doom across the Channel when they were trapped by Nazi forces early in World War II.

More, perhaps, than al Qaeda thought possible, the emotional shock waves from the tunnel explosion spread quickly throughout America. Many were afraid to pass through tunnels, even to go over bridges. The American workforce seemed to be paralyzed for several days. Americans just wanted to stay home. Later estimates put the economic cost of the subsequent absenteeism at about ten billion dollars.

⌖

When President Nimer heard the news, he was at once filled with anger and embarrassment. Anger because al Qaeda had pierced the protective net he wanted to think would always work, and embarrassed because the attack took place on his watch. Given his temperament, though, he grew tired of monitoring the vigil. The eventual carelessness began to trickle down to 10/2, the day of the Q-M-T. disaster.

Shortly after eleven a.m. on the same day as the attack, Nimer met with the civilian and military principals in the Situation Room in the West Wing, first to make certain about conditions around the United States and in its protectorates. Then, to discuss what action, if any, to take.

It was decided, of course, that the president would get on national TV to condemn the attack, and that he would visit the site on Thursday. It was decided to put off any military action until al Qaeda's role in the attack was confirmed by intelligence, and until Nimer had a chance to meet with the full cabinet in the morning at 8:00 a.m., followed by a principals committee meeting at 10:00.

The president hurried the pace of the meeting, and gave it a tone of urgency, the kind that said "let's do something, and do it yesterday."

It was not unusual for him to ask the commander of the joint chiefs of staff to stay behind for a private meeting. After the perfunctory goodbyes that ended this kind of emergency meeting, he asked Arena to wait a while.

"Well, Jeff, are you in or out? I've waited well beyond five days for your answer. And, frankly, I'm a bit pissed. Here it is eleven thirty in the morning about a billion years later, and I'm asking you where you stand."

It was the first time Arena had ever heard the president use profanities.

"It's the morning when we got hit again, hit hard again, and I'm losing my flexibility with the plan. If today doesn't get you over here, well, I'll never say anything in public to embarrass you, but if you're not with me today, I'm afraid you're against me."

Nimer was so angry with Arena's hesitancy and with the events of the day that he felt like grabbing the general by the collar and shaking him into an uncommon, yet clear, sense.

"Mr. President, I've thought about this long and hard, and I apologize for taking so long getting back to you. It's a big thing you're asking. I'm not even sure if it's lawful, although, except for the liberals, you can win the people over when they see the results of our work." He paused and added, "Count me in, sir."

"I'm relieved, General. At times like this especially we have to work together. You and I are leaders, the kind of bold leaders it will take if this earth is ever going to get back on track."

Nimer now seemed pumped up after the downer news of the attack that morning.

"Maybe now we can stop the killing. With you on my side, I think I can. And by the way, send Major Overstreet to see me on Wednesday a.m."

They left the room, chatting about the morning's numbers so far. The president felt on the verge of some great destiny, while Arena felt on the verge of throwing up. He was still not sure about his decision.

↘

It was an especially hot day in Kenya, and a lazy day in its capital, Nairobi. By the time Nimer woke up, it was early afternoon there, the hottest time of the day on the east coast of Africa.

The people were poor, yet they were proud and assertive. If they'd had an advanced notice of what the president of the United States had in mind for them, they would be ready, in their tradition, to fight him for what was theirs.

Most of the buildings in Nairobi were relatively small, although there were a few that might stand in any of a dozen western cities. It was ironic, perhaps, that the architecture reflected Hiroshima of sixty years ago with its short white buildings surrounded by flimsy houses.

The million and a half wildebeests that had come up from the Serengeti were by now settled in the north, looking for water and grass. Mixed with zebras and gazelles, they were as much a melting pot as the many tribes that made up the country.

The Great Rift Valley, perhaps the birthplace of man, ran north to south through Kenya and on down into Tanzania. It was lush with farmland that grew coffee, tea, corn and potatoes.

Hovering over the Rift Valley on Sunday was the possibility that, if Nimer's plan was successful, it might be known in the future as the deathplace of man. It's composite of man, nature and animals made that gloomy prospect a stark possibility.

The Masai Mara, a plains area with rolling hills drifting among the savannas that were home for elephants, lions, rhinos, buffalo, and leopards, was home also for the Masai tribe, a simple, yet colorful, people who lived their lives tending to families and cattle, while using everything nature gave to them. Even the dung from cattle was spread about the dirt to dry in the sun, later to be used for fires.

How simple their lives. Each man woke up this Sunday to two wives, a cow, and perhaps a child or two in his small straw and mud hut. He would put on a loose, red garment. The brighter the red, the wealthier he was, with the measure of wealth being the number of cattle he owned. He would go about his day tending to the herd, talking with his fellows, caring for his family.

It was the same for the Samburu warriors to the north who lived their lives the way their ancestors had centuries ago. To the southwest were thousands of pink flamingos living on Lake Nakaru and the land east of Lake Victoria.

Kenyan herdsmen were sweet people living in a land made poor by colonial neglect and years of struggles to find their own voice. Except for the Kenyatta International Airport in Nairobi, it was a place declared not important by the west.

For Matthew Djibouty, his wife Marlosa, and their son, Sam, today was normal by the standards of the little town of Narok.

Matthew was a Christian, and he was leaving church with his family at about nine in the morning before driving to work in Nairobi, where he was due at about one-thirty. He had been born into a Samburu family in 1964, the year when Kenya, led by the Mau Mau, an anticolonialist organization of ethnic Kikuyu, gained its independence from the British.

His father had been a potato farmer, a good and just man who had higher aspirations for his only son. When he was thirteen, his father sent him to Mombasa, a port city on the Indian Ocean, to live with his aunt. He went to the local elementary school where he was considered one of the brightest and sent on to the high school.

There he had a choice to take academic subjects or technical. His choice of auto- mechanics would serve him well in just a few years. His aunt's husband worked in a food transportation office in the city. Matthew could see the rapid pace of food and camping equipment being transported to the game reserves, and was tuned into the conversation of his industry that said soon the tourist business would increase exponentially over the "tent and hunt for skins" style that had existed in Kenya for the past one hundred years. With advances made in camera technology, vans, and wilderness hotels, there would be a satisfying place for a young man like Matthew, who was not only polite and socially adept, but a trained auto mechanic as well.

He was the whole package for a new industry, and soon grew with a Kenyan travel tourist company called Tour Around Kenya, or "TAK," that was based in Nairobi and specialized in taking tourists around the many game parks situated there.

Matthew was a natural leader in the company, always prepared and well-liked by tourists who sometimes wrote admiring letters to TAK after returning from their trips. Handsome and gracious, a natural charmer, he was well-liked and much loved by the young women of Nairobi, many of whom he sampled before settling upon Marlosa. He had met her outside a crafts shop near the post office on Haile Selassie Avenue where she was leaning against a window of the shop, the tip of her right index finger against her lip, but still as a zombie.

Matthew stopped to ask her if she was all right.

Amused, she said, "Yes, I am," immediately adding, "but how nice of you to ask." Most people who were sincere about relationships usually waited some time before getting to know each other. A lucky few knew each other fast, sometimes in minutes. Then, too, something always seemed to get in the way. A bus to catch, an appointment to keep that kept them from connecting the next link in the chain.

It was the same here by the post office. She had to go. She was only leaning against the wall, she said, because she had forgotten where she was supposed to meet her boyfriend for lunch.

When she walked away, Matthew had a feeling that started in the lower part of his lungs, expanded, then ran through his throat and into his ears, which started to ring softly with a tune he had heard one evening on his father's farm long ago. He couldn't get it or the girl out of his mind for days.

The light tint of her complexion kept running through his mind. And it was always accompanied by her face, a not unusual face but one with a perfect symmetry of parts. A nicely rounded nose fit with her brownish-red eyes, high forehead and full cheeks.

Although he wanted to get her out of his mind, as he did with all impossible dreams, he could not. He kept asking himself why her face was so exceptional when none of its parts seemed exceptional. The more he pondered the question, the more he thought about her. He even looked at foreign English magazines with models in them to try to figure out the puzzle of her beautiful face.

On the very day that he decided he would think of her no more, she got in line in back of him at the post office where he went to mail his old father a letter. She was carrying a box to mail to her grandmother who lived in Meru. When they recognized each other and said hi, he offered to carry her burden while she waited her turn. She couldn't say no, as he nearly grabbed it from her, wanting to help. Marlosa thought it was cute and let him. When it was her turn, he put the box down on the counter, and began to turn away from her now private business.

"Good to see you again," he said.

"I wonder if you'd wait for me in the lobby, and we can talk," she answered. He felt shy with her, perhaps because he had thought about her so much. Yet, he asked her if she would like to get a cup of coffee. She said she couldn't, that she had a few errands to run. In the next forty-five minutes, though, standing in front of the post office, they shared ideas about life that were more noble than either one had ever heard before.

As they said goodbye and walked away, they turned around at the same time to look at the other, each wondering if the conversation they just had could have been that real.

Matthew went to the post office every day for fourteen straight days. His father had never received so many letters.

Finally, Marlosa showed up, and they set a date for coffee. Then an endless stream of coffees over many months, until they married at his father's house in Narok, where they decided to live. Sam arrived in due time.

Matthew made the trip between Narok and Nairobi twice a month to guide small safari groups, usually four to a van, that visited the Mara and the game reserve of his own people, the Sambaru.

On his days off, he flourished with the leisure of hanging around the town with his male friends, telling stories, enjoying his life. Mornings and evenings were spent with Marlosa and Sam keeping the dirt of the front yard swept with thatched brooms, and cleaning paper debris tossed from cars and trucks passing through from Addis Ababa in Ethiopia to Dar es Salaam in Tanzania.

Theirs was a good life. Each of the three loved the other. They had a small three-room house made of wood, enough clothing to make a few changes, good friends, and ample food. They loved their God, and worshiped him on Sundays. In turn, they felt loved by others and protected from nature.

11

"It's good to see you again, Overstreet. Major Overstreet, that is. Always treat a man with respect and respect is what you'll get back," he said, trying to set a friendly tone to the meeting.

There was so much going on that the president felt like he was barely holding his head above water. He had been on network and cable news stations twice since Monday, had held a meeting with the cabinet on Tuesday to coordinate their public remarks about the attack on the tunnel, and to keep up with business as usual. He always kept up with business as usual, as he felt this was a good way to reassure his top people.

He had met also on Tuesday with the principals committee, a group of administrators, both civilian and military, in high level posts, who were hand-picked by the president to give him a more coordinated and in-depth point of view on issues than the cabinet, whose heads dealt mostly from a compartmentalized viewing point.

Intelligence confirmed al Qaeda's role in the tunnel attack. It was recommended to the president to step up the bombing of the mountains in northern Afghanistan. They knew this was only a symbolic gesture, yet they could think of nothing else. For the time being, chasing the remainder of al Qaeda was like running after a ghost, or running after smoke. There would be fire, then smoke. Once you put out the fire, the smoke would waft away.

Now, he would step on the rock called Overstreet. The major was experienced enough to be useful, and yet young enough to be idealistic and daring, energetic and simplistically patriotic.

"Young man, would you like some of that licorice tea I'm becoming famous for?"

"Yes, sir."

"Nimer picked up the phone and called Mrs. Joslin. "Two licorice teas. Make it so," he said, imitating the imperious tone of Picard, the captain of Star Trek.

When he turned back to Overstreet, the president thought to himself, "How odd that I'm about to talk with a young man pretending I'm a fictional character in order to get him on my side for perhaps the greatest decision any president has ever made."

For as long as he could remember, it puzzled and sometimes vexed him that he simply could not say to another person what was on his mind, straight out and clear, so there would be no misunderstandings. It never occurred to him that his own sensitivities were delicate, that sometimes his own emotional skin was tissue-paper thin.

He always remembered the day when he had told his mother that MaryLou, the girl down the block, was fat. His mother responded with a simplicity that was memorable. "Remember, Fletch, 'fat' girls are 'heavy' and 'skinny' girls are 'thin.' Never fat, never skinny. That way of speaking, my dear son, is only for the movies." The little lesson by his mother was the touchstone that began to round off his edges in this regard. Lots of later faux pas did the rest.

"Did you ever follow the Star Trek TV series, Major?"

"Not really, sir, I was a little too young for that. But, I've seen a few re-runs and have a general idea of it. My wife's a fan. I think she likes the way they dressed. Kind of reminds her of traditional Japanese samurai costumes."

He was trying as much as Nimer to make this meeting work.

"I have always had a great regard for bold men," Nimer said. "I know that the country is in trouble right now, and I don't mean to make light of it. But, let me, for the sake of what I'm trying to get across here, refer to Captain Picard of the Enterprise.

"He was a good man, had the right instincts. He always had the ability to remain calm, even when everything was going wrong around him. He knew that if the center did not hold, the rest of the parts would become unglued and fly away."

In an attempt to add humor, he said, "Wouldn't want that to happen, especially in outer space."

Overstreet chuckled on cue.

"Seriously, though, Major. Kirk knew how to handle situations. And do you know what always made his handling of these situations work?" he asked rhetorically.

"What made them work was his boldness, which most of the time in the politics of his time was there, not like today.

"I noticed that behind his boldness and decisiveness and the courage of his convictions, he always had to answer to the head of the Star Fleet for his actions. I swear, Major, there's always someone to answer to, even when you go up the ladder. Kids answer to teachers who answer to the principal who answers to the superintendent who answers to the board of education who answers to the people who pay the bills! And who do they answer to? Their wives," he said, trying hard again to lighten up the meeting, really his own way to handle the anxiety he was feeling.

"Excuse me a minute, Major. I've got to visit a man about a horse. I'll be right back."

He exited for his private bathroom, saying "Good morning" to the Secret Service agent before going in.

"Pardon me, sir, but will you be long?" the agent asked.

"What in hell is that about, young man?" he asked.

"Pardon me, Mr. President, but we're told to ask you that question because if you stay longer than expected, we kinda press the inner alert button. You know, a fainting spell or something like that."

Nimer instinctively knew there were several dozen good jokes in this, yet he responded with a simple one. "I'm about to initiate a leak."

It had gotten around the rooms that Nimer liked it when his jokes were appreciated.

"Good one, sir."

"What is your name?"

"Agent Henry Ginter, sir."

"Thank you, agent Ginter. I expect it will be a short leak."

"Thank you, Mr. President."

Nimer went in, closed the door, swallowed the xanax he had in his pocket, drank a small cup of water, and relieved himself, mostly to satisfy Agent Ginter's expectations.

When he went back into his office, Overstreet was sitting in the same chair, looking decidedly uncomfortable.

"Getting back to Captain Picard, do you know who he answers to, Major ? He answers to the same one we all answer to in the end. He answers to his God."

It was getting a little heavy for Overstreet. It was difficult to know how to respond to a president when he began talking about his God.

"There comes a time when every man has to decide how he is going to answer the call from God. It's a call that comes in different ways to different people. For some it's the call to answer bad habits, like drinking or drugging.

For others it's sticking out the grind of college so they can get the degree and get on with the work of their lives, what it is they are called for.

"Sometimes, for the young, like you, it's a call to greatness before their time. Greatness is usually draped on a man when he gets older. But sometimes the young get called.

"That's a good thing. Because the young have energy and boldness. Like a Captain Picard. When the older cave in, young men can step up and do their thing. They don't think as much as older people do. Thinking too much is not good for the spirit.

"Frankly, Major Overstreet, I think it's the root cause behind Alzheimer's. You know, the brain is like computer. Each of us gets a different hard drive, so to speak, at birth. A different capacity. When we clog it up with too much stuff, too much thinking, it just freezes up, gets overwhelmed and won't work any more. Can't recall a thing after a while.

"The brain needs a vacation once in a while, too. Ever notice how I spend time at my ranch, away from everything? I try not to do a thing when I'm there. Maybe morning briefings and a few decisions so the folks know I'm on the job. What I'm doing is just defragging the parts, like a computer, letting my brain cells jump around for a while, air out, rearrange themselves, so I can go back to the White House refreshed and ready to go again."

Nimer realized that he was trying too hard. Even though Priscilla, mostly in the old days, would remind him that he sometimes talked too much, he would as much sometimes forget.

He had to bring Overstreet back to the enthusiasm he'd had in his office for the plan a few months before.

"Major, when we last talked you were quite excited about playing an important role in my plan for world peace. I told you then, and I want to repeat it now, that you can go down as one of our greatest heroes ever. I want to know if you still feel the way you did that day when you said, I remember your exact words, 'You can count on me, sir.'"

"Mr. President, I feel even more committed to you and your plan than ever. When you told me to keep what you told me a secret, well, that sort of got me thinking better than ever. You know, keeping it inside myself made me deal with it myself. I had to go, I hope you don't think it's trite, well, deep inside myself to know where I really stood."

He stood up and said "I told you then that I was with you. I tell you today I am with you," he declared, adding "Sir" with a tone that affirmed the respect and affection that had grown in his heart for the president.

As he turned and looked out the bay window, Nimer seemed taken by the formality of the response. He wished his official photographer were here to capture the moment, the way they did with J.F.K. during the Cuban missile crisis.

He thought about calling his photographer to replicate the moment for history. But the secrecy of the meeting was vital.

"You know, Major, some men are born to greatness. I think perhaps you are one of these men. Some men are destined to lead others. I don't mean to put them down when I say this, but most people don't really know what's good for them. They're too busy making a living, mowing the lawn, recreating themselves, playing with their children, drinking with their friends. I hate to quote bad and evil men, but I think it was Hitler who said that governments ought to be grateful that people don't think. Well, I'm not grateful that they don't think. I wish they would. But I do know that they're just too busy and distracted by the wonderful opportunities they have. To go to the movies, watching TV, and so on.

"So, there's some men who are elected. I don't mean 'elected elected' as in politics, but selected by nature, I personally believe, elected by God, to be the leaders. These are the guys who get things done.

"You'd think that most people, like you and me, would be tired of all the killings going on throughout the centuries. Now and then it happens, but then when it does, it's usually for the wrong reasons. You take those hippy bastards in the 60's and 70's marching through the streets, burning their draft cards, and throwing their medals over walls, right here near this building we're in. Then leaving after making their chaos to smoke pot and make indiscriminate love. They are a disgrace, and we all know it.

"You take those people marching around the country against the war in Iraq. They leave their little nest in the suburbs, take the train for a day in New York City, photographing each other in their nice down jackets. Why, I'm told they don't even make up their own signs. They get off the train and a sign is poked into their ribs. All they do is agitate. Agitate against the killing, they say. They just don't think right. What they don't realize is that they are agitating against the peace. If they would just know that I'm getting this one right, Hussein, Bin Laden, those crazy Iranian bastards.

"And I betcha," he continued, his tongue sliding words together in the excitement of hearing himself articulate his position better that he had ever done before, "when they were finished with their rallies, they got back on those same damn trains, went back to those same damn houses in the countryside, drank the same whiskey as the hippies. And then, you know what, they watched the evening news to see if they could spot themselves on TV.

"No matter, they could still get the photos developed and tell their children and grandchildren they were there. And their friends who are inclined to think that way.

"The sad part is, major, that the next day they go mow their lawns, take the same train to work, do their jobs and come home. They are just too busy with being busy and enjoying the good things we've gotten 'em to follow up. They're just an irrelevant noise in the boredom of . . ." He stopped to search his mind. " . . . a desert."

By this time, Major Overstreet was a bit mesmerized to hear what used to be the most noble rhetoric on TV now turned into bitter street talk right in front of him. No matter, the principle was the same, he thought. It was good to be in the presence of a man with convictions, who was willing to act on them. And he would be a part of the action.

"Thank you, sir. It will be my privilege to serve. To help us find the way."

Perhaps it was Overstreet's tone, or the mood. It was like the mystery of falling in love, Nimer thought. Whatever that was, whatever needed to come together for someone to know the mystery of the other, Nimer now knew whatever that was in the major. It was something he just knew.

Much like a lover revealed his love, the president would now reveal his secret to Overstreet. Either he would be accepted or rejected. But, like an insecure lover who held off 'til he was certain, he was certain, at this precise moment, that he would be accepted.

"Major, I am going to tell you a few things that may seem at first frightening. But I'm going to tell you everything about my plan to bring peace to our world. Two people you know, your boss, General Arena, and Secretary of Defense Jarvis, are involved with me in developing a plan to create a war with another nation, a war to get the world thinking."

He walked a few steps to think of how he wanted to say this, as well as to gauge how Overstreet was responding to the news.

"Jarvis thinks it's going to be a conventional war." Slow down, he told himself. "And General Arena knows it's going to be . . . atomic ." He speeded up the pace because he didn't want the major to reveal his shock right away at the word "atomic." There would be more shocks to come. Overstreet might as well get a feel for the whole ball of wax, he thought, rather than a chunk at a time.

"What General Arena doesn't know, and you are the only one aside from me to know. . . . Hold onto yourself here. . . . is that, rather than the three 'possibles' we have chosen, I plan to announce a list of four countries that are on a possible hit list. I will let them hold their breaths for one day before I announce on the next day the two cities that might be bombed with a Hiroshima-type bomb.

"It will give those people a full day to think about their possible fate. I will choose the final city by a lottery."

"Mr. President. Please stop for a moment. Let me see if I understand this," the major said, gasping at what he had just been told. "You're going to have an atomic bomb with a Hiroshima-level power that only General Arena knows about, and you will have it dropped on a city of your choice after giving the people of that city a day's notice?"

"No, son, let's get the details right. Arena and Jarvis have each chosen countries for a conventional attack. Only Arena knows that it will be with a Hiroshima-yield atomic bomb. For my own reasons, Jarvis will not be told. Arena thinks it will be one of the three countries he has chosen for the attack, but he does know the bomb will be atomic. He has agreed to go along with it.

"But, and this is a big but, he doesn't know that I am going to select a bigger list of four nations that I'll announce to the world two days before the bomb is dropped. After letting them all stew for a day, I will narrow the list to two possible cities, announce them, let them stew for one day, and then have my own lottery here to pick the 'winner.' The bomb will then be dropped without any fanfare or appreciable warning. I will simply reveal the name of the city and drop the bomb."

It was impossible to explain Overstreet's reaction. Was his the slack-jawed look of a father who had just been told that his only beloved eight-year-old son was run over by a truck while riding his bicycle? Was his look the shocked stare of a small boy just molested by the village priest? Was the strain in his face the disbelief of a husband whose wife had just told him she was in love with another man?

Were each of these to happen simultaneously, they could not convey the confusion that the young major felt. He was at once shocked and outraged. Yet he was also instructed by his own inclinations, as well as by his training, to defer to authority, especially to the authority of the commander in chief.

After a thoughtful pause, which Nimer expected, Overstreet said, somewhat tippy-toed, "Mr. President, this is extraordinary. I mean, what you are proposing to me is beyond what I could ever imagine."

"You've got the point, son. It is beyond what anyone would ever imagine. That is its strength. It's not the bomb. The bomb will kill maybe eighty, maybe a hundred thousand. The staggering enormity that anyone would ever drop a bomb like that is the surprise that will shock the world."

And then he stopped to express the obvious. "You're surprised, aren't you, Major?"

"Well, yes sir, I am. It's just that what you have told me doesn't want to register in my brain. I keep wondering what city it will be and who will be killed. I know people, families, in lots of places. You know, military travel and such."

"I wish I could tell you what city it will be, but at this time I don't even know. I wish I did so I could help you out there. It depends on the lottery, which will be fair. But, let's get to the larger issue here. I know what I've told you is a surprise. Who would ever think it possible? Yet, that's why I'm doing it. It's especially important for the world to know that the president of the United States, the most powerful nation ever to exist, is doing this. By picking a little bomb, they will know, and they *do know,* what larger bombs can do. The Hiroshima one is the smallest one possible. Any smaller would be a tactical bomb used to wipe out, let's say, a village or a section of a city. We're not even talking here about thermo-nuclear bombs or neutron bombs. By not using one of these, the world will know our intention is to create peace, not war, or dying, or killing. Which we could do, if we wanted. But we don't."

Nimer was surprised at the major's silence to immediately make what he thought was the most important point. "I want to be clear that my intention is not to kill, but to create a lasting peace in the world."

Nimer sensed that his argument was beginning to be convincing.

Overstreet asked for a cigarette.

"I don't smoke, Major, but you're welcome to."

"I don't either, sir, but I'd like one now."

Nimer got on the phone and asked Mrs. Joslin to bring in a few cigarettes.

"Any kind will do," he said.

After a pack of unopened cigarettes was delivered, Nimer suggested that they go to the Truman Balcony for the smoke. They made small talk while Overstreet puffed and gagged on his cigarette.

"You can keep the pack, Major. A nice souvenir of the day."

There was a time when a pack of cigarettes received from the president would have been a remarkable souvenir to show off at his and Noriyo's parties, perhaps even give one or two smokes to friends along with the story of how he got them. At this minute, though, the thought left him cold.

Once back inside, Nimer picked up where he had left off.

"What I want to do is shock the world in the biggest way ever. Greater than 9/11, bigger than the day Kennedy was shot, greater than Hiroshima itself. You see, when they dropped the bomb on them that day, it was different."

He then pulled back a bit on his statement.

"I guess it wasn't totally different. It was during war, and we're at war. The war against terrorism has the chance to be a ceaseless war, and the killing to keep going on. I want to stop that. I want to put an end to killings. By doing it this way, my way, everyone in the world will have a chance to think about it for two days. Then some will have a chance to think about it for a day, while everyone continues to think about it.

"It is the thinking and the waiting, wondering what will happen that will make the difference. They didn't know in Japan that the bomb would be dropped, they didn't know it in Hiroshima. But, the city we will hit will *know* it's possible a day before. They'll have some time to think about it.

"I have no idea how they will react to the news. There could be some panic. I hope for their sake and the sake of their children, there won't be any. That things will be orderly. It's why I want to give only a day's notice to the last two, and less than minutes to the chosen city. More than that would be cruel. It could cause pandemonium and so on. More than minutes to think about it is cruel. Wouldn't you say so, Major?"

"Sir, I don't, I don't know what to say," he stammered.

"I can tell you're a little shocked, maybe even numb. On the surface of it, I'll admit, what we're about to do seems odd. But if you think about it as a strategy to end all wars, it does make sense. Look at it this way, for all of history, man has been killing man. Look at it in the overview, as if history is one long war, let's say.

"The hunters kill the gatherers who pick fruits and nuts from the hunter's land. And then the gatherers kill the hunters to protect themselves. Then they form tribes that kill off other tribes who band together for protection and form villages. The villagers attack each other, so more people gather, this time to form cities. At the same time, weapons increase and grow in sophistication. First you've got wooden spears, then bows and arrows, then onto guns, bigger guns, bigger explosives, and planes to drop the explosives on the cities."

Thinking he was making his case, he said, "And on and on.

"Until one day, we, the U.S., make and drop an atomic bomb on a city. Everyone sits up and takes note. For years. They've seen what the bomb can do, so no one wants to drop it again. And guess what? Every son of a bitch who has some kind of a gripe, going back to when there were tribes, starts a war. Little wars and a few big ones. Every son of a bitch who doesn't like us and what we stand for, you know, freedom and opportunity, equal rights for men and women, blacks and whites, that kind of stuff, every one of them wants to kill us off.

"We're like the big name sheriff used to be in the west. Every gunslinger was out to get him. Like Hussein and bin Laden were out to get us." The last of the pent-up righteousness he had was beginning to spin out of the bottle.

"I'm tired, Major Overstreet, of fighting little tactical wars, going just this far and no more, worrying about hurting someone's feelings. It's why I wanted to go right into places like Fallujah and blow it to kingdom come. I'm just plain old tired of this. I want one big strategic war. Not an everyday war. Wars have just been a tactic to win the peace for a little while until the next gunslinger decides to take us on. My plan is beyond war. It's a strategy to end all wars."

Shifting gears, he continued, "You watch. When they see pictures of children on the TV, walking around the city of choice dazed and alone, people with skin hanging off their arms and face, busses and trains looking like stripped-down skeletons. When that happens, people will say 'No more wars,' and they will mean it. They will force their leaders to stop the killing. You see, dropping the A-bomb on a city in this way is a strategy to end wars. It is not a tactic to end *a* war."

Slipping into his instructional mode, he said, "Do you see the difference, Major?"

Before the major had a chance to answer, Nimer said in a louder and sharper tone, "I want to break the design of wars, what the professors call the paradigm, the way things are usually done. Those ways do not work. We know that because the world has wars after wars after wars. They never stop and people never stop dying in those wars, mostly the young and innocent.

"I hate to use the son of a bitch's words, but Hussein talked about the 'mother of all wars' before we kicked his ass the last time. I want the next one to be the one everybody will remember, the one when they think about it they'll see the horror and brutality of war as it relates to them in the cruelest of ways. That's why we've got to do it in a way that some of the innocent, the children, the mothers and wives, the old men and old women, get killed and wounded in the grossest ways. We've got to make it happen so that everyone who thinks and reacts, who cares in any way about themselves or their children, will say to themselves, 'No more war,' and really mean it.

"I want every mother's son, after we drop the big one in the way we're going to do it, with premeditation and forewarning, to think the same way a wife does...."

His mind seemed to fragment, the pieces flying in many directions at once. "Let me tell you about a story," he said, "that I read in some small newspaper years ago, about a local woman who came home one day from her job at the office, and there was her husband sprawled on their bed, the same bed they made love on and slept together in, with half of his head gone, blood and brains splattered all over, on the pillows, the bedpost, the walls, the blankets." He paused, then said, "Everywhere," his hands stretched out as if he was some beseeching some god for the answer to the question "Why."

"I don't know about you, Major, but the thought of such a sight had me the next day putting out a national security action memo to the security chief about tightening up the availability of guns.

"When the chief told me that the item in question was not a part of 'the domain' of his responsibility, I nearly blew a gasket. I told him I didn't care whose 'domain' it was in, and to find out fast whose 'domain' it was in," he said with a sneer, "and as soon as he found out, if that wasn't too much of an inconvenience, to get something started about guns, a new law, or a new directive from me, whatever it takes.

"Anyway, I want every caring person to think of the victims of this one the way that woman felt about her dead husband. It's one thing for the people to know that people die in war, you know, fifty-four thousand Americans dead in Vietnam, a hundred fifty or something like that in the Gulf War, and over two thousand in Iraq, a couple of dozen in Iran. But it's another thing to see the pictures and the films of civilians dying, especially in the ways that these people will die. They will be real heroes, because through the ugliness of their deaths the world will come to a new perception of war. They will stand, as one, and say, 'No more war.'"

Nimer knew that he was exhausted. What kept going through his mind was that certain relentless awareness he always had between what he thought was his potential to convince others compared to the reality of his inadequacy when he got in front of the cameras. In fact, he was probably as good a communicator as Ronald Reagan, if he would only allow himself the luxury of smiling, of not taking himself so seriously. If Reagan could nap in the afternoons, Nimer could not.

He knew that the one big dream of his presidency was on the line right now, in the next few seconds when Overstreet would answer him.

Nimer always tried—in those most alone moments when we dare to tell ourselves the truth about ourselves, about our dreams and desires, the friends and acquaintances we like or don't, the neighbors we speak to only because by chance they live next door, the child we like best of the three, the misunderstandings we think of as signs of carelessness in our marriages that then begin to erode, the core of togetherness getting smaller before the corrosion takes place—to tell himself that the lights he followed in his presidency led him to the people and their welfare, that his country was a nation *of, by, and for* the people.

Yet, by that same instinct for inner truth that blesses the lucky ones, he knew his limitations and because of them this plan would be his only chance for greatness, the kind that historians would write about. He shuddered at how close he might be to the greatest.

And in the smallest, most inaccessible part of his mind, he actually thought he might be counted as the greatest president ever, greater than Washington and Lincoln. After all would be said and done, Lincoln only freed the slaves. He would have freed mankind.

"Well, major, what's it going to be," he asked as if he were offering a choice of small gifts rather than the opportunity to be involved in the making of history, as well as the chance, according to Nimer, for the world to have a new beginning.

"I wish I could have the chance to talk this over with Noriyo. I think that what you have in mind is wonderful, great, and even noble. I'm just having trouble with the part about so many people dying. I have trouble with the killing part. Maybe it's because of Noriyo's mother and her experience. I don't know.

"When I was about sixteen, I remember I was driving the car, our cat, Tinkerbell, had five kittens one day and my dad was pretty upset. He had asked us all to keep her in so this wouldn't happen. As a punishment, I had to take them to the local pound to be exterminated. I couldn't do it. So I pretended, and put them in the woods about two miles away. I knew they'd probably die soon, but at least they had a fighting chance. I sometimes wonder what happened to them, if any of them lived. I never told my father."

"Remember, son, we're talking about something far more important than saving cats. We're talking about saving the lives of millions of people, maybe the lives of mankind. I would like to keep the dead to a minimum. It's what I stand for. But sometimes things can get out of hand."

"Out of hand" was his way of saying that he didn't even know yet which four cities he might choose. And certainly, the "winner" of the lottery he would conduct underground was to be determined only at the moment of the drawing, which he would conduct himself. *After all,* he thought, *if I have the authority to drop the bomb, I must have the responsibility to make the choice.*

Here it was for Overstreet, the moment no one ever wanted to happen. It was a decision far beyond the theoretical ones he didn't want to think about, but crept upon him and all of us now and then, begging to be answered. The one about whether we will or won't come to the rescue of the woman being threatened with a knife on the street corner where we find ourselves simply walking from here to there. The one about whether we'll give mouth to mouth to the smelly and bearded drunk who clutches his heart-attacked throat on the floor in front of us on the train that takes us home from work.

Perhaps it was not the big stakes that pointed Overstreet's hand towards the president's, but what appeared to be a small one. He was getting older and had not yet made his mark on life. He had been a major for four years, and had very little else to show for his career. True, he had a beautiful wife and two fine sons. But so did millions of others, he was sure. He had served in the first Iraqi war, and in the role of a military consultant helped to rebuild the infrastructure in Kuwait. Now, he was stuck in an office at the Pentagon, and there seemed to be no way out.

Blessed and sanctioned by the firm and quiet authority of the society in which he lived, and passed on to him by its culture, Overstreet was convinced that his value lay in the significance of his contribution to it. A loving family life and dignified job were nice. Yet, they were less than what it took for a man to amount to something.

He never thought about these things in any other way. Here was the wall that a man had to go through, the barrier that each had to break in order to count. He would go through the wall, he would break the barrier, cross the line that separated the significant man from the insignificant. Seizing the opportunity, he put out his hand to Nimer.

Overstreet felt as if he were in a movie. Here he was, his hand engulfed by the president's two in an enthusiastic handshake. It seemed as if a part of himself was outside himself. Like he was looking at himself, the same way he felt the day he bailed out of an airplane at 4,000 feet in order to overcome his fear of heights. His heart had pounded that day, his knees shook, his throat dried up, his hands sweated. No matter, he was committed to jump. To make certain he would, he asked the jump-master to put him first at the door. In that way, he was forced to jump as soon as he got the go signal. If he didn't jump, he would be kicked in the back out the door so the rest could also jump.

When the jump-master yelled "go," and he stepped out onto the wing strut before leaping into the unknown, he was so overcome with anxiety that he became a sort of disembodied spirit watching himself jump, so great was his fear that he would fall into the tail of the plane. It was not until the chute opened seconds later that he got back into his body.

Today, it was Nimer's tight grip that brought him back.

"Good," the president said sharply. "Now, let's get down to business. Here's what we've got so far. You're in. Arena is part way in. I don't know how he'll react when he knows the rest of the plan, you know, the part about the four cities, then two, then one."

Unknown to Overstreet, Nimer did not plan on telling Arena about the lottery unless it was necessary, and even then telling him would be a gamble.

"Your contact will go by the same name as the one I mentioned to you the last time. Do you remember the name?"

"Yes, sir. Back Seat."

"Correct. What I'll need from you is this: a reliable communications man in the Command Alert room who has authorization to speak with the president, me, about an order to drop an atomic weapon. I'll ask General Arena to get me a man on the inside at the Greenbrier in West Virginia, where I'll be once we begin the bogus plan of having an atomic armed nation threaten us. Arena will make sure that's fixed also. He'll also get the Hiroshima-type bomb ready with a special order from me. I don't think we have one that small anymore right now.

"There's also a matter of having the secretary of defense confirm any order from me to drop an atomic weapon. Even though Arena will not be in on the plan, that part is being taken care of and you will know how when the time comes.

"Remember, you are to speak to no one about this. I know I told you the last time we spoke that 'Back Seat' would be your contact from then on, but I had to let you know in person first about my total plan. I had to see with my own eyes where you stood and how you stood. I know now that you stand straight up, proud to be an American. I know that one day when she knows the details, Noriyo and her mother will be as proud of you on that day as I am today."

"Thank you, sir. It is my privilege."

"There's one more thing I want you to know, so you won't be on edge waiting for the time schedule. You've got to get right on the work of getting me the inside man, but I want you to know that nothing will happen for the next few weeks. The mid-term elections will be here soon, and I have decided to wait on the plan until they are over. I've also told this to General Arena. I don't think it is proper for me to execute the plan before the mid-elections. If we should lose . . . and I might, judging by the heat right now about both the Iraq and Iran thing . . . if the party should lose its edge, the new Congress will have the burden to pick up the pieces," said Nimer, adding, "so to speak," thinking it an understatement that that particular phrase should pop into his head right then.

"It would not be fair to the American people. I want the American people to know what I stand for, to know my convictions, my heart. If they do, I know they would support this plan. I will, though, trust their voice in the elections. If they should support my brothers and sisters in the Senate and the House, I think it is their way of saying that they support me.

"I am a practicalist as well as a realist. As I've said, one way or another, after the bomb falls, I'm going to need friends on my side. I can't say much before the bomb, but I can, and will, say a lot after it. Lord knows I've tried to tell the world about the dangers of Iraq. I knew I couldn't just bomb the bastards without some excuse. We'd have looked like the Japanese at Pearl Harbor who just came swooping in without an excuse and bombed the hell out of us that day.

"We live in a world of legalisms, Major. You can't just know a man is evil and get rid of him. You've first got to have a reason that will hold up in court. If Americans support my people in the mids, I'm going to put it all on the line, this time greater than ever. I could just pick one of the three countries we could provoke into threatening us, tell Americans of the threat, an atomic one I could say, and then drop the bomb on them before they did it on us. I'd be a hero.

"But I'm going to let it all hang out, once and for all. I'll just let the world suffer the anxiety for a few days of knowing it's going to have an A-bomb fall on one of its cities. It will be the greatest strategic effort ever in military planning. Folks the world over will know the hell of war, what with modern media capabilities. I'm almost certain when the dust settles on this one, there won't be any fallout about legalism. Everyone will just know it's the right thing to do, and I really don't believe there will be any second guessing. If there is, though, I want Congress on my side."

He finished the meeting by saying, "I really believe, Major, they will see how right I've been all along."

12

Nimer's appearance in New York City was marked by rallies both for and against his administration. His national public appearances were so infrequent that when they did occur they were magnetic, drawing masses to him while repelling an equal number.

Perhaps historians someday would analyze this phenomenon. For every one drawn to the man's simplicity, his edgy and straightforward ways of doing things, there was always another one who saw him as incapable of foresight, a bull in a China shop.

The attack on the tunnel three days before created an atmosphere in the city that was a nightmare for the police department. There was a palpable buzz in the streets. The mix of presidential loyalists with those who blamed the recent attack on Nimer's agitation of the terrorists was a very real problem, made worse by the anger and fear of Americans everywhere, especially New Yorkers, who were now three times put under the gun, twice in the past several years.

Even the police were irritable. Using pens to hold in the demonstrators was a relatively recent tactic they used to keep the anti-war protestors under control. The tactic was not going well this day. The pens were set up on Third Avenue and went only to 34th Street. This would keep the rabble rousers away from First Avenue and 39th Street where the president's motorcade would arrive from the north on Roosevelt Drive.

The police estimate for the anti-war rally was 75,000 people. Its organizers claimed 200,000, a coalition of groups spun together quickly, mostly via the internet.

They were annoyed at first by being herded into the narrow pens. A small vocal crowd began chanting, "We're not animals, we're not animals." Soon the chant took hold, and in that magnificent way that large crowds have, the thousands became one voice, "We're not animals, we're not animals."

Some of the police began to get nervous, especially the young and inexperienced ones. Almost imperceptibly, they, too, as if in unison, began to cup their truncheons in the palm of one hand while gripping them tightly with the other. A few began to toss the agitators down on the ground. Others moved in to smack them on the legs or back with billy clubs as the crowds grew louder.

The people seemed like a lumbering giant awakening to the day, kneeling on one knee before assuming stature and bellow. It was like a low hum expanding into the doorways and down the side streets of New York City. Thousands of simultaneous screams filled up its caverns and echoed down its corridors. The crowd was a beast agitated, wanting its wailing to be heard on the moon.

Contrary to established procedures, some of the plainclothes police were trying to rip signs that they felt were disrespectful out of the hands of protesters, signs that read, "Nimer, the Duh Man," and, "Nimer, How Many Kids Did You Kill Today?" and, "Hey Nimer, Aside from the Incident in the Tunnel, How're the Wars Going?"

At the same time, removed, President Nimer was speaking to a more select and orderly group. He could hear the noise in the background the way a golfer could hear the screams for an opponent's great shot at some distant hole. Yet he was unaware of the chaos taking place.

Nor did he really care, except to pay attention to it as a measure of the discontent that would lessen their support. He would later refer to the unruly crowd in the distance as irrelevant as a gathering of doves.

He declined to read a prepared statement, telling his speech writers that what he wanted to say was in his heart, that he just wanted to speak from his heart and from his convictions.

Whenever he spoke about what was living in his heart, the several levers that turned him, he was effective. Today he was, perhaps, more effective than ever. He knew that the cameras of the nation were upon him, as were, indeed, the cameras of the world. He spoke with passion and uncommon eloquence, urging the people of New York City to stay the course, while beseeching America to stand by them.

"How many times must I come before you and thank you for your bravery.? How many times must I ask you to lend your courage to your fellow Americans and to this great nation of ours?" he asked.

Near the end of his speech, he seemed for just a fraction to choke back his tears when he said, "Every once in a while, in the history of man, a people is asked to give beyond measure. We have been asked to do that. And every once in a while, a particular segment of that people, because they are strong and unyielding, is called upon to make the sacrifice more than once. You, my dear friends of New York City, have been asked to make the sacrifice more than once."

Before anyone had a chance to applaud, Nimer, in a moment almost regal, held it back with his right hand raised, before completing his remarks in a tone so sincere that they had bite and resonance. With fire in his eyes, he said "I pledge to you today, more than once is enough."

New Yorkers are not to be screwed with under any circumstances. Their crap detector is sophisticated, and they can make noise like no one else.

When Nimer said these words, they also applauded like no one else could. Though the outdoors usually converted the timbre of clapping to tin, they applauded him with a super gusto that translated their enthusiasm into the homes of millions in America and billions abroad.

Within the hour, a city firm manufactured T-shirts with the slogan "More than once is enough" on the front, and "Terrorists are hiding in their own ass hole" on the back.

Little did the American people know how literally Nimer meant it when he uttered the heart-felt phrase "More than once is enough." Given his plan and his intention to execute it, he might as well have said to the world, "This is the last time."

13

There are times in our lives when in the middle of everything going wrong, many things start to go right. In this re-distribution of misfortune and good luck, commanded by the universe itself, the scales that measure injustice, once moved out of balance, are righted again. And speedily. This was not to be one of those times.

New York City, the symbol of vitality and power, was attacked for the second time on Nimer's watch. Although he spoke eloquently in the aftermath of the tunnel attack, the polls still indicated that a slight majority of Americans did not approve of his handling of terrorism.

At the same time, the war in Iraq was still not really over. It was the first war America had ever fought where more men died after it was officially declared over than while it was officially going on.

Most observers thought that the mid-elections would be decided in the last few weeks, depending on what happened in the world. Conspiratorial theories were abundant. That the illusive weapons of mass destruction would be found hidden in caves in the northern part of Iraq, justifying the war and adding new vigor to its completion. And that our troops who had searched the outskirts of Tehran in every direction were beginning to find the bits and pieces of the Iranian technology to build an A-bomb.

None of these dramas, though, were to decide the elections. Not like in the weeks and months preceding his re-election, when his opponent in the presidential race had made much about his own heroic service in the Vietnam War. As the facts about Nimer's involvement in that war were illusive, the contrast in their military backgrounds was seized upon by some as an indication that Nimer was unfit to send Americans to war, and possibly to their deaths.

A few political ads began to show up in prime time, alluding to this difference in their war records. Their general tone usually was along the lines of asking viewers if they would feel secure re-electing a man who knew little about war to guide and protect them against increasing terrorism in the world.

But Nimer's supporters were always digging to find new information about his opponent, the kind of information that might connect with the country's Puritanical roots, its predictable show of horror at a sexual indiscretion or two, especially if it had a dramatic or scandalous flair to it.

As much as they tried, though, they found nothing of this sort. What they did find, though, was just as useful, depending on how it would be divulged as well as the mood of the country when it was.

A local newspaper writer in Garrison, Minnesota, was sitting at the bar in a Veterans of Foreign War lodge talking with several veterans of the Vietnam war. The conversation eventually got around to the Democratic candidate for office. The reporter indicated how impressed he was with the candidate's war record and heroic actions in Nam. How he had turned his patrol boat around to go back along the Mekong River to rescue a wounded comrade who had fallen overboard.

The veterans laughed at this. The real story, they said, was that veterans of the war despised the man. Sure, he might have done a quick 180 to position the boat for a rescue, but there was no going back any appreciable distance to get his fellow soldier treading water in his life jacket.

"All he had to do was reach over the side and haul him in. It was as easy as that," they said. And besides, the Vietcong soldier who had shot his buddy was lying on the side of the river bank, dying of his own wound. Do you know how big a .50 caliber machine gun bullet is?" one of them asked the reporter before answering his own question. "It can put a hole through a man as big as this around," he said, making a circle with the index and thumb fingers of his two hands.

"The poor guy was lying face down when our heroic candidate, as I've said, leaned over the side of the patrol boat and just shot him dead in the back. One round straight through his back, before hauling their ass out of there."

Again, a chord with the American past had been struck. Cowboys and gun-slingers would shoot a man face to face. That was the macho way. But shooting a wounded man in the back was against the code and the Geneva Conventions. It was the coward's way.

"And besides, most folks don't know that the man only served four months in Nam. There was a rule that if you got three purple hearts you were out of there, out of country, on the first plane out. So, he was gone. Served only four months. Funniest part of it, which most folks don't know, but vets do, is that the bastard wrote up his own citations for the Purple Hearts." The men laughed the derisive and scornful laugh of those who, from experience, had separated the real from the phony.

The reporter felt he was on to something. Knowing his stuff, he immediately asked if anyone in the room had experienced this for themselves. No one had, but they said it was common knowledge among Vietnam veterans, and that they probably, given some time, could round up a few who were in the area. The network was that good.

This was enough for the local, who seized that day to make a name for himself. "Common knowledge" was quickly transformed into verification, and it didn't take long for the spinmeisters to get the story out.

A reasonable doubt was quickly implanted in the idealistic psyche of the average American: "Would you trust a man who would shoot another man in the back, manipulate the story, and then write about it as if it were heroic?"

It was just enough to give the president a few additional points in the polls. The event that leveled the playing field came the next day in a medium-sized supermarket outside of Lincoln, Nebraska.

↘

The act was simple, yet it had a profound impact on America, more than the Twin Towers or the Queens-Midtown Tunnel terrorist attacks did.

Again, the optimum time for the most devastation was chosen by another set of "sleepers" willing to give up their lives. It was 10:30 a.m. on Saturday, October 30th, just two days before the presidential election.

Two al Qaeda-trained men and one woman, who had lived normal suburban lives on the outskirts of Lincoln for five years, it was learned later, were responsible.

One of the store managers who was situated at a front check-out line, helping at busy times to fill bags with food, told investigators that each of the three had the swarthy complexion of Middle East people, though he thought nothing of it. He was trained to keep an eye out for newcomers to the store, as his company knew from experience that newcomers were often transients set on robbing a few food items before moving on.

He said that he knew the faces of the three, that they had shopped there for about a year. He did notice, in retrospect only, that in the past month or so they had been in the store shopping at the same time.

It was discovered that one of the men had lived with the woman in a rented house. In fact, they had two young children. Their neighbors of five years told police that there was nothing unusual about them, although they might have been a bit private, not unusual for this day and age when neighbors were too busy to be friends.

They were nice enough. Said "hi" when they came outside every once in a while, mostly to mow the lawn or cook hamburgers on an tiny old-fashioned barbecue grill.

Their children rarely played in the back yard. That, they said, *was* noted as being unusual. One neighbor in particular said that she often remarked to her husband when the children did play in the yard that it was unusual. They mostly speculated how sorry they were that when the children were in the house they were probably watching TV or playing video games, and that their social growth might be stunted.

Otherwise, they seemed normal. No mustache for him, no burka on her. Nothing to make them different from any other American, as they put it. Even the one daughter who was in kindergarten seemed normal.

The other man lived in a rented apartment by himself. He was in his early thirties, clean-shaven and always well-dressed. His comings and goings were perceived as the comings and goings of a handsome, unmarried man, which he was.

His aloofness and ability to deflect questions allowed him to be in the community, but not of it. This was not unusual, so no one thought anything about it. If a man was the private sort, let him be.

Confident that they were above suspicion, they had communicated in the last week on the internet. Nevertheless, their e-mail messages were always brief, always coded. Some of the messages, later found on a server, made sense only after the bombings had taken place.

"Let's meet on the 30th for a hotdog. How about 10:30 sharp." And before that, "We'll shoot for Saturday. Let's go when it's least crowded." There was a message on the 29th from the one man, who appeared to be the ringleader, to the couple, that said, "We finally get to go shopping tomorrow."

Matching these and later messages against the realities of the 30th, which newspapers called "Gloomsday," the coded understandings seemed to be based on specificity and generality. If the message had specifics, such as "the 30th," it was to be interpreted literally. If it contained generalities, such as "when it's least crowded," it was to be interpreted as its opposite. It was simple enough, yet safe if discovered. Though innocuous on the surface, the communications ended in death and suffering.

It took only a few days to put the pieces together. The couple had entered the store first at about 10:15 in the morning. They said "hello" to a few people when they came in. Then the man picked up the local paper from the rack and looked at it carefully, even opening it to an inside page to read something for a minute, then folded it back up neatly and placed it in one of the small plastic baskets that shoppers used when they were going to buy just a few items. She took a shopping cart from outside the store.

Again, only in retrospect did it seem odd that they each had a large backpack on their backs. Odd because just about everyone would leave packs of this sort in their car. One of the assistant managers, semi-trained in surveillance for would-be shoplifters, thought little of it. It was a nice day, and they probably had taken a walk before going shopping, maybe stopping to eat and drink from the pack. Perhaps they had bought a few items from another store on their way there.

The only thing he noted, he told the investigators later, was that packs were sometimes used by shoplifters. But they were regulars who had never raised any suspicion. "You just give them the benefit of the doubt," he said, "and move on."

He did say, though, that his inner alert mechanism sounded when the third person with a backpack walked in the door a few minutes later. The young man said "hello," then went immediately into the center isle to shop. The assistant followed him at a distance for a few minutes while observing him as inconspicuously as possible. He did nothing out of the ordinary. Nevertheless, the assistant manager decided to report this to the manager. While he was on his way, the bombs blew.

The woman probably placed the pack in the wire carriage. Pieces of the carriage were later found near the section where cold cuts, roasted chickens, and assorted mixed salads were sold. All other carriages were found bent yet intact because the percussion of the blast went right through the square spaces in the baskets.

As this section of the store was located near the popular pies and tarts specialties, it was where, generally speaking, the gathering of shoppers was most crowded. The terrorists had done their homework.

In all, there were three blasts. One near the pastries section, the second in the isle with freezers that contained assorted micro-wave pies, vegetables, pizzas and dinners, and the third on the side of the store that displayed meats of every sort, from filet mignons to cuts of chuck.

Some said the slaughter was well-coordinated, that the blasts went off simultaneously. Others said the bombs, analyzed later to be made of dynamite charges ignited with hand switches, went off one after the other in a sort of a staccato, like firecrackers in a string.

The force of the air being compressed was the first thing most survivors felt, then the bang and percussion of the explosion. Some of the more cogent survivors said it felt as if they were inside a tin can when a hand grenade erupted in it.

Things, food, and people were blown everywhere. Firefighters compared the scene they found to the ugliness of a sick nightmare movie. Sometimes, they said, it was impossible to know if they were picking up a large piece of meat or a part of a person. Whether fact or imagination, others said they could not distinguish bits and pieces of chop meat from bloody human flesh.

Think of an unusual slaughterhouse wherein the animals, skin-stripped and hanging on hooks, their heads cut off and their torsos sliced in two, are taken from the hooks and laid on the floor. Yet their torsos have not been emptied and cleaned of their intestines and other viscera. Nor has the blood been entirely drained from their bodies. Cut off their legs, too, and strew them about the floor.

This is what Strefano's Supermarket looked like when the police and firefighters arrived three minutes after the blast, the acrid smell of dynamite still fresh in the air.

Only the core section of the supermarket remained intact, and not entirely so. Canned goods, bottles of soda, some broken, breakfast cereals and the like, were scattered here and there in that area. A few isolated shelves seemed as neat and orderly as they had been three and a half hours prior when the market opened.

It was speculated later that the terrorists came into the store, pretended they were shopping for a few minutes in order to appear normal and not arouse suspicions. At an exact time, they walked to their predetermined spots, and continued to fake that they were shopping while at the same time setting their electric switches to ignite the dynamite in ten to fifteen seconds, certainly not enough time to be caught or stopped.

The only remains of the terrorists was the driver's license of a Mohammed Moussire, who, it was determined, was the father of the two little children.

Roughly ninety-six people died in the explosions, eighty-five of them customers. It was again difficult to determine the number of dead. That the explosions occurred in a self-contained area made the work of discovering mutilated bodies and body parts possible. The complications came from the intermingling of food products, especially the meats, with body parts. Forensic specialists certainly had the technology, but it was time consuming and the public, especially the families of the dead and missing, grew irritable quickly. It was not until a week after the election that the numbers of dead were increased by eleven when it was determined, not conclusively for all eleven, that their bodies were completely obliterated.

Evidence that nine of the eleven were at the supermarket was compelling enough for their families to request financial compensation from the government. However, relatives of the other two "missing persons" could not account for their presence at the supermarket without a reasonable doubt.

Most disturbing to America, though, was that fourteen children between the ages of four and nine had been killed. No doubt, they were out for a Saturday morning of shopping with their moms and dads, an event usually made more joyful by the small empowering acts of letting the children choose their own breakfast cereal, pick the bag of potato chips, or carry some of the purchases in the little carts provided by Strefano's.

Blowing up the supermarket appeared at first to be an act of unsurpassed brilliance and planning, especially in its purpose to defeat Nimer, who al Qaeda knew was more than a thorn in their side. Blowing it up at the last minute, though, was a miscalculation of the American people.

Nor did Nimer's Democratic opponent know the American people. Thinking that the voters would agree with his assessment that the country couldn't be trusted to a commander in chief who could neither protect them against terrorism nor get their sons and daughters out of Iraq, he pounded this theme home non-stop for most of the two days before election day. He traveled as quickly as he could in a private jet to whatever large city his staff could get him a venue by day, and appeared on as many TV talk shows as he could by night.

Somehow, though, it all backfired on him. In the several days after Nimer won the election by a small margin, opinion columnists and TV talk shows were riveting with guess work about the way the election went, comparing it to Truman's upset of Dewey in 1948.

In the previous two days, it had been thought by many that President Fletcher Nimer was trapped in the net of terrorism. How could Americans vote for him again, what with three tragic attacks and bad wars happening during his tenure? How could they ever trust a man like that?

What they didn't know was the extent of Nimer's street-smarts. Oh, sure, most insiders knew that the man had what it took when push came to shove. They didn't understand, though, the depth of his intuitive ability to calculate what might happen next. Whatever psychic dysfunctions, minor or major, were his, allowed him to know ahead of its time what actions others, just as quirky and off-center as he was, might take.

He was, for example, aware that American sports fans always rooted for the underdog. That when an awesomely talented basketball star, accused of rape, was introduced in the starting lineup the very next night after the accusation, his name would be met with enthusiastic, if not wild, applause.

He was aware that the baseball star accused of taking steroids in order to add to his home run totals was greeted with applause and even affection. Although he thought it was wrong, no one held infidelity against movie stars, or financial indiscretions against pop celebrities.

Even the peccadilloes of former presidents were met with a distant admiration by the public who found it amusing that great men are, in the end, just men.

Nimer knew that the American people always rooted for the underdog, that they were easy to forgive, and liked having a strong father figure. Even though that strength might have at times been misguided, it was strength nevertheless.

Besides, his opponent did not seem to be catching on with Americans. He did not seem able to affix a strong signature on the campaign. Many felt that they simply did not know who he was, or what he might decide to do in a pinch. Nimer also counted on the growing misgivings about the man's ballyhooed war record and the public's knowledge that he had killed a defenseless man by shooting him in the back.

Nimer quickly decided to execute an unexpected tactic in order to win the election.

He would get on prime-time television Monday night. He would do the expected by pledging his commitment once again to overcome terrorism. And he would do the unexpected. He would apologize to the American people!

With tears in his eyes and a calculated pause to catch his breath, he told the people how sorry he was that so many had died on our soil, that so may had died on foreign soil.

What made this "A Talk with America," as the press would later call it, instead of a speech, was that he meant what he said. He was genuinely sorry that so many had died "in freedom's cause." He was sick of killings, of cold-blooded murders, death and dying. A genuine hunger for justice came through to the people that night.

Enough viewers decided then and there that they actually liked him, actually felt something for him for the first time. Besides, he was now the underdog.

By a bare margin, they elected him the next day to a second term.

14

Nimer enjoyed the triumph of his re-election for less than a week. Most of the time he spent trying to get America to shop again. During the week of the attack, almost every mother stayed home, afraid to go out, especially to go food shopping. Retail outlets of every kind were at a standstill. Even school attendance was down markedly across the nation.

Suddenly the commander in chief of the Armed Forces assumed the role of cheerleader in chief of the American Economy. Every industry related to food was impacted by the terrorist attack on the supermarket. Growing, processing, trucking, warehousing and distribution. By the millions, people simply stopped shopping. Al Qaeda had shut down a large part of the economy.

Nimer knew he had to get America shopping again, both for the sake of the economy as well as for the morale of the nation. He appeared live on TV twice that week, as well as in numerous ads. He tried mostly to appeal to the national sense of defiance. If they did not shop, he said repeatedly, the terrorists would have won.

Business leaders, too, helped in whatever ways they could. One ad executive created a t-shirt he thought would improve the situation, distributing a million of them on a first-request basis to supermarkets across the land. However, its slogan, "Shop 'til You Drop," never caught on.

Before too many days went by, hunger simply brought the people back.

Not only did America resume shopping, they did it with gusto. The economy got healthier, and the number of jobs increased. Productivity and wealth were up. Economists said that even though the wealth was flowing to the rich, it might eventually spill over and down on the middle class and the poor.

The incursion into Iran was sold to the American people as a clear shot into Tehran with a limited force that had an exit strategy: to get out as soon as evidence of Iran's nuclear buildup was unearthed. The American people perceived Nimer's act as bold and decisive.

Most important of all, there were no more acts of terrorism on American soil. Nimer passed the word that he was deadly serious about homeland security, that anyone not found on the job 24/7 would be history. A commitment to make something happen, one of the extraordinary parts of America's backbone, was working. In this case, it was a commitment to prevent something: terrorism.

There was little drama in all this. Simply a fitting together of the parts. Nimer knew the recipe for re-cooking of the organic pie of America. Enough party members were elected to the Congress to insure a majority in both houses. The president had the political padding he needed.

He decided the time for the bomb was now. The one great reservation he had was cleared, and he didn't have to worry about the after-debris of the bomb.

In order to keep the circle of those who knew about the plan tight, he called on his trusted body servant, Richard, who had never failed him.

Not wanting anything incriminating to befall Richard if the plan went awry, he simply asked him one morning if he would be willing to make a few phone calls and deliver a few messages. Nothing earth-shaking, just a few messages that he didn't want to trust anyone else with. Touched by the flattery, and prompted by his loyalty to the president, he said he would be happy to do that "for you, Mr. President."

Richard found it humorous when Nimer told him always to identify himself as "Back Seat" when he was delivering messages, whether by phone or in person. He told him that whenever he wanted Richard to deliver a message, he would point to the small table next to the side of the bed he slept on. There would be an envelope.

"Open the envelope and do what the message from me asks. It will sometimes have a phone number in it. Just call from home, say 'This is Back Seat' and speak the message, which will be in writing. You might also have to deliver the message in person. "Never, I repeat, *never*, deliver the message, though, unless the other person says, 'This is Major Justin Overstreet speaking.' Only then deliver the message.

"Always ask if he wants you to repeat the message. If he says yes, do it once only. If he says no, just hang up or leave. Tell no one else, ever.

"Do you have all of that, Richard?"

"Yes, sir, Mr. President, I have it all," he replied, resisting the impulse to say it felt good to be in a James Bond movie.

"One last thing. Always put the envelope and its contents back on the same table the next time you come back into my room. You'll be doing me a great favor, Richard."

⌵

The rainy season in Hanoi was over and the evenings beckoned people to be outside, walking, often shopping for the next day's fruits and vegetables in the always buzzing market places.

The people loved to sit in little groups on the sidewalks in the evenings. One group might gossip about people in another group a half block away, while that group was talking about them. Grandmas would cook on the wok, and serve up little meats and vegetables a bit at a time, so the eating and conversation might go on to well after midnight.

Jobs were scarce, but the government had figured out an ingenious way to employ twice the number of its people than there were jobs. They simply asked employers to hire two people for half a day each rather than one person full-time. The pace of life was normally an easy one, and this method helped to slow it down even more. The ones who had the first half of the day off could stay up half the night, eating and talking. The regular rotation of hours allowed everyone periodically to catch up on the gossip.

Quan Trong Thanh lived in the Old Quarter, an 800-year-old section of Hanoi that was a crowded, noisy, smelly, yet romantic place. Its streets were a network of shops and homes combined. The second floor of these home-shops still lay bare the architecture of colonial France. Except for the lines of laundry hanging about and the strewn flower pots, they were the same porches the French built. If they were freshly painted, one could imagine going back to over a hundred years ago when they were first built.

The streets, too, were the same as a hundred years ago, tight and narrow, no longer functional for the cars, busses, trucks and motorbikes of today. It was easy enough, though, for pedestrians to cross the narrow streets. Look and dash was the method.

The boulevards down by the lakes, though, were another story. From early childhood, mothers taught their children to walk as normally as they could across wide streets. If they could just keep up an even gait, the traffic could make judgments based on the predictability of the walk and avoid collisions. It was only when someone got nervous and broke stride that accidents would occur. This was so infrequent that when it did happen, it was an event. Crowds would gather, mostly to watch how the inconvenience was handled. If nothing worse than bruising occurred, and the negotiated settlement was handled with courtesy by all parties, the event ended quickly. But, if an expected apology was not forthcoming, a long and heated argument might occur. If one of the parties was not satisfied with the level of politeness offered by the other, only the presence of the police would stop the verbal outbursts before life could go on in the neighborhood.

Thanh loved the streets, though garbage and some human waste ran down their sides. He loved saying "hello" to his neighbors who ran the little shops, and sometimes he would be invited to come into the back half of a shop, which was their home. They would sit on the straw mats they used for their beds, eat some fruit and drink tea.

In the old days before he married Huong, one or another of the young women employed to watch a store while the family was away running their own errands might invite him into the back room for tea and whatever the moment might bring.

He loved the memory of those moments, more so lately as he and his wife of six years were not getting along. It was shocking to realize with a kind of suddenness that the erosion of their marriage had been taking place for about two years. At least that is what Huong thought.

"We haven't taken a cyclo-rickshaw to West Lake in a long time," she blurted out at him. He said it was the rain, she said it was a lack of interest, and that he seemed pre-occupied.

Thanh had told her early on in their relationship that he had little patience with the jealousy she sometimes showed. He said that it demeaned him when she accused him of being flirtatious or staring at a pretty woman in a traditional ao dai dress that accentuated curved hips and breasts. He told her that he looked at these women the same way he would look at a sculpted piece in a museum.

Whenever she said that he seemed preoccupied, it was the code word for her jealousy. In fact, he was faithful to her, although sometimes the fidelity leaked a little around the edges of propriety, especially when he danced with other women at the neighborhood parties they attended. He liked to slide his free hand lower on the buttocks than was commonly accepted practice for the modest Vietnamese women.

Whenever Huong noticed this, she would begin to withdraw. When he inquired about her aloofness, she could not answer, as he would say again that she was jealous. Tension over the idea of jealousy began to take on a life of its own.

She was slowly turning away from him, using her energies to make the unique flower pieces that she loved so much. When he was unaccountably gone for more time than she had come to expect, she began to think the worst. It was now common knowledge that AIDS was spreading in the country, so she was beginning to avoid her husband.

"We don't talk anymore," he told her at lunch that Sunday.

"We never did," she retorted in a one-liner that made him angry. In their ways of seeing the world, they were both right. He always wanted to probe the depths of things. That was talk. She was satisfied with whatever, as long as it didn't have to be parsed or analyzed. Or as long as it didn't become a problem.

He was never a simple man, yet when she fell in love with him she expected that a mechanic wouldn't ask so many questions or be so questioning of the way things were. In time, she discovered a man in conflict, a man trying to get out of his head and into his heart, which was the place he liked the most, the simplest and most loving place for him to be.

Getting out of his head, though, had its exit dangers for them. He left it by talking about Vietnam, about its problems. He wanted to serve his people. That was the way he often talked. "My people" had become a catchword for the worth of his life. Huong used to kid him about this, saying that it would be on his gravestone, that she would make sure it was, even if he was killed in a car accident out in the country and they buried his broken body in the nearest patch of land, as was the custom. She would make sure he had a stone that said these words.

His excessive thinking and her predisposition to jealousy became a deadly combination over time. She wanted him back in the simple state she had found him. He wanted her to be there for him without any questions about his loyalty to her.

Maybe tonight they would take that cyclo-rickshaw to the lake. He promised himself he would not talk about polluted rivers or algae in the lakes. Nor about the sewage problems in the streets of Hanoi, or the choking smells from the cars and motorbikes. He wouldn't talk about the cynical politician in Ho Chi Minh City who told "his people" on TV yesterday, "We have given you the hats. Now give us the rabbits."

There would be no talk tonight about the poor farmers of Vietnam who were sacrificing their faith in tomorrow by accepting their government's dirty insecticides today. Or about the second generation of Agent Orange babies being born blind.

The only talk tonight would be about his wife. He would buy her a bouquet of the roses she loved from one of the many women selling flowers on the street. Thanh promised himself that tonight he would sacrifice his relentless brooding, not for his people's sake, but for the sake of Huong, the woman he loved.

※

While carrying out his many presidential responsibilities, Nimer managed with all the stealth he had learned in governing, to meet with the people necessary to accomplish his plan.

Relying on Arena and Overstreet's willingness to keep the secret about an atomic plan, he seized the first chance he had to assure Jarvis that the plan to start a conventional war was a "go," and asked for his advice as to which country it ought to be, a way to keep the secretary's focus on the wrong place.

"I've been giving this a lot of thought, Mr. President. I think it ought to be Iran. A full invasion." He waited a minute for the president to react.

"It's a good choice, Norm. A really good choice. We have some of our troops in there now. Moving more of them there won't be all that difficult. We might be a little short-handed in Iraq for a bit before the UW is up and running. But it will give you a chance to mobilize more fast-moving units from among our divisions, you know, the ones with the most technology and ability for a quick, mobile strike.

"It will give you a chance to test out your theory that quick-moving, streamlined troops packed with the latest and most efficient equipment, resources, and specialized gear is the way to go in today's wars. Norm, what shall we tell the American people about why we are ratcheting it up in Iran?"

Jarvis responded quickly, as he had thought this over to give the answer he thought was most creative and most pleasing to the president.

"We can first remind our people about the nuclear buildup, and how hard we are trying to bring democracy to that area of the world, how we are supporting a new government in Iraq, as well as standing behind the efforts that Israel is making to bring peace to that part of the world. Also, how many of our boys have paid the price. And our women, too," he added. "We have some units in Afghanistan posted on the border of Iran. There's a sort of flat land that runs for miles along the middle of the western part of Afghanistan where it juts into the eastern part of Iran near a city called Birjand.

"We've got a hundred or so troops on alert there because we think it's a place that the Iranians allow al Qaeda cells to train and prepare for sabotage in the region. We have reason to think, also, that al Qaeda members cross into Afghanistan from this spot to pay off some war lords to resist our efforts there.

"We've spotted a large contingent of Iranian soldiers in this region. They are heavily armed. I'm sure if we suck them into a firefight on the border that some of our people will be killed. You can, in your own inimitable way, convince America and the Congress of the reason for our invasion.

"I'm sure, too, that given the green light to invade with our swiftest high-tech units, the battle will be over, perhaps in a week."

Again, Nimer agreed, more to get rid of Jarvis, whom he was beginning to disdain, and to keep him occupied in the ensuing weeks when the real, and perhaps last, war would begin.

He had what he needed from Jarvis, his voice on tape running through the sequence that Nimer needed to authorize dropping the bomb.

"Again, good work, Norm. Why don't you get right on it. Better still, wait 'til you hear from me. I'll call you to set up a principals committee meeting, and then a cabinet meeting. Or maybe the other way around would be better. I don't know. I'll let you know soon. Thank you again for a great job here, Norm. We'll talk."

As Jarvis left the room, Nimer was hoping that the secretary of defense would begin to tell his confidants in the government about the impending war. If he did, the "buzz" would be on. Rumors would fly, phones ring, secret office and cocktail hour conversations would begin. Everyone would be busy anticipating the future, while few would be in the present, when Nimer and his cohorts were plotting to shape events that would take some lives in order, Nimer was convinced, to save many lives.

15

"Mr. President, I agree in theory with what you are doing. But I cannot participate. That is, I can only participate to a point."

With these words from General Arena, a sudden and startling electric surge ran through the president, starting from his heart and darting to his extremities.

Although it seemed like a jolt of lightning ran through him, it was only fear giving birth to anxiety. He heard Arena's words as the articulation of his worst fears, that someone along the line of people he needed would not cooperate.

All he could think of saying was, "What do you mean?"

The question came out more like a whimper than a reprimand. He sounded like an eleven-year-old whose father has just told him they would not be going to Yankee Stadium tomorrow, that something else had just come up.

Nimer was immediately aware of the complaining tone of his question. He was determined to rectify the mistake and take command again. Arena, though, continued. "Mr. President, I have already completed your order to have a Hiroshima-type bomb prepared. But I am backing off on the information that I gave to you verbally in this office about targeting Hotan, Jilin, or Al Bab. Frankly, I agree with your analysis of the current state of world affairs. I also agree with your assessment of man's history, that it seems to be one war after another after another, and that there seems to be no end to the killing.

"You know that I'd like to go into Iran right now with 200,000 troops with the biggest and best equipment and blow those bastards to kingdom come. They want to give themselves up for the sixteen virgins, or twenty-one virgins, or whatever, and I'd like to give them that chance. They want the kingdom, well come and get it. I'm the same as you this way, Mr. President. I have not trained myself to lead men into war because I like war or killing. No, sir. I like peace! Yet, it seems no matter what we do, no matter how hard we try, the wars continue, the killing continues. So, I agree with your thinking and will help. But I cannot and will not be an official part of the plan to drop an atomic bomb on a city. I am afraid of the consequences. I have a wife and a daughter I love. I try to see my world through their eyes. I ask myself how they might feel about me when I give an order that I know will end in the loss of people's lives, sometimes innocent people, people just like Flo and Terry.

"When I think that way, I must weigh my decisions carefully. It is one thing for innocent people to be killed in a bombing raid when the raid is justified. There's always collateral damage. It's the same thing when I give the okay for our troops to enter a hostile city to get the bad guys. We just know from experience that some innocent folks sitting in their living rooms will be killed. It can't be helped. But dropping an atomic bomb that will blow up an entire city..."

The president interrupted. "It might not be an entire city. It could very well be just a portion of a city."

"Nevertheless," Arena continued, "many people will be killed in a flash, just like that. Others will be crippled, maimed, radiated and die lingering deaths. People whose flesh is burning will drown themselves just to get out of the pain. I know, I've read the books and seen the films.

"After our last meeting, I ordered a film called 'A Mother's Love.' It is about how the Japanese mothers reacted to the atomic bombing of Hiroshima in 1945. The film in it of the disaster is so horrible that General MacArthur withheld it from the Japanese public for ten years. He was afraid if they saw it, all hell would break out across Japan, and our occupational nation building would be hampered.

"It is simple with me, Mr. President. I do not want to have my name associated with your plan. Off the record, I will get you the bomb, and I will get you an inside man at the Greenbrier. It is being taken care of in a way that is above suspicion for me. Mr. President, I am not accustomed to using my clout against my commander in chief. But I must tell you, and I must be clear, that if my name or office is ever identified with this project, this plan to provoke an attack and to retaliate by dropping the bomb, I will categorically deny it, and I will do all in my power, which is considerable, to be difficult for you.

"Mr. President, I want to put a seal on this episode for me. I am embarrassed at what I am about to tell you, and I ask for your understanding. You would, perhaps, do the same thing if you were in my shoes and in my head. I want you to know that I have kept a diary, that neither Flo or Terry know about, from out first meeting about your plan until now. As soon as I get back to my office, I will write up today's notes. The diary is in sections, and each section is stored in a different place. Each section begins with a complete summary of all the previous ones, so there's an assured continuity. Only I know where they have been placed. There's no point in any one looking for them, as they could never be located except if the starter memo is known.

"If I should die, let's say an untimely or suspicious death, the starter memo will kick in. Don't even think about how it will. It will. In the diary is a fully detailed account of my withdrawal from the plan, along with my account of each meeting with you about this. In this way, the world will know, especially my family, that I was, shall we say, a reluctant participant."

"General Arena, do you know what you're saying, and who you're talking to?"

"Yes, sir, I do. And that is not all. I want a statement in writing about my reluctance, signed by you as president of the United States. I am not going to let my reputation go down the toilet bowl if this fails."

Before Nimer could respond, Arena said, "If you want my limited cooperation in getting the bomb ready and a man inside the Greenbrier, as well as helping you with the cover story for dropping it, you'll give me what I ask. If you don't, count me out."

For emphasis, he added, "Totally!"

The president walked over to the large window in his office, looked out of it for a few minutes in a pretense that he was making up his mind about this unusual request.

Actually, he had made up his mind as soon as Arena had indicated what his "limited cooperation" would be. He was indifferent about the request. As long as he got from Arena what he needed, he was satisfied, so confident was he about the outcome.

Nimer knew that Arena was the last piece he needed, and if he acted quickly it didn't matter what the general needed from him. He would give it, he would give almost anything now, in the name of peace, to make his plan work.

He began to hand-write the following:

> *I, Fletcher Nimer, president of the United States, take full responsibility for the atomic bombing of . . .*

"Jeff, I forgot to ask you. Which of the three cities would you like me to put down?"

Arena's response was sharp. "There'll be nothing further from me about that, sir."

Nimer tore the piece of paper he was writing on into little pieces and threw it into the garbage receptacle under his desk with a sharp, snapping motion calculated to deceive the general into thinking he was angry.

> *I, Fletcher Nimer, president of the United States, take full responsibility for authorizing the release of the atomic bomb. It is my decision alone. Any military or civilian cooperation in this matter was done on my direct order as the president and commander in chief.*

He showed it to Arena, who read it and said, "Please date and sign it."

The president did as he was told, knowing that if Arena knew the full truth about the plan, he would run for help to discredit the president as quickly as he could.

16

Nimer knew it was time to act. Everything was in place, yet a few parts were shaky. Jarvis had been left out in the cold, and as soon as he found this out, he might do what he could to stop the plan, if only out of his own careful ways that precluded the boldness Nimer needed in those instrumental to executing the plan.

Arena would go along part of the way, but was still in the dark about the real nature of the plan, that it might include countries different from the ones he chose, that there would be no manipulative plan, no excuse to drop the bomb. The worst part, the lottery, the two and a half days of waiting for the world, the day of waiting for the last two cities chosen, would be unacceptable for Arena, once he knew.

As for Overtsreet, well, he was relatively young and inexperienced, a romantic idealist who could be persuaded by logic that was articulated in visions chasing dreams seen through rose-colored glasses. Anywhere along that continuity of discontinuities things could go wrong.

Nimer knew that his own transactions with world leaders, coupled with the sum total of his education, intuitions, experiences, loves, hatreds, and longings, had all led him to this day.

He knew all along that he had been appointed by some divine force to lead the world away from killing, to lead it towards the freedom he had always felt was every man's gift from God.

Asking God to embolden his hand, Nimer decided to act now.

Before secluding himself at the Greenbrier, he had to choose the four countries and cities for part one of the plan. Most of that work had already been done, ironically, at national security and cabinet meetings when he was bored or preoccupied with thinking about his plan. He had a way of doodling in code at those meetings, so that "icy place" was Iceland, "porn cap" was Vanuatu, and "rocooco" Morocco. "Goodturf" meant it was a possibility, "red light" was out of the question, "go-go" a possibility. And so on.

He always doodled on plain white 8 ½ by 11 paper, which he scrupulously took away from meetings to give to Richard to shred. He just kept paring down the possibilities until only four remained.

Nimer had only two criteria for his selection process. The first was that the choice had to be fair. "Fairness" was a vague notion he had, a kind of bag full of personal values he had assumed over the years. It included not hurting your own, which then excluded, of course, ourselves and the Canadians to the north. Russia was excluded, as they were friends, at least in name, plus they also had A-bombs of their own.

Red China was excluded for the same reasons. At first, all countries of Western Europe were excluded because dropping the bomb on any one country might mean harming other countries, possible friends, with fallout radiation. Many of these countries, such as Germany, Italy, Spain, and Portugal, although sometimes fair-weather friends, were excluded. England was out.

The concept of fairness, though, might include exceptions, based on his gut feelings about the unworthiness of old friends, as well as their geographical location, which might be useful. The concept was about as fair as giving a fox a head start before unloosing the dogs.

Besides, he thought, if he was absolutely fair the element of fear that would bring chaos to the lesson might be reduced in the equation.

His second criteria was that it must be a place that had enough people congregating together to give the world ample examples of what physical and psychological damage the bomb could do. This immediately excluded places like the Canary and Galapagos Islands. There could, though, be exceptions.

At one time or another his list of nations included Cuba, Morocco, Vietnam, Argentina, North Korea, Indonesia, Greenland, New Zealand, countries of the Mid-East, Romania, and Kenya. France was included as the exception to the rule.

Central America and the Caribbean-based nations were excluded because they were too close to the American mainland. This then precluded Cuba, which was disappointing to Nimer, who had grown up in the tradition of hating Cuba, led by the devil himself, Fidel Castro, who must be punished, no matter the cost to the citizens of his country. Castro was a splinter in the side that the president would like to extract by blowing it away. Problem was, the fragments would fall down on Miami.

Morocco would have been a good, somewhat neutral, country with a few large cities such as Casablanca and Marrakech to hit. The desert in the south would prove useful because it would be there with its unmitigated heat that survivors would flee to die. Portugal and Spain were just north across the Straits of Gibralter, too close for comfort, he thought.

He would have delighted in dropping the bomb on France, if only for the real and alleged slights of the past few years. It would be unthinkable to bomb Paris.

It was not to be. France was an ally, a part of the traditional diplomatic framework for now. Besides, bombing it would most likely spread radiation to her neighbors, many of them America's friends.

Nimer knew about Vanuatu, a republic in the South Pacific Ocean. It was the communications center of the internet porno industry, the source of the mysterious and expensive phone calls on the monthly telephone bills of thousands of unassuming and innocent American men, porno peepers, who didn't yet quite know the ropes of the internet.

The island was perfect for the bomb. It was isolated, flat enough for his purposes, and had a population of 150,000 people, more than enough to give testimony that wars had to end. What it didn't have was proximity to a bomber that might make it there quickly enough before it could be intercepted if anything went wrong with the plan. He reluctantly erased the slut center from his list.

Vietnam was perfect, an opportunity to finish old business. Nimer thought of it as "payback on a stick" for the one time that we had been humiliated as a nation in a full-scale war.

Whenever he read a book about that war, he became infuriated that we had run a scared war. Scared of Red China, scared of the Soviet Union, scared that a full-scale atomic war might break out. We should have invaded the north with ground troops, he always thought. We should have used force even more massive than we did, on the ground, right there in the heartland of the Communists. We could have marched into Hanoi, at the same time telling the other Commies in China and Russia to get lost. If they wanted the big war right then, we should have had it. At least by now the dust would have cleared, the damage cleaned up, the dead buried, and everyone would have learned that destruction, like the kind he was going to show the world, did not pay.

Argentina was on his list for awhile because it had location, population, and virtual anonymity with the American people. Its little frontier city of Ushuaia was the southernmost city in the world, just north of the Drake Passage from the Antarctic. Its small population of 40,000 would have been a perfect sample for demonstrating the damage of the bomb. Yet the principle of fairness, as he knew it, kicked in for Nimer on this one. Although he believed that nature and animals were created for the use of man, he thought it was not fair to America's grandchildren to know about whales, penguins and seals from videotapes only. As he thought of himself as a kindhearted teacher, the humpback and orca whales, the chinstrap and adelie penguins, the crabeater and leopard seals would be spared from the tidal waves and radiation that would come across the Drake if the winds worked against them that day.

Nimer would have loved to include North Korea, a key prong in the "Axis of Evil." They had always seemed like a far-away danger to him until they hinted at possessing atomic warheads and missiles that could reach the west coast of America. Without doubt anymore, they were a very real danger.

Yet the danger always lived in the shadows of the past. America had fought them to a standstill fifty years ago when they didn't have atomic weapons. It was a long and costly war. Another one would be more dangerous than when China threw their ground troops into battle like so much fodder. China, too, now had nuclear weapons, as well as long-range delivery capacity.

It was better, he thought, if their government continued to rattle sabers while starving their people to death and reducing them to squalor. Time would cripple them just like it did the Soviet Union. Besides, North Korea's atomic weapons, because of their proximity to Red China, were more of a danger to the Chinese than to us.

The hundreds of islands of Indonesia would also provide the test-tube conditions for Nimer. Practically any one of its many islands would do. For a half century Indonesia had been difficult to handle. Insurrectionists, it seemed, did not often take a breath from their struggle for freedom.

Mostly, though, they did not meet the second criteria of being consequential. Besides, he thought, the damage would be spread too thin.

Greenland was intriguing for Nimer's purposes. It was the biggest island in the world, yet had several cities with enough people in it to showcase the results he wanted. Its citizens were Danish and were dependent on Denmark for help in handling their foreign affairs. But Denmark was weak in the ways that counted for Nimer, so possible consequences were really inconsequential to him.

Most of Greenland's little cities and villages were populated by Inuit

Indians, and their loss would not be as important, he thought, as that of countries the world was more acquainted with.

On the downside was its location, much of it inside the Arctic Circle. Some polar bears might die in the after-effects of the bombing. As might whales and caribou. Unfortunately, it was a complex world, Nimer thought, and sometimes you couldn't save everyone.

He quickly discounted New Zealand, although it had possibilities. It just seemed unfair to bomb them, as they had never caused anyone any trouble, at least to his knowledge. Besides, it was too interwoven with Anglo-Saxon values, and there might be some trouble there.

There were certain possibilities in the Mid-East. Iran and Syria, for starters. But he could not go there, as the region was already too volatile. He had a mind to just blow much of it all up, and often scribbled little mushroom doodles on scrap paper with the words "Run, Sire," his own lean understanding of regional wars in the area long ago. Besides, Israel was too close, as were American troops active in the region.

Sometimes he thought about Eastern Europe as a possibility, although, in the final analysis, he didn't know enough about it to draw any conclusions regarding its worthiness for his plan. And he didn't want to begin asking any questions now as it might raise too many suspicions.

It was only in the last week or so that he began to entertain thoughts about Africa. He knew there was a grave AIDS problem there, that it had a lot of countries in and out of dictatorships, that one of its leaders some time ago was a cannibal, and there were lots of valuable mineral deposits here and there.

He did, though, feel kind of drawn to it because it was far away and thus removed from the radar screen of American consciousness. He knew that the media from Europe would move in quickly to record the event, and that photographers always did a splendid job in Africa taking pictures of wasted mothers and their dying children, so he could count on them for that.

There were plenty of opportunities in Africa. Lots of countries, small- and medium-sized cities, some mountains and valleys and little villages teeming with possibilities to show the world the cruelties of atomic death.

Nimer didn't even care about what African-Americans would think. His background had virtually shut him off from contact with them and, as they populated the underprivileged class, he quickly learned in his political experiences that he didn't have to pay much attention to them. The one time he did go to Africa, he did not even invite any of their leaders to meet with him about their concerns before he left. "Going to Kenya," he said, "was not about African-Americans. It was about Africans."

Nimer spent the last two nights in his bedroom checking and re-checking his lists. He was sincere about picking the target places and cities with fairness while still paying attention to results.

It was a difficult task that he knew could be pondered for ever and ever. Whenever he was met with this kind of a dilemma, he called upon something in a shoe ad that he had seen a long time ago and that always stuck in his mind. "Just do it" had become his mantra in situations that presented him with a struggle to decide one thing over the next. There weren't many of them, but when they came up he would say to himself, "Just do it," and then he would do it.

After two days, he had the list. He would, when the time came, present it to the world in alphabetical order. For now, he would not write them down. There would be no trouble remembering the painful process when it came time to write his autobiography.

The List:

Kenya, Nairobi
Australia, Sydney
Greenland, Ilulissat
Vietnam, Hanoi

It had been a spiritual struggle to pick these four out of about two hundred countries, although his thinking was freed up by another personal axiom: whenever there is fairness in the world, there is also unfairness. Being fair to one child only caused an unfairness to the other. He called it the "unfairness of fairness" principle. In order to echo this principle, he chose Australia as the exception to his rules, even though it had several large cities. It simply was not fair to make the drop on these people, as they had never offended the United States.

According to his calculations, four out of two hundred would be about 2% of the world's nations, and way less than that as a percentage of cities. Relatively speaking, it would only be a small number of people who would die and suffer for the good of the whole.

In retrospective ceremonies, he thought, they probably would be considered heroes, perhaps even have cities, parks, and schools named after them.

17

It was now November 11th, Veterans Day. How fitting, Nimer thought, that all the sacrifices made by our soldiers over the years in the name of peace would begin to be vindicated on this day.

"Richard, please take the envelope from my table today, and do what it says. Do you remember my instructions?"

"Yes, Mr. President. I am to take the message, read it, and do what it says. My code name is 'Back Seat.' I am never to give the message unless the other person says 'This is Major Justin Overstreet speaking.' Then I give it, and ask if he wants me to repeat the message. If he says yes, then I repeat it and cut out. If he says no, I cut out, always making sure I place the envelope and its contents back on your night table at the first opportunity. I am never to tell anyone about this. I am to call from home."

"Exactly, Richard. I am proud of you," he said, not as condescendingly as it could have sounded to an outsider. Richard simply accepted it for what it was, an expression of affection from his president.

At the end of his morning duties to Nimer, Richard left the bedroom, excited to be going to his little condo not far from the White House. He could feel the thrill of being important and of serving the president in ways other than getting his suits, shirts and ties ready.

As soon as he entered his living room, he sat down to first quiet himself before opening the envelope. Wild thoughts raced through his mind. Could it be that Overstreet was the middle man who might set up a romantic liaison for the president? It was a long shot, but he knew you could never know with men of Mr. Nimer's stature. After all, they had the worries of the world on their shoulders, as well as the weight of making decisions that could also affect the world. Who would we be to deny them their little pleasures of the flesh? It was probably the only way they had to release their tensions. Probably had nothing to do with their marriages or fidelity to their wives. Great men lived on the edge, and the edge could be tight. Affairs could keep them loose.

Richard took a deep breath, and opened the envelope. It said:

> *On November 27th I go to the Greenbrier. Prepare Pentagon communications man at Command Alert for the first announcement on November 28th. Event to occur on November 30th. Code name "Snappy." Need communications man at Command Alert for 72 hours beginning 0600 November 27th. Begin execution. Acknowledge to "Back Seat."*

The telephone number in the envelope was Overstreet's at the Pentagon. Richard picked up the phone and hit in the numbers with his right index finger. After a few rings, a recorded message came on: "This is Major Overstreet. I am out of the office right now. Please leave a message and your phone number. Thank you."

Acting more from native intelligence than from orders of the president, who had overlooked contingency planning for linking up with Overstreet, Richard concluded not to leave a number, and resolved to call every fifteen minutes.

On the fifth try, the major was on the phone. At first Richard felt a little silly when he said, "This is Back Seat," but he quickly got used to his role.

"This is Major Justin Overstreet speaking," came the response. Richard read him the president's message, slowly and carefully.

"Would you like me to repeat this message?" he asked.

"Yes, please do."

Overstreet filled in the gaps in his note pad from the first reading, and ended the conversation with a simple, "I acknowledge the message. Thank you."

⤵

Although Overstreet was beginning to experience nervousness and uncertainty, he became more resolved than ever. Hadn't the president told him that great men rise to the occasion? Here was his chance at greatness, the opportunity to say he had really done something with his life. At the moments when he felt the uncertainty the most, he simply just looked into its face, accepted it, and moved on to what he had to do.

What he had to do now was to make certain that his "pigeon" inside the Command Alert Center at the Pentagon was ready.

He immediately called Lt. Aaron Yucaneer to ask him to come to his office ASAP.

Yucaneer was a thirteen-year veteran of the army. He had enlisted at the tail end of the first Gulf War, hoping mostly to avenge his brother's death at the hands of Iraqi troops trying to make their way back to Baghdad soon after the rescue of Kuwait.

He had been manning a gun turret in a Humvee when suddenly he keeled over, a bullet through the right temple of his forehead. It was surmised that an enemy sniper hidden on the far side of the road had killed him.

Aaron was thirty-one years old, probably an alcoholic waiting to happen, although he was quite functional at his job. In fact, he was sometimes brilliant at it. Attention was drawn to him when soon after graduating from army communications school he quietly solved the married base commander's problem of contacting his lover, a subordinate, without using any of the base telephones.

Yucaneer simply re-programmed the commander's official cell phone to contact a working number assigned to no one that would automatically flip the call to his lover. In this way, there was never a trace of his calls.

After several years of slow, but sure, career escalation, he found himself assigned to a top clearance position in the Command Alert section of the Pentagon. His primary responsibility, along with two other officers, and one alternate, was to be available in case of a nuclear threat to the United States.

In this capacity, he was trained to execute the various ways to patch in the commander in chief with the secretary of defense and to help execute the codes and passwords for a nuclear strike.

Overstreet had known him for a few years. He was at first intrigued by the man because of the dare-devil way he led his personal life. This later grew to respect when he realized the extent of Yucaneer's skills, as well as his reasons for joining up.

Yucaneer's penchant for alcohol was made easier by his schedule. He had three days on, three days off. He could drink wildly, and often did, on the first two days off. He was smart enough, also, to realize that he had to cover the signs of his compulsion. He did this by sleeping most of the third day off, as well as by meticulous grooming habits. He never smelled of the gin he so liked to drink in the Black Russians he ordered at the various bars and strip joints he visited. Part of his third day "health habits" was to breathe it out while jogging ten miles, chew lots of peppermint gum, sleep and eat three squares.

The sleeping on his days off was done mostly in bed with one or another of the girls at the strip bars. Once he knew the routine, it was an easy matter to bed them, most of the times for pay, yet sometimes for the heck of it.

He could afford it, as he received food comp, and his digs were paid for by the government. Most of his salary could be used for discretionary purposes, which, in his case, were liquor and women.

Word got around about his carousing, yet he was never called on it. His work habits were that excellent. Although Overstreet had some reservations about the way Yucanner spent some of his days, he privately admired him for it. The spark that lured him to the excitement of women had never really left the major.

How they became friends was no different from how most people do, a combination of being in the same place at a time when one of the two parties reaches a bit beyond the line of learned propriety and says "hi."

Overstreet had first met Yucaneer at one of the Georgetown parties he and Noriyo were obligated to attend. They tried to get out of as many as they could, yet they were not always successful. A rule for the smart and connected set who liked to hold parties in their swank townhouses was that a certain number of people had to attend if it was to be considered a success.

As the first-liners were often invited to many affairs, they could not always attend, either from boredom or want of bi-location. Second stringers, like the major and his wife, were asked mostly in order to fill up the required number. Every now and then, everyone invited showed. These were referred to as "shoulder to shoulder" parties.

When this would happen, Noriyo would whisper to Sherm, "Let's leave; no one will miss us." She asked Sherm to think of it as an airplane flight that was overbooked. But the major knew that word of an early leaving would get around. Besides, it was rude to leave without saying goodbye to your hosts, and he wanted to stay on the invitation lists, as he thought it was good for his career, even if he and his wife were, for the time being, bit players in the cast.

↘

"It's good to see you, Aaron. It's been a while since our little talk about something special I might ask you to do. How've you been?"

"I'm good, Sherm. Just the same ol' same ol'. Nothing much. How're Noriyo and the boys?"

"They're fine. Getting along. You know, no problems. Everything's good."

Now that they'd had a full personal masculine exchange, they were ready to move on to business.

"Aaron, have a seat, please. I don't know if you remember the last time we talked. I put it this way because you had had a few drinks, and I didn't know if you remembered our talk."

"Sherm, I do remember the conversation. You asked me how my brother died in Kuwait. And then you asked me if I ever wanted to avenge his death. I told you I did, that I would like to avenge the death of every American soldier in every war. And that I'd like to do something for every little innocent kid who ever died in a war. You also told me that some day, perhaps after you've retired, you'd like to go to Africa to do some work with orphanages, or something like that."

"Yeah, I would," the major responded.

Then quickly, before Overstreet could say anything, he said in a tone that suggested he was annoyed, "I know that I drink. I know that I drink too much, and I'm a bit of a slut-monger. But I want you to know, Major, that I always conduct myself with integrity. I know when a conversation is important and when it isn't and behave accordingly. I know when to have fun and when not to. When you talked with me about my brother that night, and asked me if I was ever presented with an opportunity to do something great and important for my country, would I do it, I said 'Yes.' I said it without flinching, without asking any questions, without any hesitation. I said 'Yes.' When I say 'Yes,' I mean it, you can count on me. I don't have a lot of things I'm proud of. My service to my country, my brother. No matter what else you think of me, I keep my word."

He added emphatically: "I am never too drunk to not know when I have given my word."

Struck by the moment, Overstreet responded, "Thank you, Lieutenant.

"I am about to ask you to keep your word. I cannot give you all the details of what I am about to ask you. What I can tell you is that I am authorized by someone high in the chain of authority, higher than our own boss, to give you this information and to ask for your cooperation."

Yucaneer sat up straight in his chair.

"A country, unknown to you and me at the moment, is about to rattle its sabers, maybe atomic ones, at the United States. We are going to respond before they have a chance to drop their bombs. You know, our pre-emptive policy. The first time with any part of our atomic arsenal. We need someone in Command Alert to handle the code traffic for significant parties. You know, the ones who can authorize that kind of war. I can tell you that what will happen will happen quickly."

The major was now stepping onto a new slope for him and it was a bit slippery. He would just get on with it and hope for the best.

"I think I better tell you now that it will happen on November 30th. That is, on that day we will drop an atomic bomb on the country that is threatening us. You will be instrumental in the execution of the plan." He stopped and said, "Reaction so far?"

"Negative."

"Okay, let me go on. President Nimer will go to the Greenbrier on Nov. 27th, the Saturday after Thanksgiving Day. We will be threatened on the 26th. You know about the Greenbrier, I assume?"

"Yes, sir. West Virginia set-up for our government in case of nuclear or bio-chemical attack. But, please, sir, let me stop you here. How do you know we will be threatened on that day?"

"Yucaneer, it's time to lose your innocence. There are times when in the national interests, we have had to, shall I say, manipulate things a bit in order for democracy to prevail. We don't have time to go into it now, but in the past the government has had to stack the deck, so to speak, so we could beat the bad guys to the punch. We've done it in South America and in Central America. We've even done it in southern Africa, as well as in Vietnam, Gulf of Tonkin." Again, he asked, "Reaction?"

"I knew about some of these things, but I guess we had our reasons."

"Yes, we did. You can be sure of that," Overstreet said. "In addition to your working the codes for us, we need you to make certain that your shift at Command Alert is on November 28–29th and 30th. You must arrange this. If you can't, let me know and I will tell General Arena who will take care of it."

Yucaneer had another question.

"Major, if the bomb won't be dropped until November 30th, why must I be certain about a three-day schedule? Why not just two?"

Overstreet was not smooth enough or experienced enough to handle the question. He was never good at lying, and really not good at keeping secrets. He quickly went to the place he was most used to, even if it was the last resort—the truth.

"Aaron, I can't bullshit you any more. There is more to the plan than I've told you. If I told you the rest and you weren't willing to go along, I'd like to say I'd have to kill you, which, of course, I wouldn't. Yet, if I don't tell you the rest, I think the plan has every chance to fall apart or be aborted. If that happens, it would be a terrible blow to peace in the world. What if I told you that the president's plan has a very good chance of insuring world peace for the foreseeable future?"

"I'd like that. My brother died for peace and it didn't last too long, did it?" Yucaneer said with a certain bitterness.

"I think, Aaron, that the plan has a very good chance to bring peace to the world for a long time," Overstreet indicated in the formal way he tended to speak when he was under pressure.

Before he said anything else, he went to a side drawer in his work desk and took out a bottle of Chevas Regal and a plastic cup. He placed them both on a table next to Yucaneer. "This might not be the drink of your choice, but feel free to knock a bit of it down.

"I haven't been authorized to tell you this. And I don't know everything, so help me out here, and take a drink."

"I'm still on duty, sir. But I will take a little sip." He opened the bottle and poured about a third of the little cup, and drank it down in one gulp.

"I'm ready, Major."

"What I can tell you is that a walkup to manipulating a reason for us to A-bomb a nuclear armed nation is underway. Something the American people will believe. And here's the kicker. I hope you're ready. You are the third person who knows what I am about to tell you. Even General Arena doesn't know this.

"On the 28th of November the president will announce from the Greenbrier the names of four countries that he might drop an A-bomb on. On the 29th the list will be narrowed to two countries, and on the 30th the target of choice will be bombed. I don't know how much time the actual target will receive before the drop. Before you say anything, let me explain the president's rationale as best I can. I won't be able to do it with his eloquence, but let me try."

Yucaneer poured himself another drink, this time two-thirds of the cup.

"Wars have been going on since the beginning of man. Let's say from Adam and Eve fighting with the Lord. There have always been killings. The president is tired of it all, and thinks that an atomic bomb, the size of the Hiroshima bomb, small by today's standards, will shock the world into knowing the horror of war. He is depending on today's mass communications to spread the word quickly about the bomb, especially by video and photos. Once reminded of the horrors of Hiroshima, which he thinks is the only reason there has not been WW III, the world will demand absolute peace from its leaders."

The silence in the room scared Overstreet. He took it as disagreement. The real surprise was when Yucaneer said, with the simplicity of a convert accepting an offered faith, "I can do that."

Pumped with a new enthusiasm, the major asked him if he was certain and, if so, did he realize how secret he must keep the information.

Yucaneer was certain, and he knew the boundaries of secrecy.

"All I need to do," he understated, "is to arrange for my schedule to include November 28–29 and 30th, and be available to communicate and forward the president's directive to drop the A-bomb on the city he commands."

"Well, yes, that's the nub of it," Overstreet replied. "However, there is a possible kink in this, you must know. The secretary of defense will be out of the loop. There is probable cause to think he will try to abort the president's plan once it is revealed to the world. His voice running through the affirming procedure to drop the bomb has been recorded by experts. I'm not really sure how, but we can guess.

You will be given that recording, so that when Nimer starts the countdown procedure, which needs the Secretary, you will be prepared. You must run the drill through in your head—the timing, etc.—so it will go off without a hitch. The plane carrying the bomb will be out of communication with everyone but you, President Nimer, and your counterpart at the Greenbrier."

Even for the likes of Overstreet, who could talk compulsively when excited about a subject, it was time to stop. "Any questions?"

"Not yet."

"One last thing then, Aaron, and I think we've got it all. Tell me if I'm right about this. There is a certain section beneath the Pentagon that is reserved for communications in case of a nuclear threat. Am I right?"

"You are. I've only been there a few times, mostly so we can see the placement of the equipment, things like that. We're told it's duplicate equipment, so we'll be just as familiar with it as the stuff we practice on upstairs."

"Okay. Good. You must go there just before dawn on the 28th before President Nimer reveals his full plan. You must lock yourself in there and open for no one, especially not for General Arena. I've received from Back Seat . . . that's the coded person who gives me messages from the president, a message that Arena most probably will bolt when he knows the full nature of Nimers's plan. So, under no circumstances is he allowed to enter. He might very well want to shoot you dead."

For some reason, it struck Overstreet as funny to think of the general shooting another person, especially one who had pledged to defend his country. With a sort of manly laugh, he said to Yucaneer, "Reaction?"

"Major Overstreet, I don't have a lot to live for. My brother was my best friend and he's dead. My mother and father are both dead. I'm not in love with anyone. Fact is, I really don't think I'm capable of it. You might be the only friend I have and, let's face it, we're really not that friendly. I know I'd feel bad if anything happened to you or to your family. But then I'd just go on doing what I do. If there's anything that makes me go around, it's that I'd like to shove a plug up the ass of anyone who keeps on killing. If I can help stop that, I'll do whatever I have to. You can count on me."

Overstreet felt good that things were working. He had taken a chance on telling Yucaneer about the president's plan. Yet, like some sort of preoccupied ingrate, he simply said, "Thank you, and stay out of jail," before dismissing the lieutenant.

His thoughts had turned to his wife, Noriyo, and what he would tell her. He had to tell her something to account for his absence during the crucial days to come. For all he knew, she and his sons might be in danger once the president's plan was revealed.

He had to tell her something. But what? When?

18

Although it occurred in late November, Thanksgiving Day always seemed to be on the cusp of good and bad weather. There were years when moms and dads dressed their children in light sweaters for the visit to Grandma's house, and other years when they looked like the Michelin Man upon arrival.

This day was one of the warm and sunny ones. That was a good thing because it somewhat neutralized the gloom that had been hanging over the land for the past six days.

Rumors were flying about in the media that North Korea was making threats again in response to the American demands for nuclear weapons inspections. What started as another order from Nimer to them to open up their borders to U.S. inspection had begun to escalate.

First, North Korea demanded, in turn, a meeting with high level U.S. officials, hinting at a deal that would have them cease their nuclear weapons program in exchange for a multi-billion dollar economic aid package from America.

Nimer said no, that they not only had to stop making any further warheads, but would also have to dismantle any existing ones under the supervision of American appointed inspectors. They refused.

Then, under a constant verbal barrage and harassment from U.S. diplomats in Seoul, General Arena finally got the outcome he was seeking, an equal barrage of verbal accusations from the North Korean government.

Lee Joo-Chan, outraged at the American demands, began to talk with a tongue loosed by tension and alcohol. He countered, by way of a major speech in P'yongyang, that the United States was perhaps the most deceitful and power-hungry nation of modern times, and who were they to tell anyone else who might be their next victim to stop making weapons of self-defense, they whose promises meant little any more.

And then he went over the line into the territory anticipated and needed. No one would ever know if Lee's threat would have been carried out. Or if, in fact, he even had the real capacity.

His exact words were: "If we are to be attacked by the warmongering government of the United States, we are ready to fight fire with fire. We are armed with weapons of destructive force beyond imagination. We also have the capacity to deliver these to parts of the United States. We are armed and ready, and our forces wait only for my word to release the trigger."

Nimer didn't believe that North Korea had the capacity to deliver these weapons to the United States, although intelligence informed him that Joo-Chan had about six medium-strength atomic bombs at his disposal. There was no evidence in their missile program that they had the capacity to target anyone but Manchuria, South Korea, parts of Japan, parts of eastern Mongolia, or the Chinese coast north of Shanghai. If we were only lucky enough, Nimer thought, to have them shoot a bomb onto China. Within hours, North Korea would be annihilated by their powerful neighbor, and there would be crazy leaders minus one to worry about.

Over the course of a few days, verbal sparks flew between diplomats, senior officials, Nimer and Joo-Chan. All the while the president continued to have his people escalate leaks about the Communist threat.

First, it was that harsh words were being spoken. Then the first evidence of hear-say about Joo-Chan's speech. Then the threat itself.

Meanwhile, mostly for his own purposes to throw everyone off the track about where he was going to take this context of war, Nimer continued to react in patriotic ways, making pronouncements about the "immediacy of the threat," as well as the "sacredness of U.S. soil," so that before the end of the week, most Americans were ready for war. Reluctantly ready, yet ready.

There was some talk, too, about the ability of America's missile defense program to protect the west coast against a North Korean attack. There were five missile interceptors on alert at Fort Greely in Alaska, and five at Vandenberg Air Force Base in California. NORAD's radar system that tracked inbound missiles coming across the Pacific Ocean would identify the missiles, intercept and destroy them.

The problem, however, was that the chief of the system, Lt. General Tim Cupat, wasn't sure yet if it would work. He needed more time to test the new system.

All of this fell right into Nimer's hands. He merely had to talk up the rationale for a first strike. A pre-emptive strike on North Korea right now was what his approach was about. The policy of deterrence had proved right for its time—when only one bad guy, Russia, had the A-bomb. But once its availability proliferated, it was time for America to sock it to 'em before they socked it to America. It was a lesson Nimer had learned from his circle of advisors, who taught it to him at every possible opportunity in the White House, War or cabinet rooms, even at the cocktail parties that he and Priscilla rarely attended. The threat was imminent and Nimer, as president of the United States, must respond.

⌖

Thanksgiving day at the Overstreets was more than a good day. It was a splendid day. They observed it in the way that they had for the past several years: by themselves. Noriyo's mother, Satoko, would help with the cooking, mainly gathering the fruits together in little bowls, stripping the peas for cooking, peeling the potatoes, and making sure there were enough cans of cranberry sauce, which Aki and Nobu loved so much they ate it like it was candy. On this day, contrary to the usual disciplined ways they were taught by Sherm and Noriyo, they were allowed to eat all they wanted at the dinner early that evening.

Thanksgiving Day was their special day, and they made it a point to decline invitations from other families, mainly friends in the military. They would spend the day together, not just because they loved being together but as a sort of unspoken symbol of their love for each other. They never spoke about the day as a symbol. That kind of talk was not their way. They just knew it in the places that symbols take up residence: in their hearts.

Sherm's job was to make the turkey ready, or so they all pretended. That meant he was responsible to buy it at the local supermarket, a still skittish place to enter all across America. Most shoppers would practically dash in, get what they wanted and pay in the lines devised for five items or less. Store managers noted that verbal spats in that line had increased since the al Qaeda attack because shoppers wanted to get in and out as quickly as possible.

A new custom seemed to be developing. Instead of shopping once a week, as had been the custom, many were going every few days so they could get out as fast as possible. Backpacks were being checked at the doors, and extra security guards were being hired across the nation. Although this was costing money, optimists saw it as a good thing that more jobs were being created.

Shopping for the Thanksgiving turkey, Sherm noted how other shoppers didn't seem friendly anymore. Their eyes would dart back and forth along the isles, seeking objects of their choice, and at the same time looking for possible terrorists.

More and more, Americans with a swarthy complexion shopped at the local food store where things cost more rather than going to the cheaper supermarkets. They were willing to pay higher prices in exchange for not being objects of the quick and jabbing stares of the many.

Overstreet began to feel the pressure of all this in the days before November 27th, when the plan would kick into high gear. Here he was, he thought, shopping for the holiday that always brought his family together. Yet he could feel separation all around him. In the market place, at work. Even Noriyo had asked him earlier in the week if there was anything wrong.

As they sat down for the big dinner, he had much to be thankful for. Their custom was always to ask Grandma to say a prayer. For the first several years Noriyo would translate her mother's gratitude, mostly for being alive, and to Sherm and Noriyo for allowing her to live in their home. She knew such kindness was a traditional Japanese custom, but in the modern world it had become a gracious happening.

Of course, she would always end her prayer with a grandmother's tribute to the apples of her old eye, Nobu and Aki.

At times like this, she and her daughter talked about Jiro, Satoko's first love who died in the war.

On this day, Noriyo said the expected, an eloquent and sincere appreciation of each member of her family. When Sherm heard these kind words, he wondered if she would appreciate him now if she knew what he had gotten into.

In just the few seconds it took her to say her prayer, the major's introspective nature seized his psyche, taking it for a sleigh ride down the slope he was on.

Would he be responsible for helping the world, Noriyo, his children? Or would he be an agent of more killing? He was sure only of the latter, and it was beginning to bother him, especially on this day.

He began to wonder how many families somewhere, in a country and city known only to the president, were eating meals together today. Would the father of those families be grateful that he and his loved ones were going to be sacrificed for the good of others?

Or, if he knew, would he stand with a defiant fist in Nimer's face and curse him to hell?

The sobering breath of his inner conversation was upon him. And Noriyo, as always, could tell. As they put the freshly cleaned dishes from dinner on the shelves in the kitchen, she turned to Sherm and whispered, "Let's have our own little thanksgiving upstairs after the children and Grandma go to bed."

He was eager, more for the intimate conversation they usually had after sex than for the sex itself, although he always loved that with Noriyo. It took him awhile at first to accept that she never wanted to talk during sex. He always wanted to talk with her during foreplay, which he called "the pre-nups" when they were dating, a term that had stuck with them. He didn't realize for awhile that it was a one-way conversation.

Her natural reticence to silence him, plus the rigor of her childhood training, prevented her from letting him know how she only wanted to enter a dream state during sex. It was her place to go for quiet and peace, a place to realize a renewal of her body.

Some people had a spot in their garden by the bird feeders, others the open space in the woods nearby, even a mythical place of grace they might retreat to in their mind on demand. For Noriyo, that place was sex with Sherman.

He had learned to wait for talk until after the love-making was over. Try as he might for awhile to let Noriyo know that good, close, self-revealing conversation with her made him "hot," he eventually gave up on it while making love because he knew that was what she wanted. Ironically for him, the conversation became like a reward for sex given.

Noriyo had many times used his after-lovemaking habit of talking to feel him out about what was bothering him. It was easy to tell when he was preoccupied, as his general demeanor spoke volumes about his inner discord. The missing smile, the lazy gait, perfunctory conversation, and a self-imposed isolation in his study, all or any one of these let her know that he was self-absorbed.

Even though the natural gaiety of the day had somewhat neutralized his distraction, she could tell that whatever it was had been festering. It would take some effort tonight to get him to talk openly.

After the children went to bed and Grandma Satoko to the temple room in the house to converse with the dead, Noriyo asked Sherman if he would wait for fifteen minutes before coming up to the bedroom, that she wanted to take a quick shower after the work of the day so she would "smell extra nice" for him.

He decided to watch the evening news on CNN for a few minutes while waiting for his cue. There was little else on the news except for the many ways the drama with North Korea was playing itself out. Interviews with medium level government officials trying to settle things down, retired generals ratcheting things up, nuclear scientists predicting, in the most objective ways possible, outcomes for a nuclear war, mostly as how it might affect North Korea. It was a way the media used to deflect startling reality.

Most of the news was coming from the west coast. The governors of California, Oregon, and Washington were on, repeatedly assuring citizens of these states that the probability of a Korean missile reaching them was one in a million, and that our interceptor missiles were on red alert, just in case.

Nimer, too, was scheduled to be on live at 9 o'clock eastern time, but that was re-scheduled for the following night, as the president thought his appearance would highlight the drama and ruin Thanksgiving Day for Americans.

Commercial air traffic was prohibited from flying into west coast airports from any place west of 120 degrees longitude. Outbound flights to Asia were grounded until further notice.

Although every effort was made to eliminate panic, including a prohibition that the three governors agreed to enforce on the population of any city of more than 50,000 people from leaving the city by car, bus or truck, many began to leave on foot with their families, pushing all sorts of homemade carts and garden wheel barrows along the roads out of big and little cities, clogging some of the main roads. Local and state police were having a hard time trying to keep the roads open for emergency vehicles.

It was an odd feeling for Major Overstreet. Here he was, sitting in his living room waiting for his wife to call him upstairs to have sex, when at the same time there was a near panic in the western part of the country.

Knowing that the doom hanging over the nation was an artificial one concocted by the president and his boss, Arena, made him feel queasy, like he was living a lie. He had never lied to Noriyo, and now, by not saying anything to her about his role in the plan to drop the bomb on an unwitting nation, he was, in fact, lying to her.

Being with his children all day long, something he hadn't been able to do in a while, made him think about the many children who would die in executing the president's plan.

And when he put on the weather channel, he began to feel like throwing up as the experts talked about barometric pressures and expected wind shifts blowing towards the east from the west coast, possibly endangering his own family if there was a strike from North Korea.

He knew that he would have to tell her something if he was to plan for their safety before the 30th. He was so into himself that he did not hear Noriyo calling him upstairs. She came halfway down the staircase and, in a sort of whispery voice so as to not wake the children, she said, "Major Overstreet, your wife is waiting for you in your upstairs office," a joke they had referring to the many "quickies" they'd had over the years when he would go home on lunch breaks.

When he walked into the bedroom, she was standing near the foot of the bed, its blankets folded down the way he liked them when they were in the warmth of their mutual desire.

He had always known enough about love to realize that he was a lucky man to be loved by her. What made it really good was that she felt the same way about him. He just didn't feel about her the way many of the guys he knew talked about their wives. It wasn't so much that they had disrespectful things to say about them; it was more about the inferences stemming from remarks like "I'd sure like to get into that waitress's pants" at the diner, or "Look at the hooters on her" at the office. Or the constant prowling eyes that many men his age had, the longing for something else, the dissatisfaction with what they had.

When she looked the way she did this night, he wanted to pinch himself so that he could tell she was real. His strict up-bringing excluded the idea that romantic swagger might be exciting to women. And there was no room in it for a dalliance of any sort, certainly no room for one night-stands, although he had managed to bypass that standard several times before he met Noriyo. He was, even in the dozen or so times he had sex with women, highly selective, towards a sort of genetic ideal, he had always thought.

So he knew beauty of body, but no one could ever match that with delicacy of soul the way Noriyo had. Sherman was a refined man, and was attracted to refinement and courtesy. Not the sniveling kind that sprang from over-cooked manners, but the courtesy of gestures that came from true regard for another.

In itself, that was a beautiful quality that, for him, indicated actions that began in a place deep within. He envied that. Although strong in character, many of his own standards were set by an external and forceful reference. It probably accounted for why he joined the army.

He admired Noriyo's mastery of her own spirit even more because it came in a small body. He had a certain masculine disposition about strength and will. That these came in men was the encouraged way to think about these things. When they showed up in a small woman who was also beautiful, he was dazzled.

Everything he loved about her was here this night. He always liked the way her body smelled. He even asked her early on in their relationship not to wear too much perfume because it hid her natural body odors, which he reacted to as if they were a mild drug that made him feel good, warm, and secure.

"Please just stay right there until I get my clothes off," he asked. Maybe it was the proximity to the expected magnitude of events soon to be, but he couldn't take his eyes off of her naked body as he undressed, almost stumbling trying to get his right leg out of his pants.

Time ran by him this night in a strange way. He went back in his mind to the little hotel room outside Tokyo where they had first made love.

He had been going out with her for six months. Her mother was older and old-fashioned compared to many of the younger Japanese women who became mothers after the occupation. As a result, most of their dating was in Satoko's home with the mother lingering about.

Even with these precautions, they managed to allow their strong attraction for each other to play out in the little ways which create sexual friction that turns to fire when rubbed enough. Hands held tighter, a bare arm fondled, a press of breasts through summer shirts.

One Friday night—he remembered it well—they simply decided to cover going to a hotel by telling Noriyo's mother they were off to the movies to see the latest epic American film, "Gandhi," and would be back in three or four hours. It was a long film, and Sherm explained the plot to Noriyo, in case she was asked.

That night, like this one, she stood before him in a long white nightgown made of silk, tied together at the waist by a tiny belt. As she began nervously to disrobe, he asked her if she would just stand there, still and quiet.

"I want to just admire the way you look, and dream of how you are when I take off your robe."

He always wondered how he had restrained himself that night from ripping her belt apart before snatching the nightgown from her body. He knew why, really. He was so comfortable with her that making love with her was as natural as breathing is to a spirit relaxed in its body. It was done without effort.

What happened next took place in Tokyo a long time ago as well as in the suburbs of Washington on Thanksgiving night in the year when the great organic pie of America was ready to re-cook itself.

"Is it all right if I undress you, my sweetest heart?" he asked. She nodded, comfortable that whatever he did he would do gently.

First he untied the soft knot in her belt, and let it fall to the floor as the sides of her robe slipped outwards, revealing a tiny part of her small, firm breasts. He kissed her, first on the lips, then let his tongue touch hers, now willing to twine with his.

"Please turn around so I can see you from behind," he said. When she did, he put both hands over her shoulders to release the robe which fell to the floor. He first cupped her shoulders and stroked them before letting his hands slide down the back of her arms to her elbows. Then up again to her shoulders in a soft massaging that felt as good to him as it did to her.

The major had always thought of a woman's upper arms as the touchstone of her beauty. If the arms had enough body to cover muscle, but not so much that he began to wonder where the muscles were hiding, then they were perfect, "female fleshy" as he liked to think of them.

Sometimes, when he was really in the mood, fleshy arms appealed to him. In general, though, "female fleshy" was the rule. Noriyo's felt the same to Sherm tonight as she had on that first night.

He had discovered long ago that she liked a soft touch, and tonight, he took the fingertips of both his hands and softly ran them down her tightly muscled back from the nape of her neck to the top of her buttocks. Then up again.

"Do you like what I am doing?" he asked, knowing the answer already.

"Yes," she said with a slow movement of her head to the left that Sherm took advantage of to kiss her again on the mouth.

He stopped his hands at the top of her shoulders before running them down the sides of her back through her small waist that curved in, then out in the tiny arc of her thighs.

In that methodical way that had made him a good military man, he let his hands, palms fully opened, run along the upper cheeks of her behind. It was an area he had appreciated from his earliest days as a teenager when the boys in his school would refer to it as the entirety of a particularly blossomy girl.

Over the years of their marriage, Overstreet would rub her backside when passing by her in the kitchen. A sign of affection, a rub for good luck, copping a feel, a way to stay in touch.

"Noriyo, Noriyo. I love you."

If flesh to flesh could be love, he was, indeed, in love, never more so than at this moment when the tension of the week seemed to disappear for them both.

As they lay in each other's arms, he told her how lucky he felt. That, hard as it was to explain, he thought about her as his buddy and as a best friend. And then when he would realize that she was above all else a woman, he felt happy and grateful beyond anything he had ever known that she was his lover, too.

The intensity of the love he felt for her at that moment overcame the code of his professional conduct, which was to say nothing about the president's plan to anyone now except Yucaneer. But, how could he go on and not say anything to her? Really, she and the children were his life in the most literal sense of the expression. He knew that without them nothing else meant much. No accomplishment he would ever achieve, or importance and recognition he might ever have would make him or his life worthwhile without them being at the core of it.

This meant to Overstreet that he had to risk breaking his word to the president by telling her what he was about to begin in earnest.

"Noriyo, I love you. I love you in some spiritual sense that I don't really understand, except in the sense that I always want to be with you. Sometimes when I'm away on duty, even in what might seem to be an exciting place, I always long for you. It's not that I can't do my work or anything like that. It's just that I have this conviction that life doesn't mean much to me except when you are in it.

"That even if everything else in life disappeared, not the kids, of course...." Then he remembered to say "and your mother." He stopped himself, looked at her and said, "You know what I mean. For the sake of what I'm trying to say, just think of you and me. You know I love the kids and your mom, but for now, let me talk about you and me."

"Sherman, say what's on your mind. Please."

"What I'm trying to say is that if everything else in the world disappeared, went away, or even never was, that as long as you were in it would be all that mattered to me. That where ever you were, well, that's where life would be.

"Sometimes I think about you, especially when I am away, and I'm busy with this and that important matter, and there's people moving all about me on the streets or in offices where I'm working, that the only place that really matters is where you are. That the sun, I mean as more than just a metaphor, shines wherever you are, that it's the only place to be. That if I was in that little circle of sunshine with you I'd be as happy as any man could be in this life. You see, wherever you are is where it is. What I mean by 'it' is happiness, joy, satisfaction, completion for me. I don't mean to get philosophical, but it's only where you are that I want to be."

He kissed her again and held her cheek against his for a long time before saying, "Am I making any sense? I'm trying to tell you as best as I can what you mean to me. It's just how I think about you. I hope I can explain it."

Noriyo put her hand over his lips. "Shush now. You are heart of my heart, and have explained your love to me. I am blessed that I am with you. And I will always try to be worthy of your love. To return it as best as I can."

"I will never be able to say it as well as you," he said. The beautiful silence in the room would now be broken by what Sherm was about to tell her.

He thought it best just to tell her, straight out. The moment was soft, so perhaps the exchange could be gentle. He first had to let her know what he was about to do, and then make certain she followed his instructions for herself and the children.

Sherm placed his left elbow next to where she lay, then held his own head in his left hand so he could look Noriyo right in the face. It was their favorite way to talk after they made love.

Some people smoked a cigarette after sex, others went to sleep. Sherm tried to summarize his feelings towards Noriyo. At times, it was a bit forced, especially when he was in the middle of a busy spell, or when the sex was more lust or relief than love.

But, ah, there were moments like this evening when the love he felt for her expanded from the core of his soul working through a place between his lungs, then into them and out into his shoulders, through his neck and into his brain from where it articulated itself.

"Noriyo, my love. I am here with you. It is the one place in the entire world that is real and valuable to me." Unlike Nimer, who sometimes scorned men who spoke with formality, the major went there when he wanted someone to know that he really meant what he was saying.

Noriyo knew her husband, and accepted his ways. Sometimes she had to suppress a giggle when he spoke like this to her because it made her a bit nervous. Although she had the same feelings about him, she grew up in a tradition of light expression, mostly agreeable things that would prevent anyone else from being embarrassed. Expressing innermost feelings, like love, was not fostered. So whenever Sherm told her how he felt, she would scan her brain for something nice to say back. She was still learning what to say and how to say it at moments like this.

"That is a cute way to tell me these things," she said. Although being cute was not an aspiration for Major Overstreet, he knew how she struggled with the words of intimacy, and he knew his own deficiencies in that regard.

"Thank you," was all he said.

"Noriyo, I have something to tell you, and I think we better sit up for it. It's not exactly romantic. It has to do with my work."

She reached over to turn up the tiny lamp light before sitting up.

"What do you want to tell me, Major Overstreet," she said, trying to lighten the moment, which she could tell from his tone was going to be serious, maybe even heavy.

"A while back, President Nimer asked me if I would do a job for him. He also asked me not to tell anyone. No one. Well, I think I have to tell you now. For a couple of reasons. First, for you and the children to be safe while I am doing this job. And also because I love you."

Tears were beginning to well in him as he looked at her, knowing there was a chance that they would never have a moment like this again. He might be arrested soon, even dead.

He wanted right now to burn the picture of her beautiful face onto his spirit so that even if he never saw her again like this, he could always picture her in his mind. His picture-taking mechanism, however, was more like a photographer's than a poet's. *Silk hair on shoulders, eyebrows slimming towards temples, oval eyes, raised curves of top lids, spark in green eyes, nose symmetrical, high cheek bones, full cheeks, strong chin, light yellow skin tinted brown.*

Typical of Overstreet, he brought all the parts together with one last soulful thought, *The brown reveals itself at certain times of the day, mostly in the evening when the shadows begin to fall.*

After letting the image burn for a bit in his brain, he continued.

"I am going to be one of a handful of people involved in a great venture, one that will affect the world. It's complicated and I don't want to tell you everything. I've been asked not to. Beside, the less you know, the better I will feel about telling you anything."

"Sherm," she said, "tell me only what you feel you must."

"There will be series of events starting this Saturday when President Nimer will go to a place in West Virginia called the Greenbrier. It will seem like the United States is being threatened, which it really won't be. It's just an excuse for the president to do something very bold, very startling. This is where I come in. On Sunday he will announce to the world a list of four cities that will be possible targets for a U.S. bomber to drop a small atomic bomb on. He'll narrow the list to two the next day and then on the third day, next Tuesday, he will drop the bomb on one of those two."

Noriyo got up from the bed, picked up her bathrobe from the floor and put it on.

"Sherman, is this a joke? Please tell me it's a joke."

Still nude, he took her by the arms. "No, it is not."

"But, Sherm, many people will die. Some will live and then die, just like mother's husband did at Hiroshima. This is a terrible thing you are going to do!"

He was not surprised at her reactions. But he had to steel himself against them, perhaps the hardest thing he'd ever have to do. He felt trapped.

There was his commitment to the president, and wanting to make a difference. And there was his love for his family, as well as the matter of not wanting to harm anyone else this way, death on top of cruelty.

Yet he had told himself endlessly since the president had asked him to be a part of this that a lasting peace might come out of the plan. That countless people might live because all the smaller wars would stop.

He had even figured it out mathematically on his calculator one sleepless night. If a hundred thousand people died in the little A-bomb blast, that same number would be saved in fifty small wars over the next ten years. And then every saved life after that would be gravy, so to speak.

He had concluded, in every way he had to question it, that the plan would be worth it in the long run

"Noriyo, it only sounds like a terrible thing on the surface, I mean on the face of it. I know it's a terrible thing that people will die. But think of how many will live. You could even think of it as a justification for your own father's death. If he and others hadn't died from the A-bomb, there wouldn't be the same respect that everyone will have for this atomic bomb. It was only because we bombed Hiroshima that the world knows how bad it can get. All President Nimer wants to do is to remind the world how bad it can really get if the United States grows sick and tired of their antics and starts to really flex its muscles.

"And besides, I'm not doing it. The president is. I'm just helping."

"Sherman, I disagree with you. If I could change your mind I would. But it is clear to me that you are into something that is way beyond me. There is only one thing I could do to stop this. I could call the newspapers and tell them."

Before she began to cry softly, she said, "And you know I wouldn't do that."

With this, the major began to feel a thrumming in his loins. So he could stay on the task of explaining things to Noriyo, he put his pants back on.

"Thank you, Noriyo, for your understanding. I think when all the dust clears that you'll be proud of what I am doing. At least, I hope so."

"Sherm, you emphatically do not have my understanding. So please don't thank me for it. I think what you are about to do is disgraceful. It is evil. Have you even thought about how many children will die?"

"Well, yes, I have. And I've also thought about how many children will live in the future if we drop the bomb."

With this, Noriyo took his face into her hands and said, "My dearest heart, you are so like a little boy sometimes. You think about how many will live because of what you are going to do, but you don't think of how many are going to die. You play with the idea of how many might live, and forget about the certainty of how many will die."

The major seemed stunned by Noriyo's response. In all their marital disagreements, she had never reached this level of assertiveness.

"Dear, Sherm, think of our own Aki and Nobu. Think of them going to school in a city that you will bomb. And you will bomb it as certainly as the president will. You can't lay the blame on him and say that you are just helping to make it happen. Imagine yourself watching the bomb fall on their school. See them incinerate before your eyes, just like the man in Hiroshima saw his own little boy vaporize in his back yard. Yes, the bomb will remind people of how terrible it can be if the full horror of war is unleashed. What you seem to be forgetting is that real people will die. Akis and Nobus will die.

She continued, "What you think is some experiment in ending wars, some do-good intention you think will end killing, is really and simply killing. Just plain old killing, as ruthless and brutal as any other killing has ever been. What you are telling me is just plain wrong."

"Noriyo, I don't know what to say to you. I understand your thoughts about the children. I do. I hope it doesn't come about that children will die."

For the first time since he had known her, Noriyo screamed at him in anger. "Stop! Stop kidding yourself! You know that children will die. You know it, so just stop."

Who knows why he wouldn't stop. Male ego? Momentum? Conviction he was doing the better thing? Inability to change in mid-course? 21st century machismo? Whatever his motive, he was not going to stop now. Hoping that sometime down the road Noriyo would return to her tradition of compliance, he simply changed the conversation, and said, "Noriyo, I've taken the liberty of renting a house in a tiny village in Vermont where I'd like you and the kids to go until you hear from me. It's called Post Mills. I picked it because it's not far from the Dartmouth Medical Center, where I know there are excellent facilities and doctors in case you'd need them."

No sooner had he said these words than he wanted to call them back. She was too smart not to know what they implied.

She stared at him, a bit confused. "Sherman, are you telling me that there might be retaliation?"

"No, it's just that I'd like to feel secure while all this will be going on. I'd like to know that you and the kids are in a quiet, secluded place, you know, somewhere where there's not much going on, or where there's not much that any terrorist would want to strike."

He had stumbled into a good excuse for sending them there. At least he thought so.

"Sherman, you can't fool me with that," she said emphatically, adding, "I want to know what you know. I don't want to stand by while Aki and Nobu might be killed. I want to know what is going to happen?"

"I'm not really certain. All I know is that the one bomb will be dropped next Tuesday. I'll probably only know what city at the same time the rest of the world will know. I'm just trying to take precautions here. Who knows what'll happen. It's not like when we dropped the bomb back in the 40's. You've got about a dozen countries now that have the bomb, and not all of them like us. I can't predict what will happen. Please try to understand."

Noriyo sat down on the bed. She was sad for her husband, sad for the children. She loved her husband, and she loved her children. She was also angry that the peaceful life they had together had just been given a death sentence.

They would lose in this, no matter what. If the plan failed, who knew what might happen. She could tell there was something fundamentally unsound about this plan, no matter what light Sherm tried to cast on it.

What would happen to them if he went to jail? Where would they go, how would they live?

Even if things succeeded, the nice life they had would come to an end. He would suddenly be in the spotlight, either as a hero or as a demented outcast.

Sherman came to her side, and kissed her on the forehead before holding her in his arms.

"I'm really sorry it has come to this. I'm sorry I've waited to tell you on this night. I just didn't know how to tell you. Even if I should tell you. I did promise the president. . . ."

Never before had Sherm felt the stiffness in her body as he felt it now.

"Yes," she said. "Let's go to sleep."

19

Friday was a busy day for Nimer. To keep up a semblance of order and security for the nation, he had to take care of business as usual, conduct emergency meetings at the White House about the Korean threat, and at the same time prepare to leave the White House the next day.

He had asked Richard to come in early.

"Richard, I'd like you to take the envelope right away, go home, and do what it says. I know it's only 5:30 a.m. Please just do it now."

"Yes, sir, Mr. President."

Richard enjoyed doing whatever it was he was doing. He was every bit as street smart in his own way as Nimer was in his. Although he had dropped out of college to join the Marines, his travels and experiences in the Corps more than made up for a degree.

He was one of those fellows who had read more books, more historical biographies, had seen more movies than most formally educated people. Besides, he had shared more of his thinking with his pals over the years than most people. And since he was almost without ego, his willingness to reveal his deficiencies drew the same honesty from his friends. He knew a great deal about the world and the ways of people.

Richard knew from the odd context of his role for the president that he was up to something big, something when he was released from the seal of secrecy he could tell his pals.

He went straight home and opened the envelope. There was something a little different about this one. It instructed him to call Overstreet at his home number rather than the usual one at the Pentagon.

The message read: "Confirm to Back Seat all set at Pentagon re communications. I will confirm the Greenbrier's readiness to you tomorrow, Saturday. Beware of Arena."

A haggard Overstreet picked up the phone.

"This is Back Seat. Who is this speaking?"

"This is Major Justin Overstreet speaking."

"I have a message for you. Are you ready?"

"Yes."

"Confirm to Back Seat all set at Pentagon re communications. I will confirm the Greenbrier's readiness to you tomorrow, Saturday. Beware of Arena. End of message.

"Would you like me to repeat the message?"

"Yes, and please hold 'til I get a pen. It's early in the morning, you know."

He fumbled in the desk draw to get a pen and a piece of paper. He knew this was it.

"Re-read the message."

Richard did as he was told.

"Tell the president that all is set at the Pentagon. I am aware of Arena disposition problem. Essential your Greenbrier man confirm to Lt. Yucaneer at the Pentagon."

There was a pause at the other end. Then Overstreet said, "That's all," and hung up the phone.

᭞

The meeting in the war room was tense. General Arena had played the angry and irresponsible speech of Joo-Chan as much as he could towards getting Nimer what he wanted—an excuse to start a war.

Arena had live press conferences on successive days. The networks and major news channels carried him. Fox News especially used the opportunity around his appearances to feature several in-depth specials about how we could bring North Korea to its knees in a matter of hours with nuclear warheads. It even estimated the number of deaths and casualties from a triangular drop of A-bombs on P'yongyang, Sinuiju and Kimch'aek. There wasn't much worth bombing north of Kimch'aek, they suggested. Besides, these three cities were far enough away from Red China and the spit of land that came down from the extremity of southeast Russia.

Of course, the many people trying to go inland from the west coast were inundating the major highways. Coverage of the exodus was carried extensively. The traditional telephone lines couldn't handle the traffic of worried family and friends trying to contact those who might be victims of the missile warheads. Many, though, did get through on their cell phones. Yet the urgency and anxieties of these communications only served to worsen the dread all over the country.

It was in this context that the president called a meeting of the key players in his government—the commander of the joint chiefs of staff, the secretary of defense, all other cabinet members, the national security advisor, and several security chiefs—to discuss the interconnected ramifications of a nuclear attack.

Nimer started in his usual way. "You know why we are here, ladies and gentlemen. So let's get started. General Arena, please."

"Thank you, Mr. President," he said as he turned halfway to point his red laser at a large map of North Korea on the wall in front of them.

"Intelligence tells us that the nuclear missile potential of the North Koreans is located in the area of Yongbyon, a relatively small site on the west coast of North Korea and east of Korea Bay, about sixty miles north of Pyongyang. We are in luck with this location. A small-yield A-bomb, let's say the size of the one dropped on Hiroshima, will be enough to wipe out the totality of their atomic warheads, while at the same time being far enough away from both Japan and China so as not to affect Beijing or even the Mongolian area north of it.

"With a small yield like we are contemplating, there is little chance that the radiation from the explosion would find its way into the Sakhalin Islands or that small slice of Russian territory situated on the extreme northern coast of the target area.

"We have a bomb ready to be deployed on one of our three covert B-2 bombers with a normal eighteen hour range. And, as some of you people already know, these bombers can re-fuel at high altitudes, so they can stay airborne for over a day and a half."

Jarvis was the first to respond.

"Mr. President, what do we know about the legitimacy of the threat, and what are we doing on the diplomatic scene to defuse the situation?"

"Norm, we can't just sit around and wait for the North Koreans to do something that we'll later regret. If we do and they drop a bomb on the west coast, we will, as an administration, be irresponsible in our greatest duty, that is to defend the lives and property of our citizens.

"As for diplomacy," he continued, "you know the U.N. will sit on its ass and discuss this from now 'til doomsday . . ."

"A good way to put it, Mr. President," Arena interrupted.

The president responded, "And then when doomsday happens to Los Angeles or San Francisco or Seattle or Portland, they'll sit around on their fat asses again and talk about a couple of hundred resolutions they'll want us all to vote on to condemn the actions of North Korea," pointing the index and middle fingers of both hands in the air as if he were writing these mocking words in the air.

It was clear where the president stood on the matter, and only the bravest people in the room would contradict him.

The silence in the room spoke to an agreement that several felt compelled to hedge, as they didn't want history books to treat them poorly if a U.S. strike went bad, or even if it was considered in hindsight another preemptive attack on our part. The Iraqi war and the Iranian "situation" were present in the room, and no one wanted to look bad.

The Secretary of State, Frank Daniels, spoke up.

"Sir, I agree in general with what you have just said, that we can't stand around and wait for doomsday to come to our people and our country. Yet, hadn't we ought to get our best people over there to North Korea to let them know what might happen to them if they attack us. Not to give away our first-strike plan, but to tell them about the collective might of our arsenal, and what that could do to them?"

Nimer knew that Daniels was making sense. But he knew, too, that Daniels always covered his own ass, that he always made sure he looked good. He knew that Daniels made it a practice of not even attending functions where the main speaker might be someone whose views were not consistent with his own. He didn't want the public to think his presence meant that he agreed with the speaker.

The president also knew that Daniels conveniently disappeared from the public eye when things got a little rough around the edges of his credibility. He would be in Africa talking up AIDs prevention when the heat was going to be on about his remarks regarding the presence of weapons of mass destruction in Iraq. And he would be in Haiti when a book or two came out saying that Daniels was left out of the loop about a critical decision because he couldn't be trusted. Daniels wanted to be thought of as a team player, as far back as his high school days when he was on the basketball team and captain of the football team. He wanted to be liked and Nimer's street smarts could always pick up on that.

"Thanks, Frank, we've already started a move in that direction, and I'm glad you've brought it up here so everyone will know," Nimer said.

True, Nimer had started a move in that direction, if that's what a casual conversation with General Arena could be called. A conversation that ended in no diplomatic action being taken.

Now it was Chief of Staff Bender's turn. Normally, he wouldn't necessarily be invited to this kind of meeting, but he was today because Nimer thought it was necessary, in order to keep the cover-up intact, for all the big players to be at this meeting.

"Mr. President, of course I agree with your thinking. Let us be clear about that. I just would like, for the record, to know if you've brought all parties together for a discussion of the possible ramifications on the Asian world of this particular kind of strike? You know, an atomic bomb."

"George, be realistic, please. How in hell am I going to have to worry about the whole Asian world right now when one of its people is about to drop an atomic bomb down our throats? How in hell do I have time to worry about that? The threat is imminent."

"Yes, sir, I understand. I just wanted to point this out in case it hadn't been considered. The Mid-Eastern world is a bit down on us now, and if the Asian world might feel the same way, well, our prestige might suffer."

"Thank you, George, for your concern and for your insight. Let's just hope that won't happen."

Nimer waited to see if there were any more problems from the room. By now he was so focused on the big plan that he was indifferent to their concerns about the present one, which he knew in all its dimensions.

"Okay, ladies and gentlemen. I will be going to the Greenbrier tomorrow, Saturday. I want all of at your posts here in the capitol until Monday when I will re-join you.

"On Sunday, I will broadcast to the people of the world that, should circumstances make it necessary, I am about to authorize a nuclear weapon to be dropped on Yongbyon in North Korea. I will explain that we have chosen this site because it houses all of the nuclear weapons available to North Korea, and that, of course, once the drop has been made, the threat here will be over and normalcy can be restored.

"As there might be some concern that I am broadcasting from a place outside Washington, I will explain that it is a cautionary measure only, and that I will be returning to the White House on Monday. Are there any questions now?"

He left no room for any by saying quickly, "If not, then, the meeting is over. You all know what you have to do. I want you each to know how grateful I am to you, how grateful the people of our nation are to you, how fortunate I am to have you on my team during these dangerous days. No man could be prouder."

First General Arena stood, then the rest, to applaud the president.

He made a slight bow to them, before saying, "Thank you. Now let's get down to business. And remember, make your business appear to be normal. There must be no leak of what has happened here to anyone in the press. Watch out for the trouble-makers, the Feerys and the Fosters. Leaks are bad. Even though sometimes they might help us, a leak about this great adventure would absolutely be a bad thing. People could die unnecessarily because of it. Lots of people. And their deaths would be on your conscience."

A line formed as they each wanted to shake Nimer's hand before going off to do their parts in saving the nation. He had created a camaraderie in the room that was like the one men in foxholes felt for each other. They were in on something big, something that mattered, and in a special way they each depended on the other one.

They shook Nimer's hand as if they already had the dirt of combat on their own. The look of resolve was in their faces, and a pride in their stride. They knew that however they would conduct themselves in the next day or two would define their lives. Most would be more than footnotes in a thousand books written over the next one hundred years. It was their time to sign their signature.

As they left, General Arena waited on the president for any last-minute exchange he might want.

"How do you think it went, General?"

"Just fine, sir."

Abruptly, the president said, "Jarvis is out. He can't be trusted."

"What did you say?"

"I said that Jarvis is out of the plan from this point on. He can't be trusted. He's always been one to negotiate. Always one to talk his way out of a paper bag. I swear, if the man was confronted by a bully in the street he'd ask the guy 'why?' before he did anything. Or, he'd probably run as fast as he could in the other direction.

"When I first met the guy years ago, I thought he was really something. I guess I misunderstood the talk for the man. He's grown soft. Tell him only what he needs to know. Then cut him off."

"Okay, Mr. President, I'll do that." He hesitated before saying, "I want to let you know that I have done everything that you've asked me to do, but from this point on, as I've indicated to you, I've nothing anymore to do with your plan."

"You know that I appreciate your loyalty, General. A regret I feel immediately is that when it's all said and done, there won't be any record of your involvement. You won't receive any of the credit. And that's too bad."

"I want you to know, sir, I am very okay with that."

"Then it's done."

As Nimer began to shake Arena's hand, he said, "One last thing, General, who is our man at the Greenbrier?"

"All I want to tell you today, Mr. President, is that the communications man who will be there can be counted on for his loyalty and expertise. You will know him when you get there, as he will be the only one assigned to you. He has all clearances and will do what he is told. I've spent a good amount of time looking over the service records of men under my command, and I assure you he is the very best. He is a man who's been through the thick of it with me over the years. He's the best."

"Another thing, General. We've got Jarvis's voice on tape verifying the code and password approvals for dropping an atomic weapon. I can't trust him in a pinch. Don't worry; he doesn't know about the tape."

Arena was reeling when the president said "Thanks, General, for everything. Please tell Florence I said hi."

20

White House beat reporters were everywhere asking questions of everyone. They were a funny lot to figure out. Sometimes they were right on top of a story, but more often they lagged behind the more informed public.

Everyone knew that the large newspapers were in bed with big business, and big business was in bed with Nimer. In a way, that was understandable, if not right. It was well-known that certain businesses did not give their ad accounts to firms that did business with this or that newspaper or television station.

If, for example, a newspaper had a liberal leaning, it would not get Republican-oriented business. And since the world had lost its innocence when the economy went global, it became more important for a business to align itself with the powers of government that controlled profit.

Perhaps more important, though, was the lack of real detective work among the White House reporters. Old-fashioned snooping seemed to have gone out with the Watergate expose. Certain big name reporters hired novices to hunt down information, but most of what they gleaned was of a personal nature, stuff for the rag magazines, which, ironically, often outdid the mainstream papers in exposing information about personalities that impacted the perception the public had of them, and sometimes even their authentic contributions.

Perception in the image-conscious world counted for much. And Nimer had an extra sense for how the media formed people's opinions. Almost without exception, he portrayed himself as the strong, silent type, a sort of John Wayne that could be counted on.

He figured if he sounded monosyllabic in public, had a clear vision of where he was headed, and didn't allow the press to see much behind the scenes, he could convey the image of strength and trustworthiness. A man of few words type.

Despite contrary opinion, many informed citizens had lost patience with the mainstream press. They were often too soft at the beginning of a presidency when first policy decisions were being made, and couldn't or wouldn't see the hand-writing on the wall, as if they were playing out an accepted scenario that presidents deserved a honey-moon period before they could be criticized, even if its fountainhead smelled bad from the beginning.

Everyone who knew anything about history, for example, knew that Nimer wouldn't be able to build a democratic nation in Iraq. Here was a people with a long history of in-fighting. Shi'ites, Sunnis, and Kurds all would be playing for power once their dictator was toppled. And they played hard-ball, kicking around the American army that was built for speed and power like a heavyweight boxer being crippled by midgets who were experts at karate.

And yet they didn't say anything to warn the American people what they were getting into for well over a year when the coffins began to return to Dover with an uncomfortable frequency.

The media seemed afraid, perhaps cowardly, to say anything outside the box, although every now and then one or another of them would be vaguely critical of Nimer.

They left important interests, like the environment, clean water, and the air they breathed, to less powerful and sometimes impotent organizations to monitor. It wasn't just that the administration was neglecting to enhance the fiber of quality that Americans enjoyed. They were unconsciously undermining it. Some said they were doing it deliberately, though others thought that they were just hopelessly unaware people. Still others thought that what they were doing was criminal.

But the press liked drama and these were dramatic times. If the lights stayed on late at the White House, speculation went unchecked. Sometimes, because of the lateness of the vigils, the reporters had time to get together at one of the area bars to talk about their thinking and what they had heard. The stories that ensued were more often the results of their imaginations than of good, solid footwork.

What the public got from this were stories laced with soft imaginings and little fact. Certainly, for the administration, that was a cozy way of doing business. Unlike many of the European and Mid-Eastern news outlets that featured hard news and stark photos, the American industry pandered to the superficial sensibilities of the American people. They would not turn off one reader with edgy stories or photos that might reveal the horror of war, a horror that was an inevitable part of the price paid to war. Those who thought it was a big price paid by a few so that many pockets might be filled were dismissed. A cynical currency, though, was beginning, over time, to grow in the public.

Nimer had a difficult time going to sleep that night. He talked with Richard for an unusually long time, as if to stall before going to bed. He knew from experience that if he didn't get enough sleep, he would be irritable the next day and not at his best. At a time like this, he would be tempted to stay up all night, tending to little things, anything to wile away the time . . . a book, magazine, newspapers.

He had stopped writing in his personal journal a long time ago after learning that these little notebooks, designed to record our deepest thoughts and secrets, were being used more and more in evidentiary hearings and criminal procedures. Public figures could no longer afford to record themselves in any way, unless it made them appear eligible for human rights awards.

Nimer often wondered why the Nazis would record names and numbers, even photos, of their victims. Or how American jailers in Iraq could take pictures of themselves embarrassing Iraqi prisoners made to pose nude and in compromising positions.

The president wished that what he was about to do could be recorded by photographs and video. All of his last minute phone calls had been placed, including talks with old cronies in the business world, as well as allies in the political one.

It would make great historical documentation of his plan if there could be some photos of him on the phone. He always loved the photos of the Kennedy brothers talking through the Cuban Missile Crisis. And Eisenhower speaking with the Apache-haired warriors about to drop over Normandy. Yet the only evidence of this action he could bequeath to posterity were the photos taken earlier in the day in the war room by the official White House photographer, John Romber.

"Richard, get me packed for four days. Just one set of formals. The rest just like the stuff I wear at Camp David. I've made arrangements for you to be with my wife and children in the morning in a safe place during the next several days. When you leave here, see the secret service agent at the bottom of the stairs and he will point you in that direction where you'll be given instructions. If all goes well, I'll be seeing you sometime next week.

But I want you here at 5 a.m. in the morning. Things will happen fast, and we won't have a chance to talk."

Richard was too smart not to know, from his own relationship with Nimer's work as well as his own sensibilities, that something big was in the works, something that might impact world events.

He wanted to say something and, on a hunch, said the perfect thing. "Mr. President, it has been my good fortune to be your servant. Thank you, sir, for the privilege."

Feeling the greatness of his office and what he was about to do, Nimer decided that he wanted later, when his plan would be assessed and judged by reporters, professors and historians, to be able to say that he didn't lose a second of sleep over his decision.

When Richard was done with the packing, Nimer forced himself to go to sleep.

21

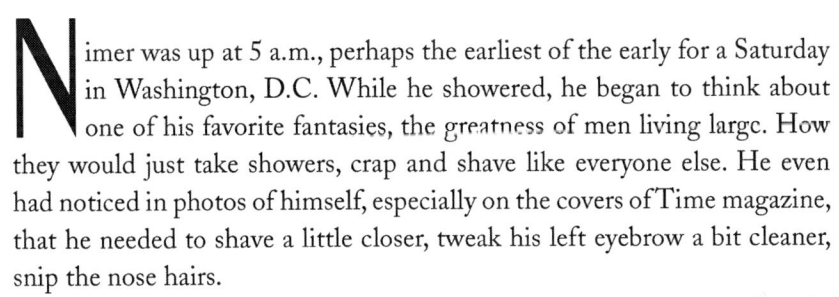

Nimer was up at 5 a.m., perhaps the earliest of the early for a Saturday in Washington, D.C. While he showered, he began to think about one of his favorite fantasies, the greatness of men living large. How they would just take showers, crap and shave like everyone else. He even had noticed in photos of himself, especially on the covers of Time magazine, that he needed to shave a little closer, tweak his left eyebrow a bit cleaner, snip the nose hairs.

He was different in his private moments from what the public thought about him as the solid rock of ages. He thought a lot about philosophical things, why things were the way they were in the world, why anyone would want to hurt another, where God was in all of this, although he didn't want to think about that too much. It was simply easier to assume that God was on his side.

Because he thought of himself as an instrument of his God, it was his style, in times of crisis, to ask his Lord to help him along the way. This was easier now than in the days when he was trying to find himself, when it seemed that every day he fought with the idea that so many others found easy to accept, that there was a God.

He had clung to an idea of God for many years, not out of conviction, but from a sort of fear that if he disposed of the idea and was wrong, there could be terrible consequences for him down the road.

Gradually, he realized that every friend or acquaintance he had, including Priscilla, seemed to believe in the existence of a God. He found consolation, too, in a book about one hundred Nobel science winners and their belief in a higher power. Of the hundred, ninety-nine said they did believe.

As soon as he showered, he knelt on his knees to pray. "Lord, grant me the serenity to accept the things I cannot change, the courage to change the things I can, and the wisdom to know the difference. That's my wish today, God."

He always started his prayers this way in the morning. It was fitting and covered most of the bases, he concluded years ago. At the same time, he prided himself that he was honest in all his undertakings. Most important of all, that he was honest with himself.

In that spirit, he would also talk with God every morning about what he really wanted to see happen, never mind the acceptance of things he couldn't change, or the wisdom to know the difference between what he could and couldn't change.

If God was an all-knowing God, then he knew what Nimer wanted anyway. So why try to hide it? How could he hide it from an omniscient God? He couldn't. He might as well, then, just talk openly and honestly with him, the way Nimer thought he liked others to talk with him.

It was all very confusing, actually. He had spent years trying to figure out if there was or wasn't a God. And if there was, was he a personal God? Was God a male or a female? Would he or she listen when you wanted to have a conversation? Did it make any difference that it was you speaking, or were there so many "you's" that it didn't make any difference?

What if God wasn't a man or a woman? What, then, would he or she be? Nimer disliked the old-fashioned paintings of God as an old man with a beard. He figured that if God got old, well, then he wasn't God. After all, how could a God get old?

He eventually concluded that God couldn't even get angry at humans for their failings. If he got angry, then wasn't he dependent on our being good for his own happiness? If that was the case, God would be a dependent being, certainly not God.

There were things moving around inside him about what God was for him. Perhaps God didn't even have a gender. Maybe it was just some kind of force or energy that could be understood. More and more, it became silly to think of God as a man.

It was very difficult for Nimer to relate to God as a form of energy. Too many ghost spoofs were in his mental camera to even contemplate that one. The best he could ever do ended in frustration when he tried to talk to an imagined Ghost God. It was like talking to the wind, and when he made the Ghost God green just so he might see what he was talking to, it seemed like a frame from "Ghostbusters."

For the longest time, he simply put his own energy into asking for courage to change the things he could. Then one day as he was jogging along a track talking with God in a little town in Texas where he had been staying for a couple of days, he felt very tired. So tired that he could hardly even walk, much less run.

Nimer realized with an insight what was happening to him. He had become fatigued trying to figure it all out. He realized in a flash of understanding that he had never really been seeking faith in a God he could not understand. He wanted something he could understand and comprehend. If he could receive understanding, he would be enlightened. Yet, without faith.

Faith was different. It was what the friends he admired had. They didn't know with any certainty that God existed. They simply believed, mostly out of intuition. Most of them were smart, too, some very well educated. Yet, they didn't believe out of a place of smartness. They believed from seeing a sense of intelligence and order around them.

Sure, he told himself, that order was being screwed up by men. He even used this thinking to convince himself, at one time, that God was a woman. Everyone knew they were naturally more compassionate and loving than men, less inclined to screw it up. Men were screwing it up by war and killings. This was a first glint into the plan that he would begin to execute this day.

From that point on, Nimer, too, began to see the order. Mostly in little things like the shape of a baby's ear, and perfect little fingers that would one day help shape the world. Of course, these thoughts troubled him for awhile, too, especially the five fingers. Why five when four might do? He even tried for a while when no one was paying any attention to do little tasks with four fingers only. When he quickly discovered how hard it was, he knew why the five.

He began to wonder if the five had evolved from a directive by God or nature. If God, that was one thing, and if nature, well, that was another. But, then, maybe they were the same thing.

Fatigue was the only way out. Who knows, maybe the fatigue was the voice of God talking to him. In any case, that was the day that he surrendered to some higher, more peaceful voice in himself.

"God," he said while entering the last turn of the quarter mile track for the eighth time that day, "I'm really tired of trying to figure out who you are, or even if you exist. I am making a declaration now that you exist. I ask that you be a personal God to me, and that you tune into me when I call upon you. I'm not asking you to do everything I ask, but I am asking you to intervene every once in a while in the laws of nature when you see fit that what I ask, even if really outrageous, is worthy of your intervention. I might ask you once in awhile to make a sick friend better. That's all, God. It's pretty simple, but it's all I have to offer to you today."

From that day on, Nimer kept his part of the bargain. He had never really tested God on the sick friend part, but he didn't get tired any more when he thought about or prayed to God.

He called on the God of his declaration this morning.

"God, I'm gonna ask for a few things today. You know that I'm about to do something we know is different. Something that probably will harm a lot of people. Well, not probably. It will harm a lot of people.

"I think you know that my intention is not to harm anyone. My intention is to bring peace to the world. When you left us long ago, you said to your apostles, 'Peace I leave you, my peace I give you.' I know that's what you want. I'm asking for your help in the next few days, that everything goes right. I ask you to watch over and keep my Priscilla and Casandra and John safe from harm."

He stopped for a moment so that his God would really understand what he was about to say.

"What I want most is for you to protect the children in the city where the bomb will fall. I don't really know what life and its purposes are all about—why some live a long time and have a great life, free from harm and worries, and why others die young and sometimes brutally. My guess is that it's all okay the way things go down. That the ones who die young come back fast, maybe that very day in some hospital somewhere, even far away from where they die.

"At least I'd like to think it's that way. But I'm not sure. Whoever dies in the bomb on Tuesday, please let them die fast. And whoever does linger, if you would just give them a little sense that what they were going through will save millions of others from being killed in maybe hundreds of other wars.

"That is why I am doing this. I thank you for placing me in a position to do your will, as I know you love those to whom you give life, and I know that you want us each to love our fellow man. Please be certain that whatever I do, I do in your name, Father. I ask these things in the name of Jesus, your son. You once said that whatever we want we should just ask you in the name of your son, Jesus Christ. I ask Jesus Christ, your son, to give us the gifts we need today.

"Amen."

"Good morning, Richard. It's a nice day, isn't it?"

Richard, remembering that Nimer expected him to respond to perfunctory questions with "yes" or "no," said, "Yes, sir."

"As soon as we get dressed, have Priscilla come in. She's up early, so we can say goodbye before I leave. We've decided to let the children sleep. Wouldn't be much of a goodbye anyway with sleepy teenagers. You know how they are about sleep. Do you have me ready for four days?"

"Yes, sir, I do."

"As soon as I'm done here, tell the agents in the hall to be ready, and get Priscilla for me."

Richard completed the last minute packing while the president finished dressing.

"Mr. President, you are ready for four days away. If that will be all, sir, I will get the First Lady."

Nimer gave him a quick hug, not unusual for him to do in private, took him quickly by the shoulders and, holding back an urge to say how grateful he was for Richard's loyalty, he said simply, "Goodbye. I'll see you in a few days."

He stepped back into a presidential posture and directed Richard to bring in the First Lady.

This was quite early for Mrs. Nimer. She was in her nightgown. She entered and closed the door, alone with her husband.

"Hey, babe," he said. It was term that few Americans could imagine a man of his conservative bearing saying, yet one he used often in private. She had told him once long ago that it made her feel special when he called her by that name. In one of her endearing moments, she told him that she'd always wanted to be thought of as a "babe," but no one before him had ever called her that. From that day on she was his "babe."

She put her arms around his neck, observing that he needed a haircut.

"I need something more than a haircut. I need some of your sweet potato."

He had a penchant towards ruining the romantic moment with fast innuendos about sex. But Priscilla knew it was his way of avoiding what was really going on in him. She had learned to allow time to go by for a few seconds, and then he would reveal himself to her.

"Priscilla, I'll miss you the next few days. I'll be televising sometime today to the nation about our plans." And then, without even a brief hesitation, he told her, "We will be dropping an atomic bomb on North Korea."

As he said this, he could feel her shrink.

"You and the children will be safe. I'm sorry I couldn't tell you this before. but I was advised not to, as your movements might tip off our plans and possibly panic the country."

As if she was used to his discordant moments, he looked her in the eyes, and said, "I hope you understand."

Ever the obedient wife, she responded, "I don't, really, Fletch. For now, though, let it be."

She hugged him again, this time for a long time.

Nimer was on the edge of telling her about the four cities, but couldn't bring himself to do it. Not from any sense of keeping the security of the next few days. His decision was based on a lack of trust, the fallout from years of not confiding in his wife.

It was time for the business of saying goodbye.

"If I can," he said, "I'll call you. By now, Mrs. Joslin will be at your quarters to fill in you and your close staff about where you'll be taken for the next few days."

Then, they simply kissed quickly on the lips.

↙

Nimer was on the presidential helicopter for the quick trip to West Virginia. His inner combativeness began to roil as he looked over the landscape when they took off from the White House lawn. The loud roar of the chopper's big engine pounded, a tuning fork resonating with the cavity of his lungs, pulsing in and out like an angry drumbeat of pride in what he was about to do.

It was a thousand to one shot, he knew. Everything had to work just right, everyone had to do their part. Most of all, the system had to work for him. Once he went into "Lockdown Mode" with the technological resources he had organized, it might just work. The world might be scared out of its wits and realize, finally, that the killing must stop once and for all.

For some reason, he felt small compared to the greatness of his mission. It was by letting himself feel small that he could get past the boldness, the outrageousness of his mission. If he could shrink and still go on, he would simply go on and do whatever it was he had to do.

Beneath him on the way to the Greenbrier, he could see the bounty of the land he loved. The slopes of the Blue Ridge, Shenandoah, the rise and fall of the Allegheny Mountains. His commitment to the mission was reinforced.

Once he was settled, he spent the rest of the afternoon and evening speaking on the phone to other heads of state, throwing them off, too, by alluding to the bogus plan to first-strike North Korea.

After an early lunch, he asked the commander of the small staff to show him the communications room, and to introduce him to the communications officer.

"Mr. President, this is Lt. Pedro Romero, U.S. Army, our communications leader."

Lt. Romero stood at attention in a stiff salute to his commander in chief.

Nimer put out his hand, which the lieutenant shook awkwardly.

"What do your friends call you, son?"

"They call me Peter, Mr. President."

"What are your instructions, Lieutenant?"

"General Arena has instructed me to do one straightforward duty, 'a simple one,' he called it. My duty is to do what you, Mr. President, and only you, order me to do. He said that my duty here is a delicate one and that there might be some in the civilian sector, as well as in the military, who might try to dissuade me from doing what you order, and that my only priority is to follow your instructions, no matter what. Sir, he stressed the words 'no matter what' to me."

"Excellent, Lieutenant."

Nimer continued, "Although this might seem awkward to you at first . . . we are going to spend a lot of time together over the next several days. May I call you Peter?"

"Yes, sir, Mr. President, you may."

"Good. And I wonder too if you could loosen up you tie and not always refer to me as 'sir' or 'Mr. President'?"

He stumbled to find the right place he was seeking in this relationship. He never liked the formalities when they were excessive or blatant. He liked the respect due to him as president, yet found it awkward when it became repetitive.

"How about it, Peter, if you only now and then use those words. When you don't have to repeat them, please don't."

"Yes, sir, Mr . . . I'll do my best, sir."

"I'm sure you will. Let's do a little business here.

"I want, first, to be certain that you have been trained in the sensitivities of what you may be asked to do."

"I have been, Mr. President. I am aware of what is going on in the world, and what your expectations of me might be."

"And what might they be, Peter?"

"Possibly to drop the big one, an A-bomb, on wherever you direct me."

"Son, that's a big order. And I need to know right now if you'll have any reservations if I ask you to drop the big one, as you say."

"No, sir. I would only have reservations if you asked me to drop it on our own country, which I know you won't. I am without any other reservation."

"How intent are you to follow General Arena's order that you answer only to me?"

"Absolutely intent."

"That's what I want to hear, Peter. You're a good soldier."

"I try to be, sir."

As Nimer walked towards the equipment in the room, he began to question Romero about it.

"I'll be doing two things while I'm here for the next three days. I'll be broadcasting by radio to our country about my intentions for use of the A-bomb. Naturally, the broadcast will be played around the world. For the moment, it will have highly sensitive information in it that I will reveal to you when the time comes. For now, let me just say that the information might surprise you.

"I will also, of course, want to speak with Command Alert at the Pentagon regarding the dropping of the bomb. I want to stop here for a moment to see if you have any questions."

"No questions so far. I can set up the radio broadcast. No problem. About the bomb, though, I think I do have a few questions."

"Go ahead, son, shoot."

"You might know, Mr. President, that there is a highly coordinated set of instructions I must follow to set the communication mechanisms, or technology, into motion. There are codes and passwords both for you as well as for the secretary of defense to follow. I've brought the Code Red Book with me, as I must first verify these codes and passwords before I can allow you to give an order of this magnitude."

Nimer interrupted with a glib comment. "So, Peter, for a minute there you will be in charge of the president of the United States."

Romero had his own sense of humor. "Yes, sir, I'm afraid so. But, don't worry, I won't take it seriously."

Immediately, he thought that was the wrong thing to say.

"What I mean, sir, is not that I don't take the responsibility seriously. I do. What I meant to say is that I don't take myself seriously about the matter."

Nimer was finding Romero absolutely perfect for his part.

"I understand exactly what you mean, Peter. I like your attitude. Let's continue. I will be asking much from you in the next several days. Much in the way of your patriotism, and much of your physical stamina. I will try to let you know when you'll be off duty. When you do know that from me, you must get rest and sleep as fast as you can because you might be called upon again for many hours of work. You have noted, I am sure, that you have no back-up."

"I have noted it, sir."

"Also, once we start the procedure tomorrow morning, we will go to a communications lockdown. I must be certain you know what that is."

"Yes, sir, it means that two-way communications proceed only if you order it. It's a precautionary method to prevent jamming and/or foreign sources to be on the line."

"Good. One final thing. This is a big one. There is some chance that all hell might break loose here. I mean gunfire. These are desperate times and you don't know what could happen. We have a minimum force here to protect us, so we might have to close ourselves off from the world until further notice." Nimer liked this young man, and wanted to re-assure him.

"You know that we have ample food and water for several months here. We even thought for awhile during the 9/11 days about setting up here," he divulged, adding, "when we didn't know the extent of it."

"I understand everything you are telling me, Mr. President. I want to assure you that I will stand by your side at all times."

"Thank you, son. Are you married, kids?"

"No, sir, I was close once. Girl named Maria. But no cigar. What I mean to say is that it didn't work out. I prize loyalty first and foremost. I wasn't certain of hers to me when I was away, so I broke it off. No point in being married to someone who is still looking around, is there, sir?"

"No point, Peter. No point at all."

22

It was an abnormal Sunday in the United States. The mood was reminiscent of, yet worse than, the Cuban Missile crisis, when an overarching fear covered the country. Today's fear was more specific, and it had a target, a 1500 mile coastline. Back then, Cuba had short and mid-range missiles. And, although the Soviet Union had long range ones, there were no specific targets identified.

On accurate assessment, North Korea could hit one section of the population. Yet the solidarity in crisis that had always been a hallmark of modern America was sparking all across the land. While the California, Washington, and Oregon governors were doing an extraordinary job of keeping order, the rest of the country was keeping watch and waiting, in many cases waiting to see what might happen to their relatives who lived out there.

The television and print media were focusing on the positive. How the roads heading east were filled, yet moving, thanks to the exceptional job being done by local and state police as well as units of the National Guard in keeping order. How so many stores remained open even in the face of desolation. The many stories of courage, the abled caring for the disabled, mothers for children, fathers for families. It was a time of great national pride and togetherness. No one was more proud of the country than its president, Fletcher A. Nimer. The nation was poised to hear from her leader.

"People of the world, this is President Fletcher A. Nimer of the United States of America. I have a special broadcast to you all this morning. Some will hear it as I speak, yet most will probably find out what I am going to say through other means of communication.

"This radio broadcast is not originating from Washington, D.C. As our government and our nation has been threatened by the Premier of North Korea, I have left the White House, and I am in a secure place away from it. What I am about to say is startling. In two days I will give an order to drop an atomic bomb on one of four cities which I will mention shortly."

General Arena was sitting on his bed in his bedroom away from home at the Pentagon, ready to hear the news that the president was going to drop an A-bomb on North Korea. He would hear the news live, take a quick shower, then rush to the readiness room.

When he heard the words "four cities," he turned up the volume to make sure he could hear what came next. His inner system was on red alert.

"I want to be clear about my intentions. I do not wish to harm anyone. On the contrary, I seek to end wars. There are many nations now that have the capacity to deliver nuclear weapons. Weapons that are far superior to the ones dropped on Hiroshima and Nagasaki.

"It is my belief that there is a slow erosion of the human spirit happening in our world. We all live under a cloud of terrorism and the threat of nuclear annihilation. We must stop killing each other.

"It is only because the world saw the consequences of the two bombs dropped on Japanese cities in the 1945 that we have not had a nuclear war. Unfortunately, we have replaced nuclear war with conventional wars more powerful than man has ever known. Technology is awesome and the killing is great.

"The world has gotten more vicious and hateful than ever before, so that even when there are no technological weapons of destruction the hatred makes do with whatever is handy, such as machetes and shovels that can kill hundreds of thousands of innocent people. I am saddened, too, that terrorism is rampant.

"Even as some die in a nuclear explosion two days from now, the world will take note, I hope finally, that war is the way of the beast, and that it is time for mankind to grow up.

"The four countries are: Australia, Greenland, Kenya, and Vietnam. Their respective cities are Sydney, Ilulissat, Nairobi, and Hanoi. I have chosen these cities, again, not to kill others, but so that others might not be killed in a continuation of the attrition of the human spirit.

"Tomorrow, Monday, I will narrow the list to two countries, and on Tuesday, after I conduct a personal lottery, I will name the city that will receive a low-yield Hiroshima-type atomic bomb dropped on it.

"The bomb will be dropped soon after I make the announcement on Tuesday as I do not wish any undue terror on the peoples of that city, especially the young."

As soon as he said the last sentence, Nimer mockingly cut his throat with his right index finger to direct Romero to stop the signal.

Nimer was relieved that he had finally done it. Even if the plan failed, the world was sure to sit up and take notice that human consciousness was taking a turn for the better.

Arena, though, was beside himself.

"The sun of a bitch said he was going to drop a bomb on North Korea and I helped him do it. I even got things arranged for him," he thought.

He dressed quickly without taking a shower, and rushed down to the readiness room to call Secretary of Defense Jarvis, who had already been awakened by five calls.

"Hello, Jarvis. Did you hear?"

"Yes, I did, but I don't know what to make of it. Don't be too concerned. You know that I have to verify the president's order to drop an atomic weapon. I simply won't do it."

For now, Arena thought it wise to not say anything about the tape. Jarvis, too, wanted to avoid his role in the plan to drop an A-bomb on one or another of the countries he had recommended to the president.

"I'm going to get Vice President Rickert on the phone. Stay there and I'll call you right back."

Jay Rickert was as confused as Jarvis and Arena. He was usually a man of action, but this one was too complicated. He immediately leaped to the question of whether a president had the right to do what Nimer planned to do.

"He might, as commander in chief, have a right to drop a bomb as a tactical maneuver," he told Jarvis, "to further an already approved action such as the fight against terrorism and its accompanying invasion of Iraq.

"On the other hand, if preemptively dropping an A-bomb on another nation amounted to a declaration of war, then he might need congressional approval; unless, of course, the War Powers Act gives him the right as president to do what he needs to do in the interests of the nation's sovereignty. From a long-range point of view, this rationale could hold up if terrorism could be interpreted as a force that was a continuous attack on our national integrity."

Yet none of the four countries was an apparent harbor for terrorism.

Rickert tried to call the president, but Nimer was, of course, incommunicado.

He did the next best thing, calling a full principals committee meeting that he would chair in one hour.

As soon as Arena received word of the meeting from Jarvis, he went to the Command Alert room to see if the communications man on duty could shed any light on what was happening.

Within half an hour of Nimer's radiocast, word of it was quickly spreading around the globe. As people woke up from sleep across time zones, the chatter was unbelievable. The telephone wires were so stressed that most people who relied on old-fashioned dial-up could not get through to loved ones and friends who lived in far away time zones.

Correspondents of the major newspapers were awakened to write their columns as quickly as possible. The major news magazines such as *Time*, *Newsweek*, and *The New Yorker* churned out special issues as soon as they could. Most of the stories were inadequate as there was little or no background available.

The announcement was grist for the mill of speculation as well as the liberal's disdain that Charles Feery of the *New York Times* had for President Nimer. Feery's instinctive contempt for the president was mostly couched in the nicely coded appropriateness that was the signature of his newspaper. On this day, though, there was no holding back.

His page one column was an example of high-blown writing at its worst:

> *Only those still asleep in their beds have missed the news that President Fletcher A. Nimer announced early this morning that the United States of America plans to drop an A-bomb on one of four countries of his choice.*
>
> *His radio announcement was given at 6:00 a.m. EST. It was brief and to the point, yet without reason behind his decision, except to say that he was tired of wars, and wanted to make a point to the world about the terrible consequences of atomic weapons, which, at the last time noticed at Hiroshima and Nagasaki, do terrible things to people.*
>
> *The news is stunning and without precedent. At press time, Nimer was incommunicado somewhere in the Unites States.*
>
> *We who are awake might be better off going back to bed again in order to take a good nap before the impending holocaust takes place.*

Television was the most useful tool of all. By the time Nimer had finished his announcement, every major TV station was announcing the news with an odd combination of information and disbelief. The old retired generals were dragged out of bed for live interviews about the why's and wherefore's. Past speeches were replayed for possible clues about what his intentions might be.

The slightest nuances about his attitude regarding the Vietnam War were played and replayed. There were a few contextual clues about "the incompleteness of things" when he referred to that war in his campaign speeches, and that the nation ought to always think twice before embarking on such an enormous effort. But nothing much else.

Africa hardly ever appeared on the radar screen of Nimer's concerns, and Australia consistently came across as being America's ally and friend from far away, people we could count on when we needed them, grateful people who remembered what the U.S. had done for them in WW II.

Nothing could be found in the archives regarding Greenland. So it was a complete mystery why he picked it.

Reputable psychologists and psychiatrists, as well as a few fledglings with a knack for self-promotion, were in demand. As there was little to go on, the interviews became a field day for psychic spin.

Dr. Sylvia Smith thought that he might have picked four nations "quite eligible" for the attack, and since none of them were on the list, the president was trying to give us "a message of opposites"; that is, a hating of what you love, or its opposite. Could it then be that the speeches of Nimer in which he praised Australia, for example, were in fact diatribes of hatred?

Other, more existential types, said it didn't make any difference why Nimer picked the four, but we should concentrate on the fact that he did chose these four. And see where we go from there.

A few at a table of psychoanalysts quickly assembled for a Sunday special that night thought that Nimer was, perhaps, a cruel man, whose reason was that he didn't have a reason we were looking for. After all, isn't a cigar sometimes just a cigar?

Others noted that none of the four had a nuclear arsenal. Marian Foster had used this angle in her nationally syndicated column that day to suggest that the president of the United States was perhaps a calculating coward.

In all, no substantive reason could be discerned. Soon, it dawned on most that seeking a reason for Nimer's actions was a futile search, and, besides, it didn't matter except in a theoretical sense that we wanted to know why.

It did matter, though, to the diplomats and high administrators in

Nimer's hierarchy. One of the first decisions made at the principals committee meeting was to appoint a task force of selected individuals as delegates of the vice president to the targeted countries. Their first task was to call the leaders of the four nations to explain to them that they didn't really know what was behind the president's decision and, because he could not be contacted, it was indeterminate when they might know.

All these delegates could say was that they were calling on behalf of the vice president to explain a presidential action that was a mystery. They told the leaders that they would be in constant communication, but yet, in the most awkward diplomacy imaginable, were obliged to say that they might also support the president's decision once communication resumed and the president had a chance to explain his actions, which might be justifiable. It was really diplomacy gone haywire. It was saying, "We're sorry that you have been chosen for possible execution, but we'll try to find out why. And we will call you when we know." One delegate commented that he felt like a Kafkaesque figure in a bizarre story.

General Arena was not used to having his authority questioned as when he approached the M.P. on duty at the communications room of Command Alert in the Pentagon.

"I'm sorry, sir, no one is allowed in the room. The steel guard doors have been closed and locked. On the president's own orders. Lt. Yucaneer is running the show in there."

Arena looked him straight in the eye. "Son, I see from your tag that your name is Sergeant Fullman. Well, Sergeant, if you don't order that door opened in five seconds, you will become Private Fullman."

"I'm sorry, sir, I can't do that," he said, still staring straight ahead.

Arena shouted up in his face, "Do you know who I am? I am the commander of the joint chiefs of staff. When I give you an order, it's an order."

Never before had he had to explain himself like this to a subordinate.

"My order is the highest of orders you can get. Now open that door!"

"Sir, I'm sorry. I can't do that. Lt. Yucaneer has received a direct order from the president, telling him to lock down this communications facility until further notice." And then he said, "May I speak freely, sir?"

"I suggest you do that now, Fullman."

"General, I know what is happening. I have heard the news about the president's announcement. I know that some are shocked by it. I am not a politician, sir. I am a trained military policeman. I take orders and do my best. I go with the highest authority. I know, General, sir. . . . please don't take this personally, but I am under presidential orders here. Again, sir, without meaning anything personal, the president is my commander in chief, and I will obey him."

"Private Fullman, you're relieved, and I'm ordering you to stand down in your quarters until further notice."

"I will do that, General, sir, but I will not disobey the president's order."

Arena picked up the phone and ordered another M.P. to take up duty at the communications room. It did him no good, as the replacement could not access Yucaneer by phone.

Wanting to make good without really knowing what was going on, the new M.P. suggested to the General that he could get an explosives expert and have the door to the communications room blown out.

It was at that very moment that General Arena realized the extraordinary and complex dimensions of what was unfolding in the life of the government there at home and, by extension, in the lives of governments around the world. He would have to tell Jarvis about the tape.

Yet he was in a quandary. Unknowingly, he had helped the president organize what he needed to execute his intention. He had experienced him as a man of good faith. And now he felt deceived.

Not only that, he couldn't know yet whether what the president was planning to do was unlawful or whether he had the authority as president to do it. He was in the middle of a legal, constitutional, and moral morass. And he was alone. The president had asked him to tell no one, and he had kept his word. He even knew about the Jarvis tape. Now that things had taken a different turn, he could be implicated if what the president was about to do turned out to be illegal, perhaps even contrary to the wishes of the American public.

If he didn't get into the communications room and prevent the impending execution of the president's plan, and the plan turned out to be perceived as unacceptable, he might be accused of complicity in an unlawful act of the most grievous consequences.

On the other hand, if he did break in and stop it, he could be accused of interference with a presidential order of the highest importance to the security of the nation. In which case, he could be found liable of obstruction, and have to pay the price.

Arena's career was on the line and he knew it. Yet, he was bright. Not only bright but with that remarkable facility to leap quickly to the end result of an action.

Storming the communications room, at least for now, was out of the question.

With cunning, he chose to break some of this information at the principals committee meeting.

"Gentlemen, the news of the president's decision is not a total surprise to me. Several months ago he ran by me an idea he had, a fuzzy idea, about dropping an A-bomb on someone to show everyone that he meant business about, I think he said, bringing democracy to the world as a way to stop killing, which we know he abhors. I didn't think much of it at the time, and kept to myself what he told me." Jarvis squirmed in his chair. He might well have fallen off it if he knew everything.

Suddenly Arena spoke with a formal tone. "Less than an hour ago I went to the communications room at Command Alert in the Pentagon building to find out more about the news. I thought, too, while I was at it that I'd try to talk with the president about his broadcast, to find out what was on his mind, in his intentions. Unfortunately, the communications room is locked down, as is the Greenbrier.

"My first thought was to break into the room with use-measured explosives. I did not because I think, ladies and gentlemen, that we have a constitutional crisis on our hands this morning." He paused, not certain of what to say.

"Let me be elementary for a moment."

In a tone that was unusual for him, he said, "I beg pardon of anyone whom I might offend by being fundamental here.

"The people have elected President Nimer and we are accountable to him, in these times especially when, for example, we are being threatened by North Korea. He is our commander in chief, and under the Constitution we are lawfully bound to obey his orders."

With that, a pandemonium of protests broke out.

"Order in here! Order," yelled the vice president. "If we cannot have order here, then leave. I mean, whoever cannot be orderly here must leave."

Almost at once, the yelling stopped.

"Remember, we are a democracy with rules and order, not some excuse, excuse for one.... Now let's get down to business."

"Mr. Vice President," Defense Secretary Jarvis broke in. "We are not even sure if you are not usurping the president's authority by having this meeting. Even making decisions that affect national security. Is there something in our laws somewhere, or in the Constitution that allows us to do what we're doing here?"

George Bender, Nimer's chief of staff, responded. "He's right, Mr. Vice President. There is a law that allows you to take charge, to be in effect the acting president, but only if the president is incapacitated. Which he is not. He's here in our country, a short helicopter ride away. I would like to go see him ASAP."

The general roar of approval made Rickert's decision easy.

"George, why don't you leave right now and see what you can find out. Get back to me as quickly as you can."

With that, Bender was out the door and on his way.

Just as quickly, Jarvis broke in again. "Mr. Vice President, as we are sitting on top of some legal and constitutional issues here, let me suggest strongly that you call for an immediate meeting of both houses of Congress. We can set it up in the Senate auditorium to get everyone in at once."

"Norm, what good would that do?" Rickert asked?

"I say this with a sense of urgency," Jarvis responded. "It is something we don't often say, yet it is the foundation of our government. General Arena has said it well. We are a government of, by and for the people. It is the voice of the people that should count when we are in danger. I know they express that voice through their elected president, yet when he is not available, as is the case right now, we must go directly to them. At a practical level, we must meet with their elected representatives in the Senate and House." He could sense he was onto something acceptable, and he loved it.

With great confidence, he added, "We simply must act with an unprecedented boldness."

It was almost as if the room had been struck by a lightning bolt that someone among them dared to frame the problem as one that should be decided by the people.

Speaking immediately, Rickert the politician said, "I think the secretary of defense has a plausible idea. We must do whatever we can to cover every protocol possible. I'm for setting up a full congressional meeting tonight, or if we must, as early in the morning as possible if rounding up a quorum is difficult. It's vacation time and many are in far-flung places."

The quiet in the room that Rickert took for consent was more a numbness founded on not knowing what else to do. Sure, they could barge into the Greenbrier and arrest the president, but ought they? Right now, it was a question without an answer. Certainly, the Constitution must be upheld. If they made the wrong move, it might be fractured, and hard to repair. Each one of them knew that a tear in the fabric of democracy could easily be torn into a wide open hole.

↘

Chief of Staff Bender might well have stayed home. His chopper landed at one of the Greenbrier's many open and well-kept fields. For many years, the underground bunker was a secret known only to a few. Off a few thousand yards and out of the eyesight of the wealthy patrons who came to this exclusive hotel in the fields of West Virginia, it was stocked with food, water, alcohol, bed rooms, a recreation room, and a small auditorium that could be used for meetings as well as for showing films and slides, both strategic and recreational.

When the Cold War was over, the identity and location of the place was revealed to the public, and opened for a small fee twice a week for public viewing. The government took its time to develop a new and similar place, thinking that once the struggle with the Soviet Union had ended, there would be little need for such a place. Our superior nuclear and conventional forces would preclude the need for our government to go into hiding. This was before the advent of terrorism and its lethal nature and, more importantly, before smaller, what the White House called "rogue nations," began to flex their muscles and beliefs that suggested one day they might be willing to risk all to establish their own right to dominance. More and more, these smaller nations had been articulating an attitude of belligerence about America's justification for keeping others out of the nuclear circle when, some of them said, the United States might be the most dangerous nation of them all.

The entrance to the Greenbrier was a tunnel with access through an enormous steel door. The entrance was cordoned off today by a phalanx of Marine M.P.'s whose orders were standard: allow no one in without the permission of the president or his designated authority. Nimer had made it clear at the outset the day before that no one was allowed entrance until the president himself initiated it. In effect, it was a total lockout.

Bender was cordially met by two captains who immediately gave him the news that he could see the president only with his personal permission. And that, since Lt. Romero had been ordered to maintain the telephone lines with outgoing calls only, permission was impossible.

Although the chief of staff used every means possible to change their minds, from calling on their patriotism to threatening them with courts martial if they did not let him in, they would not budge. It was a fail-safe security system not intended to be used this way. The system was based on a model of predictability that everyone on the friendly side would communicate with each other.

By the time Bender got back to the capitol, some senators and congressmen were already gathering for the meeting with the vice president, who knew it would be, at best, an awkward session.

Rickert was an experienced politician whom Nimer chose as a running mate because of his superior people skills which could offset the edginess of Nimers's style and the relative poverty of his public speaking skills.

Rickert knew that the meeting might end in chaos if he didn't have a compact agenda. It was critical, too, to have the precisely correct issues on that agenda.

He had to avoid at any cost a discussion of why Nimer wanted to drop an A-bomb. It would end up going nowhere at a time when a discussion had to lead them somewhere. The members of his party would support him, and the opposition would not. Yet, there was little room for predictable conversation tonight.

He decided to place four items on the agenda, but only the last for a vote. The results of that vote, either way, might lead them down the road towards actions that could change the way America had always done business with foreign nations. At least, Rickert thought, they would be upholding the democratic process by meeting, talking, and voting their consciences.

These items, he decided, were critical:

Does the president, as commander in chief, have the right to unilaterally direct the military under his command to attack another nation, even though that nation has not provoked the attack?

Must the president have the consent of the Congress before ordering such an attack?

Does the War Powers Act give a president the authority to war on another nation without the consent of Congress?

Given the consensus of answers on the first three items, what action ought the Congress take now about the matter of the president's announcement?

Rickert knew that discussion on each item had to be limited. How limited, he didn't know. He thought two minutes per speaker would be enough, yet he knew that would never be enough for the old timers, inveterate smoke blowers that they were.

⇘

Nimer was watching CNN for most of the morning. He didn't like that he was taking satisfaction at the confusion in his America, as well as the growing chaos around the world. He had hoped to make the world squirm. That was beginning. Yet, there was little or no discussion about his rationale, the whole point of the exercise.

He thought at one point, when reactions were shown from Nuuk, the capital of Greenland, that he might as well call it off as simply a bluff, and then explain his motives.

Most Greenlanders thought that it was a joke by those funny Americans whom they knew mostly as tourists or business men trying to capitalize on the new awareness of money-making opportunities there. At least, that was the spin being given to it by the major networks, wanting, perhaps, to make the reality go away.

It was 7:30 a.m. in Eirik's little city when President Nimer had come on the radio to tell the world that the United States might be dropping an atomic bomb on it in two days. The 64-year-old paper boy was delivering the bulky Sunday issue that would take him several hours. He didn't have much in the way of material things, but he had always been grounded in the inevitability of life's difficulties. While most of the townspeople were negotiating with small boat owners to take them as far away as possible, the Danish government, which had responsibility for Greenland's defense, was asking the people of Baffin Island and Iceland to sail as many large ships as possible to the city to take its people and the people of its next door neighbor, Qasigiannguit, out of the area as soon as possible. Unfortunately, though not very far away, Denmark would not be able to get its large ships there for four or five days.

Comments from the people on America's streets ranged from speculation that Nimer must be crazy to guessing why he chose the four countries he did. One old lady in Omaha, Nebraska, said, "He must have his reasons. He always does." A young man in Greenville, South Carolina, told an interviewer that his dad had served in Vietnam, and that it was about time they got what they deserved.

Reports were coming in from around the world. Australians were stunned that an American president would even think of doing this to them who had always been staunch allies. There was an almost haughty and dismissive attitude developing. They called Nimer "stupid, and doesn't he know that we're the world's best sailors? No worries, we'll have Sydney cleared out in twenty-four hours with everything that can float, including our bathtubs."

And with that defiance that had always characterized them, they practically shook their fists at Nimer, vowing that someday he'd get his. There were several reports of American tourists being pummeled in the streets.

In Vietnam, the reaction was ugly and angry. For many years, American veterans had come back to help build schools, churches, and orphanages as a way of reconciliation with the people. Contrary to the horror stories that came out of the war, the Mai Lai's and village slaughters, most soldiers had treated the Vietnamese they met in the cities and hamlets with compassion and kindness.

Horror stories, though, lingered in the minds of the aggrieved. How could it be otherwise? The stories were passed down to the next generation, and became like raw pimples on the skin, something you cover over, try to hide while giving time some time to heal them. Nimer's announcement was like ripping off a Bandaid from the old wound.

A school and an orphanage, both built by American veterans, were summarily burned down by angry crowds outside Saigon, now Ho Chi Minh City.

In Hanoi, the people were already packing their belongings to leave. Although the older crowd was used to emergency circumstances, it would only be a matter of hours before the normally crowded streets became a knot of moving vehicles and people, with the knot getting tighter by the minute. The only realistic hope of getting out of the city was by walking, bicycles, and motorbikes.

As usual, little was coming out of Africa. Because of distance from the United States, it hardly ever appeared on the horizon of American political or business interests. American coldness towards Africa had a long history. In more recent decades, the government had watched, in the name of money and business interests, the ugliness of Apartheid fester in South Africa, and then looked on from afar as the Hutus massacred 800,000 Tutsis in 1994. The apparent indifference to the bloodletting was made more clear the following year when the Tutsis turned the tables. There was very little America wanted in Rwanda, so it again stood by and watched. It was only months later that the American citizenry were apprised of the atrocities.

The ultra-right American press was quick to say that in some ways the Africans made it easy to give up on them. Perhaps we stood by and watched the blood-letting in Rwanda because we had been so unappreciated in Somalia, where a contingent of U.S. troops was ambushed in 1993 and several American peacekeeping soldiers were dragged through the streets of Mogadishu. The indignity was unacceptable, and the troops were soon withdrawn. The incident left a bitter taste in the mouth of the American people. They had sent their sons to help and they were murdered for their efforts.

The few stories that did get back to America this morning indicated that many Kenyans were heading south towards the plains of Tanzania. The least startling news was that the Nairobi story was practically a sidebar piece compared to interest in the fortunes of the other three. Africa might be raped again. And no one seemed to care.

※

There was little time for peace organizations to mobilize. Citizens for Peace was too old-fashioned in its organizational structure to make anything happen quickly. The best Move On could do to organize a rally for the next day was to use the Internet links to call for demonstrations in Manhattan and San Francisco.

Because of the immediacy of the situation, the rallies would have to be handled in a radically different way. There was no time to get the usual permission from the NYPD or the SFPD. Courtesy calls were placed to the police chiefs just to let them know what the plans were, and to ask their tolerance of possible disruptions.

They explained the obvious: tensions were high everywhere, the rally would be somewhat disorganized, and it was a workday in those two cities. So there was a good chance that traffic would be tied up and tempers would flair. The rally organizers begged the police to act as a keeper of the peace rather than a confrontational force that might incite trouble.

It soon became apparent to the organizers of the two rallies that the turnout was going to be enormous, that most citizens did not plan to go to work that day anyway. "How can I go to work and pretend it's a normal day when somewhere on Tuesday thousands of people are going to die, to be killed deliberately?" was the main response.

Even though the demonstrators were being warned about how loosely organized the rallies were going to be, they were ready to mount their own attack against a president they had disliked almost from the beginning.

When asked, very few of them could articulate why they had such an intense dislike for Nimer. Some gave glib answers that he was a most dangerous man. Others talked about an attitude they called arrogant, or his inability to be spontaneous, or "real," as some liked to say. A few said they were embarrassed that such a "light-weight" could have been elected president. When asked what that meant, they were a bit stymied to give a clear answer, mostly making reference to his inability to talk on his feet. When pressed what that meant to them, they said it meant that he had not thought enough about the issues that affected them, or worse, that he didn't care much about them or their problems.

Even the way he walked affected some attitudes towards him. For every one that said it was a strong and manly gait, others called it pretentious and showy. It was mostly the loner quality he had that affected the way people thought about him. Many people thought it lent him the John Wayne sort of aura of a resolute man who would not be deflected from his purpose, no matter what. He knew, by golly, where he was going and didn't have to talk it over with many people how he was going to get there. If others wanted in on the action, they just had to do it his way, a kind of "my way or the highway" point of view. This coming from a man who didn't seem intellectually endowed was hard for the well-educated or those enlightened by experience to accept. Whether accurate or not, it got around that before he was elected that Nimer had gone to Scotland once for a few days on a hunting trip, and to Rome for a weekend. That was the extent of his travel. When asked about why this should stir up a resentment when, after all, travel experience was not a requirement for the presidency, the response was, "When he has the power to send men to fight wars in foreign lands, he ought to at least be able to point them in the right direction."

Perhaps it was the lack of personal warmth behind why many could not identify with him. He even annoyed some when he played with his dog on the White House lawn. One man said that he cringed when TV cameras caught Nimer saying to his dog, "Come on, Bennie, we've got to go in now and do the work of the people." It was so constructed, so uneasy.

Whatever, he certainly wasn't going to make them feel at ease in the next forty hours.

"I've got to know if we have enough for a quorum," Rickert asked the sergeant at arms on the phone.

"Mr. Vice President, apparently we do not." At that moment, 6:30 p.m., only two hundred and thirty congressmen were present. "We have been working the phones to contact as many as we can. Unfortunately, sir, most are out of contact, or not answering their cell phones. It's holiday time and many are on vacation."

"Vacation my ass! The cowards are out of town because they're afraid to be here to work on this puzzle Nimer's got us in.

"In any case, get who you can and have them at the auditorium tonight at 8:30 sharp."

"Ladies and gentlemen," Rickert addressed the assembly, "I have called you all here tonight for one purpose: that we might as a body representing the people of the United States make a decision about how to handle the crisis presented to us and to the world this morning by President Nimer.

"Let me up-date you. We have tried in several ways to contact the president in order to have his thinking regarding his unilateral decision to drop an A-bomb on one of four nations. And also how we might assist him in this endeavor if we deem it lawful under the Constitution and other enactments governing a decision for the United States to go to a state of war.

"Unfortunately, because we lack a quorum of either and both chambers of our Congress, any decision we reach tonight cannot be binding. Nevertheless, as the present circumstances are without precedent, we must provide some structure to make a decision."

Several senior senators, including Tom Melarnowski from South Carolina, were about to interrupt.

"Let me finish first, please," Rickert pleaded.

"No, I will not," drawled Melarnowski. "I have an important question to ask of you. A structure to make a decision, you say. I ask you, Mr. Vice President, to make a decision about what?"

"I'm not sure. What I am sure of is that, in the absence of a quorum, we can at least have a consensus of this group of men and women who represent the people of the United States.

"Now, if I may continue," Rickert said sternly. "There are four basic questions we must satisfy here tonight. In order to keep a tight schedule for answering these questions, I have set a few rules to govern us. They are not the usual rules that guide our discourse. But as the circumstances of this meeting are very unusual, I have taken the liberty to amend the usual way we do business.

"In order to expedite any decision or decisions we reach this evening, I suggest that this meeting lasts no more than three hours. That would be 11:30 tonight. I also suggest that each speaker have the floor for no more than two minutes."

Another round of upset voices filled the air.

"I know this is unusual. But, this is an unusual day. Let me begin. The first question to be discussed is this: 'Does the president, as commander in chief, have the right to unilaterally direct the military under his command to attack another nation, even though that nation has not provoked the attack?'"

It was soon clear that the discussion would break down on party lines. Loyalty was going to smother reality once again.

"It's clear to me, with the clarity I get when I look through a clear pane of glass, that the president has no right to do what he is doing," the Democratic senator from New Jersey thundered. "How anyone can condone what the president is about to do, is doing, is beyond my comprehension. We had a long and wonderful history, before the ill-advised war in Iraq, of attacking another nation only when we were attacked first. I'm talking about the important wars here. Pearl Harbor, Gulf of Tonkin, that kind of stuff. It is beyond the boundaries of logic here to think that Vietnam, Australia, Kenya or little Greenland fall into being in any way categorized as threats to the United . . . States . . . of America." The emphasis on the last four words was a clear effort on his part to show his patriotism.

Senator Denton's words were met with an applause that was more protocol than approval.

Rickert would try to pick alternate speakers to represent their respective parties. In that the meeting was an attempt to draw a consensus on what to do next, he would give equal weight to representatives as well as to senators.

"Speaker of the House Cobbleman, the floor is yours for two minutes."

"Ladies and gentlemen, members of our august bodies bound together today by a crisis we have no precedent in handling, we have a heavy weight of responsibility on us. A responsibility to either support our duly elected president, or to conceive a plan to abort his undertaking. Let there be no doubt about why we are here.

"I have known President Nimer for over twenty years. And I must say that I have never known a finer public servant or a better man. I just know in my heart that what he is trying to do is informed by the best and most noble instincts a man can have. He must have his reasons for doing what he is contemplating.

"Let us take a good look at the first question presented here by our esteemed vice president, Jay Rickert, who asks us if our commander in chief has the right to unilaterally direct an attack on a country that has not provoked the attack.

"Perhaps there was a time when that was not true, as the senator from New Jersey has pointed out. What was true once is no longer true. A new precedent has been set in this regard. In March of 2003, as a Congress we authorized the president of the United States to attack Iraq because we had some evidence that Iraq was a threat to the physical well-being of our nation. Although we have not found a great deal of evidence that they had weapons that could do significant damage to us, we do know that they once had these weapons and probably got rid of them when they knew we were coming. It's a whole new world out there..." he uttered when Rickert interrupted that his two minutes were over.

Without missing a beat, Cobbleman said, "As I was saying, it's a whole new world out there today. Weapons can be small, held in a suitcase. That's right, what our president is contemplating doing in a clean way, a suitcase can contain and let it go in a dirty way. I ask you, does anyone in this world know any more about who is and who is not our enemy than our president? Does anyone have more information to act on than our president? Is there a better, more honest man in this nation's capitol than our president?

"We know that the answer to each and all of these questions is, without question, *No.*" He knew that he had already taxed Rickert's patience. Yet, he continued.

"We know that there are committees on foreign relations and armed services. I grant you that. But, we don't know what the president knows. To abort his plan before we hear from him is the exclamation point behind this hearing—yes, hearing—that we do not trust our system of respect for the office of the presidency. Some of you might not respect the man because he is not one of your party. That is understood with honor. But, if that be the case, I beg you to respect the office.

"Finally, my friends, I spoke late this afternoon with the chief legal counsel of the Republican party whose opinion is that the first question the vice president presents to us today is a moot point in that it has already been decided, in the case of the U.S. attacking Iraq, that a president of the United States, as commander in chief, does, indeed, have the right to unilaterally direct the military under his command to attack another nation, even though that nation has not provoked the attack.

"And where does he get that right from? From you, my friends, in March of 2003. As this gathering is not a duly constituted meeting of both houses of the Congress with quorums in attendance, we can do nothing more than debate the issue and nothing less than support the president."

Cobbleman's speech was as convoluted as the nature of the circumstances, yet it received a loud round of partisan applause. Even those who disagreed with him knew, too, that he had focused the question.

He had taken more time than there was to give. It was already late in the morning of the next day in Australia. *We must do this faster,* thought Rickert.

"Let us turn to the second question, must the president have the consent of the Congress before ordering an attack on another nation?"

It was difficult for Rickert to pick one over another. Yet his eye first found a Democrat who was less than a star, then a Republican not yet graced by celebrity. He figured they would not be so caught up in themselves and might be able to keep their remarks to the prescribed time.

Perhaps the first-term Republican congressman from Minnesota summed it up best when he said that ideally the president had to have the consent of the Congress, yet there might be circumstances when that ideal could not be met. That it was a changed world compared to the days when it was written into the Constitution that war could be declared only with the consent of the Congress.

He went on to speak about the slow change of the nation's foreign policy and the ways that it conducted war. Where once the bombing of civilian populations had been off-limits for the government, considered illegal and immoral, the tide had turned during WWII so that now it was acceptable. And whereas the Geneva Convention was once applicable to all combatants, military and civilian, there was now a new classification, the terrorist, "illegal combatants" they were called by the Nimer administration, who, because they were illegal, were not under the umbrella of the Geneva Conventions.

"We have come to a place in our history that is unlike yesterday and the rules that governed it. Whereas once we deliberated the declaration of war in congressional sessions, we have recently made, in effect, the same declaration through a congressional bill that authorizes the president to spend money on the object of our wrath. Perhaps now, without fully understanding his reasons, we must place our trust as never before in the wisdom of the president. One might say, as an analogy to the pre-war ability of Iraq to hurt us deeply, that the world at large is potentially a terrorist setting primed to do us harm, and we must do what we can to tell that world in the hardest way possible that it must not. If it does, what might happen in the next few days is only a hint of what might be down the road."

The rhetoric was stimulating, but the logic was not. The assembly did not know whether to clap or remain stunned in silence. Straight thinking seemed to have gone out the window, floating around out there for someone to rope in and make shape of once again. Unfortunately, there didn't seem to be anyone in the meeting capable of doing that, so divided were they, and so full of fear to even let anyone try.

As more and more spoke to the issues, the two-minute rule also began to go out the window. What was clear, though, was that the discussion wore on along party lines, Republicans defending Nimer's right to strike an atomic blow, Democrats opposing him and suggesting he had to be stopped.

By 10:00 p.m. it was clear that the group consensus on Question 3 about the War Powers Act was a resounding yes, that it did give the president the authority to declare war in an emergency. What was not clear to the group, though, was if Nimer had invoked it. The radio broadcast was replayed. He had said nothing in it about using the authority of that law to justify his actions. The question, like the meeting and the nation, was in a state of limbo.

The buzz in the lobby at the break was unlike any ever heard before. One of the lawmakers lit up a cigarette, thereby breaking the law. But no one cared this night, and others followed suit. Before long, the lobby was as smoky as an old-fashioned lizard lounge along the Circle.

It was time now to tackle the most important question—what action ought they to take? In addition to the security of the nation being at stake, reputations were on the line. Every possible decision seemed to present dilemmas. And there was the question of North Korea's threat still hanging in the air.

"Ladies and gentlemen, let me quickly summarize so we might set the context for our decision about what we ought to do now. Frankly, and not to waste our valuable time, the only thing we seem able to agree on is that the War Powers Act does give the president some authority to declare war, yet, as he has not officially invoked it, the point is mute. Given all of this, let me hear suggestions from the floor regarding what our next move might be."

If a witness could have hovered with wings over the auditorium at that moment, and if that witness had the capacity to listen into the minds of the audience, he might have heard the frantic cries of children screaming in the night.

It was their worst nightmare come true. And more. They had, at one time or another, discussed in civilian and military committees what might happen if a conventional war turned nuclear, or if a rogue nation would attack America. But never anything like this.

"Mr. Vice President, I take it that the president is in a lockdown and cannot be reached," blurted four-time Senator Barbara Murtaugh, a Democrat from Tennessee. "Why don't we just get him the hell out of there, even if we have to blow the doors down! We've got enough problems right now without this mess. I am, as I am certain others are here today, embarrassed by his typically bullheaded approach towards bringing peace to the world. I know it is frustrating to continually experience wars and deaths and killing. But this is not the way to end it. Killing to kill war brings more killing. There's got to be another way. Let's just go in there and get him out."

Rickert replied, "I have been informed that all civilians have been removed from the Greenbrier facilities, and there is a 24-hour perimeter watch by the West Virginia National Guard. We wouldn't have to worry about injuring civilians. But we would have to worry about injuring or, possibly killing, the president. That possibility would be tragic both for us and for the foundations of our government.

"It would not look good to the people of America," he continued, "or to the rest of the world that the president of the United States was accidentally killed on the orders of the vice president. I don't think Mrs. Nimer would like it, either."

"How about cutting off his communications, so we can have some time to deal with this?" shouted another poorly informed congressman.

Before anyone had a chance to answer the question, a new voice from the back yelled, "How about we just support our president?" It was Priscilla Nimer.

↘

"Mr. Vice President, may I have the floor?"
"Yes, Mrs. Nimer. Please."

Her walk to the platform was different from the usual sauntering way she had, as if she had decided to draw on a new source of energy and will for herself.

"I know you all must be wondering what I am doing here," she started. "Some of you who do not support my husband probably would like to think that he just left me here in Washington. Well, he didn't.

"President Nimer has made provisions for both me and the children to be in a safe and protected place. The children have been escorted there. My husband does not know that I have chosen to remain behind, the same way all of you here have when others have left the city.

"I thought I would come here today and speak on his behalf. I know who he is and I know what he is doing. When you live with a person as long as I have, you get to know things about that person.

"I know how he grieves over the senseless killings that take place every day on our planet. He sees no let up, no transformation of man into someone good."

The buzz had ceased and there was silence in the auditorium.

"There are good men and women, for certain. Many are here in this room today. But there aren't enough. So he has taken it on himself to put an end to the killings once and for all. Not every one might agree with how he's going about it. But be certain that he will grieve two days from now when the bomb is dropped. I know that he does not want anyone to suffer, especially children.

"What he needs now is your understanding and your support." She began to think about more to say. But her usual shyness in public took over again. Simply, she lifted up her hands as if in supplication before saying, "Thank you."

If the room was not fractured before she spoke, it was now. There was some applause, but many more boos and hisses. "How can we support a crazy man?" one irate senator shouted.

"You're over the line, Senator," another shouted back.

She had made a hit with some. "Let's support Mrs. Nimer by supporting the president."

"The meeting's over. Let's go home and support Nimer."

These shouts were mixed with, "We're being led by a maniac," and "He's a threat to the world, a dangerous man."

On and on it went until Rickert realized that he had lost control of the day, at least this day.

The back and forth shouting seemed to echo into the night when in many homes on the east coast of America folks were ready to go to sleep, tired of the scramble they were in, angry with the president, admiring the president. But all tired nonetheless. Rickert adjourned the meeting until the next morning at 9:00 a.m.

Issues had been aired, but the decisions made were insignificant. For the time being, Nimer was having his way against the clock.

23

It was about noon on Monday in Hanoi when Rickert's meeting ended, and three in the afternoon on Monday in Sydney. They would have about six more hours until the list was narrowed to two.

Most Greenlanders stayed up the night, some partying, some praying, while in Kenya people were beginning to get out of bed to look once more for what the day might bring.

Living under the immediate threat of dying was dread changed into a thing that could be heard in the ticking of a clock and seen in the face of a spouse. In effect, everyone was a piece in Nimer's chess game, and every one in the four nations was in a lottery. There would be two winners the following day and two losers. The losers would rejoice in their hearts, while the winners would feel bewildered and hopeful. Bewildered because they could not answer the question "Why?" and hopeful that on the final day it would not be them.

Nimer was up early. In fact he had gone to bed early and lost no sleep. He took a quick shower, got dressed, had some toast and coffee, and called Lt. Romero to see if everything was ready for the morning's radiocast, when he would reveal the identity of the two remaining nations.

Romero said there were some signs that jamming was being attempted, but the power of signal there at the Shadow Command post was so strong that even sophisticated attempts at blocking the signal did not work.

Nimer was in the communications room at 5:55 a.m. and went on the air at precisely 6:00.

The world, of course, was anxious this morning, although most of the people who lived in countries not on the list of four continued their regular sleep hours. Those in countries bordering the four were anxious, though, that they and their children might be endangered by radiation fallout.

"Good day, ladies and gentlemen. This is the president of the United States. Let me at the outset say how sorry I am for the worry and probable torment that has come to the people of the four nations whose names I announced yesterday as possible targets for a small-yield atomic bomb, which is scheduled to be dropped by an American bomber tomorrow morning at 6:02 a.m. U.S. east coast time.

"Let me reiterate, too, my intention. It is not to kill, not to maim. What I am trying to do is a natural progression of the ways in which wars are fought. Because of bad faith on the part of the German government in WWII, civilians were bombed by them, then by us. Conventional bombs turned to napalm over Tokyo, then to A-bombs on two cities of Japan. We did this not to kill civilians, but to prevent the deaths of American soldiers who would have had to invade the Japanese homeland.

"Before and after that great war, there have been genocides too numerous to mention here, some of them in the cruelest ways imaginable. Then after some time, the way wars are fought took another turn with terrorism. Those who engage in that pursuit are outside the law.

"America itself in the immediate past has had, on the heels of 9/11, two significant terrorist attacks on it, one in the tunnels of New York City, the other in a supermarket in Nebraska.

"I am tired. Better let me say that my soul, my spirit, is tired, is fatigued by all the killing we've seen in the past several years. So, it is time to do something about this.

"I am hoping that by dropping a small atomic bomb on a nation of my choice, a nation I do not have an issue with, the world will see just how stupid and cruel war is. And it will know that what will happen tomorrow is but a foot of devastation in the miles of land that the power of the United States can scorch to its roots if we so choose.

"I will leave you for today in sadness when I tell you the names of the two cities that remain on the list.

"But first I want to tell you about tomorrow. I will be on the air at 6:00 a.m. U.S. east coast time, precisely. I will say only the name of the targeted nation, and then leave the air.

"As soon as I go off the air, I will give the order to an American airplane, already in the sky, to drop the bomb on that nation's city. I am doing this to preserve the people of that nation from excessive dread and fear.

"Here are the names of the final two cities: Ilulissat, Greenland, and Hanoi, Vietnam. I will speak with you again tomorrow."

↘

Screams, movement, joy, fear, regret, anger, instincts, near and remote conversation.

Mainly talk, then movement. Or movement, then talk. It depended on where you were when the announcement was made.

Although it was 9:00 p.m. on Monday in Sydney, the streets were filled with revelers. People took off their clothes and swam nude in the waters of Biondi beach, where not a few made love in the sand. They simply didn't care what anyone thought.

They were alive, and expressed it in the ways they wanted. For them, it was neither hell nor high water.

Narelle Hailey and Ray Evans lay in each other's arms where they had been for over a day, talking and making love and talking and copulating. They couldn't get enough of each other, so strong was their affection, so mighty their hormones peaked by the impending doom of the past two days.

They had talked about a future they weren't sure they would have. Barriers seemed to break down in the face of death. They told each others things about their past that they might not have under normal circumstances. The very intimacy of the conversation stirred Ray to erotic heights he had never known before.

When they heard the good news that Sydney had been released from the flash burn of the atomic noose, they hugged and made love again. Then they laughed hysterically. For over thirty hours they had eaten only from the plate of sex seasoned with anxiety.

↘

Matthew was back home in Narok with his family listening to the radio when Nimer announced the news, which was relayed to Africa within seconds. He kissed Marlosa sweetly on her beautiful forehead. Then he picked up Sam and kissed him, too.

"Do you mind, my beautiful Marlosa, if I take the ride into Nairobi to see my friends. I must rejoice in the streets with them."

"Go, Matthew, and when you come home, I will have much of a pig cooked for us to eat together. I will ask your father to join us, and to bring some of his wine you like so much."

He kissed her again and left, knowing fully how lucky he was now, likely not to be claimed pre-emptively by death.

↘

When they heard the news at 6:00 p.m., Quan Trong Thanh and Huong were gripped by fear. He was finally beginning to understand himself these days. He was beginning to take on a certain commitment to Huong and to his life, and trying to stop the endless analysis of Vietnam and its problems.

And now this. His ancestors had fought so hard, with such courage and nobility to evict his country of the outsiders who wanted to take from them what was theirs. Now they wouldn't even have a chance to defend themselves against the aggressor.

He was especially angry that it was the United States that was going to drop the bomb. He had left work that day a little earlier than usual so he could be at home when the bad news came to the world.

When he came in, he asked Huong if she would sit with him to find out the news. They spoke about going south towards the central highlands if Hanoi was chosen by Nimer. They would take the most powerful of several motorbikes Thanh possessed, the one left behind by his friend Vinh when he had been arrested by the police for selling illegal copies of CD's he had obtained to the Chinese market.

When he heard the news that Hanoi might be bombed on the next day, all of the unexploded rage about the inequities of his countrymen, which he had recently suppressed for Huong's sake, suddenly began bubbling to the surface like a volcano ready to erupt. He knew that when he began to feel that way, there was nothing he could do about it. Every time in the past when he would get like this and try to stop it in its tracks, he could not. It was just a matter of time.

"Huong," he said, "I want you to take the motorbike I've been getting ready for us to leave on, and go south as quickly as you can, before the roads get even more crowded than they have been for the past two days. I want you to go to Hue. First get a room, then check in with the police department and give them the address where you'll be staying. As soon as possible after things are over here, whether we are the target of the insane nation or not, I will come to you."

Before she could respond, he said, "I'm sorry that I have to do this, stay here and send you away. I want you to know that I love you, that I am trying hard to be a good and faithful husband. I know that we are different in many ways. For a few months now there has been a stirring in me. I don't know what it's about. I know that I'm trying to come to some place in me that's good for you and for me.

"I've tried to forget about Vietnam and just concentrate on you and me. But, I'm sorry, I can't do that. It's like something comes over me, maybe the same way that a man picks what he wants to do with his life. I don't know where that comes from. Maybe my father's being in the war, or watching my mother working so hard to keep things together on our little farm without receiving any thanks, or not having the things that she wanted. Just little things like a good haircut instead of my father cutting it.

"Have you ever noticed that my father wears long-sleeved shirts, even in the summer? His left arm was severely burned in a napalm attack by American planes early in the war. He told me once when I asked him about the shirts that if it were not for his warnings to the surgeons about what he would do to them if they cut off his arm, he would be an amputee. They did what he asked and left him to rot and die. The shirts, he said, were the least of his worries. Keeping the farm intact, and providing for me and my mother and two sisters was his biggest worry.

"Huong, when this is over, we'll find a way. I fell in love with you because you are warm and gentle. You love the small things in life. I love that you are like this. Sometimes when I see you wearing an ordinary sweater I fall in love all over again. You are like the earth to me. I love you in my hands. I love the way you smell."

He began to cry a little. Huong realized that she had never seen him cry before. Seeing him this way made her feel good, very good. It affirmed her impulse about him when she had first met him. *He is a loving man,* she thought.

Brushing from his cheeks the few tears he allowed, Thanh let her know that he had to stay in Hanoi to help his people, especially then.

In a way not typical of Vietnamese women, she came close to him and held his face in her left hand. "We are together again, you and I."

Although she was a Buddhist and had never read the Bible, she more breathed the words on him than said them, "We have been lost, and now are found."

She kissed him on the lips, and they held each other for a long time.

"You must go now, my love. I will see you in Hue," Thanh whispered.

᭦

It was 7:30 a.m. when Eirik Narsaq heard the news. He was a little less interested in it than most Greenlanders. His life was tough and he was old now, so a few years now cut off from his life didn't make as much difference to him as it did to others in Ilulissat.

There was, though, the urge to live. He even at times wondered about that, though it was becoming less urgent lately. He, like many others in this tiny city, was a proud Inuit. Although the Danish there treated him and his people well, he had a feeling that he didn't belong any more. The old ways were fading fast. Even when some continued to go fishing for seal along the coastal waters, they used an assortment of new fishing gear. Others used high powered rifles and shotguns to kill the fish. On a good day it was like shooting fish in a barrel.

The relief payments sent from Denmark didn't help much, as they made some hard working people lazy. They were caught in a cultural trap that held them fast while the rest of Ilulissat and similar places were moving fast to the next level, one that Eirik did not like. More cars, TV sets, drinking, snowmobiles.

His life would have been easier if he was as stupid as most people thought he was. There were times, of course, when he felt like he was living in a vacuum, a place where all meaning had been sucked out. When he sometimes got on line at the soup kitchen for the ones who didn't even want to use the government tickets to purchase food in the little "supermarket" in town, he did so because he thought it might bring him back into contact with the world he had once known in Uummannaq. He could find real people there who valued friendship and the mutual interdependence he had once known, unlike the way he lived now, on the dole and delivering newspapers for some extra cash, a way to deliver himself a bit from being dependent on the indifference of bureaucracy.

Eirik found it amusing. Here he was leading a most ordinary life, yet asking extraordinary questions about it just when it might end for him. It all seemed quite ludicrous to him. Then again, what the president was about to do was no less incredible than his son's suicide. It was all bordering on being pointless for him now. Like many others that day, his capacity to ask questions superseded his ability to answer them.

➷

Once he was finished making his next-to-last announcement, Nimer went into a personal retreat in his quarters at the Greenbrier. He had counted on his own government being in a state of mass confusion regarding the legal and constitutional questions his action would cause.

He was also a bit gleeful over some of the news that Lt. Romero was giving him. That many congressmen had left Washington for safer pastures, and that the ones who had remained to meet the night before were hopelessly bound up by the unprecedented nature of the situation so that nothing amounting to anything had been accomplished. Nimer loved it.

Yet, he was bemused by statements coming from the U.N. about legalities and moralities, treaties and pre-emptions. More scary, though, were veiled threats coming from the Peoples' Republic of China. The diplomat in him felt them like tuning forks echoing from his sense of fear to his need to act and back again.

Romero was an excellent choice to bolster his resolve. He was not only loyal and unquestioning in his duties, but also superb in his craft as a communications man. To hear his voice was a constant reminder of duty. Besides, he was a very good cook.

After eating a small breakfast of bacon and eggs, Nimer took a second cup of coffee back to his room. He wanted to spend some time thinking about the possible choices for the following day. He would go over some of the last-minute details that night with Romero.

How did a man think about making a choice between one city and another that would mark it for death? He first thought about Truman and how he had made the choices of Hiroshima and Nagasaki.

There was not much help there. Hiroshima, too, was one of four target cities for the first bomb, and it was chosen more because of the good weather over it that day than any other factor. The thought that he could get weather reports on Hanoi and Ilulissat struck him as absurd. Besides, it wasn't as if there was a specific aiming point the way it was over Hiroshima, where the t-shaped bridge over the Motoyasugawa River was the precise target.

In tomorrow's case, the instructions would be simply to drop it on the city of choice. There was no need for precision. The president wanted only general destruction and havoc.

Since he couldn't get any guidance from history, he decided to think about it not as a choice of one over the other, but as a decision that would kill one and not the other. If he could only think clearly enough to know which one's demise would be more helpful to his goal than the other.

He thought little about Greenland except that it was far enough away not to cause any damage to the continental U.S. by way of wind-blown radiation. He wasn't sure, yet he'd never heard of any country around Japan complain about the effects of radiation from the two 1945 bombs. Additionally, he wasn't aware of any mineral or oil deposits around Ilulissat that might be harmed.

In a general way, Nimer knew there was lot of ice in the area and that it was sparsely settled, at least compared to the U.S. He still thought of the Inuit people as Eskimos, as Nanooks of the North who slept in igloos, tight up against each other to warm their nude bodies.

Most importantly, Nimer knew that he didn't know much about Greenland and its people. What he did know, in a vastly underestimated way, was that the icebergs, animals and openness of the place would make it an excellent target to effect good results. Most importantly to him, the loss of Eskimos would be tolerable.

Vietnam was a different story. He knew about this country because he was once eligible in his youth to serve in the war there in the 60's. He was going to the University of Arizona at the time, and had no desire to fight in a war that had no discernible purpose other than to prop up a domino called South Vietnam lest it change into a Communist block that would topple onto another country to keep it under the Red thumb.

He had covered all his bases back then, beginning the paper process of joining the National Guard before his lottery number came up, allowing him to continue his education and stay out of the war.

Nimer knew about the war through several of his contemporaries who served before returning to the university. He was befriended by an African-American student named Ray, a wizard in mathematics, who was part of the Tutorial Center staff. Ray was assigned to help Nimer pass the statistics course required for graduation.

They gradually got to know each other, even sharing confidences. After awhile, Nimer sensed that it was okay to tell Ray that he thought some of the black girls on campus were beautiful, that he had even thought of dating one, but knew that it wouldn't be acceptable to his father.

He began to ask Ray about the war, what he really thought and saw. At first, the young man was uncomfortable, but gradually began to open up. He even shared, with some measure of pride it seemed to Nimer, that he was still under orders not to share the clearance that allowed him to execute a mission into Cambodia long before these incursions became known to Americans.

It was mostly, though, the stories Ray told him about going into the little villages in central Vietnam that marked Nimer's soul. At first, Ray was general about what went on. Gradually, he told his friend "Fletch" some of the details. How a few of the men would look into the huts for the young females, take them forcefully into the nearby bush to put the fear of God into them by raping them. How they would later laugh and brag to the other guys. Ray said he always felt ashamed of himself by not saying or doing anything.

Once Nimer asked him if he still remembered those things. "I will always remember those things," he said, asking Nimer if he would never tell another.

He said that he never experienced it himself, but he had heard stories of American soldiers going into villages and burning them down in front of cowering families whose homes were going up in smoke.

One time, he said, the story got around that one of the men in his patrol went into a hut where the family was huddled like a ball of flesh. The soldier fired a burst into the center of the ball and then, as the knot of arms and legs unraveled like a precious sculpture being violated by a gun spraying red paint, he continued firing until the screams died down and no one moved. Later that night, when the guys asked the soldier why he had done it, he said he didn't know, that it just seemed to be the thing to do.

When Nimer heard the story, he closed his eyes and breathed as deeply as he could, vowing some day to do what he could to stop this kind of cruelty.

For weeks after, the future president spent time by himself, mostly in the little rustic settings around the campus, thinking about what he had heard. He could see the teenagers' fear, hear the yells of babies, and smell the stench of the blood, so keen was his hatred of all things cruel. It was an admirable trait, yet one he never learned how to handle.

Nonetheless, his instinctual feel for Vietnam was ambivalent. He also knew about the almost 60,000 American men and women who had lost their lives there. And he had heard or read about the cruelties of the other side, how they would sometimes cut off the penises of dead American soldiers, or leave their beheaded bodies in the woods.

The worst part of it all, he had always thought, was the residue that war left in the hearts and minds of the young soldiers after it was over. They had been taught to kill. Some, in the absence of law and order, learned how to be murderers. It was all a part of the crazy cycle that had to be stopped.

Nimer concluded that it was fruitless to make his decision based on what he knew or even on what he felt.

He would go to the argument of maximum impact for his purposes, which target would present more physical evidence that might be captured by photos, film and video.

Certainly, Ilulissat would present better evidence, he thought. The openness of space might present a certain kind of desert-like atmosphere in the wake of the bomb. There were the icebergs melting. This would give the world a bit of evidence about how a larger bomb could melt parts of the Jakobshavn Glacier, or even blow football field-sized icebergs from its sides. Maybe water levels would rise a bit around the world, not too much to cause permanent damage, yet enough to put the world on notice.

Dead seals, walruses, and whales floating onto the shore would fire up the environmentalist organizations to broaden their scope of interests to include world peace.

A most interesting part, he thought, was that the brown colored Inuits would remind people of the Japanese of Hiroshima and Nagasaki, perhaps raising the world's awareness, a kind of deja vu that could remind people that they had not come far from their beginnings.

His mind wandered back to Hanoi, and how crowded he knew it was. Its broad lakes, interspersed around the newer and taller buildings put up since the U.S. bombings, could present opportunities for victims to jump into in an attempt to try to stop the burning sensations caused by the bomb. Just like Hiroshima.

The older sections of the city housed most of its ordinary people and were the centers for everyday food and clothing shopping. Nimer hoped that the Old Quarter would not find its way into the bomb sight. Instructions would be given in haste to drop the bomb as close to the center of the city as possible. He did not know if that included the densely packed Old Quarter.

The city was populated by almost three million people as compared to Ilulissat's nine thousand. Certainly there would be more casualties in Hanoi. Nimer knew he wanted some, but how many was still a question for him. In the case of Ilulissat, would nine thousand be enough?

He thought, again, about the collateral damage the bomb might cause to nations nearby. Ilulissat was almost 3,000 miles from Maine, enough distance not to do any damage to Americans. It might send some radiation to the large island of Ellesmere to the north, or to Baffin island almost directly west. Both of these islands, though, were thinly populated.

Vietnam bordered Laos, Cambodia, and southern China. He knew little about Laos and Cambodia, and cared less. His education, travels, conversations and briefings hardly ever included them. The southern part of China could be a critical problem.

Nimer, though, was in a mood to finalize whatever tensions fell into his thinking about this undertaking to stop war forever. If China wanted war, or if it wanted to go to war over the proximity of the bomb, then perhaps it was time to go to war with them, once and for all. Now was as good a time as ever, he thought, because at this moment America had more and bigger nuclear bombs, as well as an infinitely more capable delivery system. Perhaps it was a blessing that Vietnam was close to China, he thought.

In the end, he could not make an easy decision. For every plus there was a minus. He had long ago anticipated the complexity of picking the final city. He always knew that a personal decision would be difficult, that God or a lottery would have to do it for him.

24

At the same time Nimer was brooding about the final choice, an estimated one and quarter million people were gathering in Manhattan to rally against "Nimer the Crazy," as the dominant poster of the day put it.

An additional half million marched in San Francisco, as well as cumulative millions in cities of every size across the United States. Without anyone having to say it or declare it, there was a national holiday from work and school. Most people were bright enough to know how pretentious it would be to go to work or send their children to school on a day that might very well change the world.

The rally in New York was the most difficult to handle. It was almost spontaneous and by its wild nature almost immune from the attempts of the police to inoculate it with billy clubs and mace. Most policemen and women did not have their hearts in it anyway. They would rather have been on the other side or at home near their families.

In the end, more harm than good was done. Many people were hurt by the police in a knee-jerk reaction to civil disobedience. Others were trampled by the crowds, especially at the intersections where it was difficult, if not impossible, to get ambulances and medical help. Even paddy wagons could not get through. The only way the police could handle matters was to cuff the disobedient and lay them down in the streets until order could be restored, which happened only in the early evening.

The streets of Hanoi seemed as chaotic, yet more so. Most citizens were trying to flee in whatever way they could, without any help or hindrance from the police.

By early afternoon, most of the townspeople from Ilulissat were gone south along the west coastal waters of the Davis Strait towards Nuuk, the capital. Every fisherman with a boat helped. There really wasn't any problem to get out. Most just flat out left, leaving behind their belongings, which, in many cases, were meager.

Nimer never asked for information about these events, and so Romero never offered it.

"Norm, things are beginning to heat up. I thought if we could have resolved the current situation more quickly, I wouldn't have to tell you this."

Feeling the anxiety of the past few days mounting in him, Jarvis blurted out, "Tell me what?"

"When the president announced his plan on the radio yesterday, you told me we didn't really have to worry, as your response is necessary for him to complete the sequence for ordering an atomic weapon to be dropped. Of course, I already knew this, and figured you have been biding your time, hoping, I suppose, your part in choosing targets for an A-bomb would not come out, that an easy solution would be found.

"Well, there is no easy solution. There is only a hard solution. The president has a tape of your voice that verifies his order with the codes and passwords necessary. The communications experts at Command Alert have it and will use it to complete his plan.

"The only way we can stop him is to get in there and destroy the communications center."

It wasn't necessary for Jarvis to respond.

At 10:00 a.m. Vice President Rickert began a last-ditch effort to hold a meeting of those senators and congressmen who remained from yesterday. About a third had left the city immediately after the last evening's meeting had been adjourned.

Rickert got right to the point.

"My friends, time is running out on all of us. Our president is about to drop an atomic bomb on an innocent nation, and there doesn't seem to be much we can do, or . . ." he deliberately paused for a long time, "we have the courage to do."

This was met with a medley of boos. Everyone present thought of him or her self as a person of courage, if for no other reason than that they showed up today.

"Mr. Vice President," shouted Senator Manfredi from Illinois, "what would you have us do? Tell us what you would do."

"My friends, I thought you'd never ask. Decidedly, we must *not* follow in the president's steps." This came as a shock to the assembly, as Rickert was known as a "Yes Man" around town, a guy who would support whatever Nimer would say.

"We all know that President Nimer is a man of peace. Fact is, his greatest contributions have been in the area of peace. He has rid the Iraqi people of an evil dictator, and he has set the tone for peace in the Mid-East. Already, several nations in that area of the world are 'playing ball' with us as never before in the fight against terrorists, as well as in their willingness to talk about their own atomic capacities. As we speak, he is in the process of unearthing the Iranian nuclear threat.

"We are all grateful to him for this. As you know, I see him and talk with him often. So I know how tired he is of war and the cruelties of dictators. I know that he wants to end wars, and I know what he is doing now. He is trying to have the war that will end all wars.

"And, again, we are grateful for his intentions. But he is going about it in the wrong way. Acting by himself, he has disdained the Congress, and he has brought distrust upon our nation. We have always been a nation that in principle tries to do the right thing. Even in the midst of our wrongdoing . . . and there have been many. We all know that. This is not the time to recite them.

"Even in the midst of our wrongdoing," he repeated, "we have tried to right ourselves from our wrongs. We have always done that from within. It is the greatness of our nation that from its inception its people have lived according to the principles of right and wrong.

"We were wronged by the British, and tried to right that wrong. The Revolution was the planting of that seed of trying to do the right thing. The right thing for the people of our great nation.

"We must abide by the principle that we are a nation that exists for its citizens. And so the question here today is: what do we think the people of the United States would have us do today?"

He stopped. Every face in the room, some of which had started the session by reading newspapers on their laps, or answering their e-mail on laptops held low and out of view, was looking at him as if to say, "So what?"

The silence ended with Representative Esmaralda from New Mexico making an odd statement. "Mr. Vice President, do we go into the streets and ask, take a straw vote, do something if they say so, do nothing if they say don't? What you are saying is preposterous. With all due respect, silly. Senator Manfredi asked you what we should do. I ask you, in the name of everyone in this auditorium, in the name of every American, what do you think we should do?"

This question became the sound byte on the evening news, as it epitomized the state of print and television news: questions that had few answers.

Before Rickert could respond, General Arena took the floor. He was military and a known leader. Just what everyone needed today.

"Gentlemen, we have about nineteen hours before the president orders release of the bomb. I have a proposal to make."

There was a palpable joy in the air when he said this. No one knew what to do, so when anyone decisively stepped up to the plate they were immediately perceived as a leader. Several even stood and applauded Arena.

"What I propose is that we go to the communications room at Command Alert in the Pentagon building, arrest the M.P.' s guarding the room, blow the door down, and arrest the two men who are in there, Yucaneer and Overstreet. By doing this, we can stop the president's completion of the complex and coded signals that must be executed to drop an atomic bomb. We can then take it from there."

At last, here was a plan to avert an impending disaster. The room suddenly got lighter.

"Let's take a quick straw vote on the general's proposal," Rickert said. All the assenting murmurs, nods and applause said, "Yes, let's do it."

"All those who approve of us going to Command Alert at the Pentagon and arresting the two men in the communications room to stop the president from dropping an A-bomb, say aye."

"But, Mr. Vice President, we must first have a discussion," a young congressman blurted out.

In a tone of annoyance, Rickert blurted back, "This is a straw vote. We are not in the Congress here. We're trying to get something f... we're trying to get something done."

He continued, "All in favor, say aye."

A loud noise of approval.

"All against, say nay."

A few scattered nays.

"The aye's have it. General Arena. Let's get on with it."

Arena ran from the room where he was met by hordes of television cameras. He simply plowed through them to his waiting staff car, which sped him to the Pentagon.

Nimer's solution was to pray and then listen to the voice of his God to let him know if it should be Vietnam or Greenland.

True to his fashion, his prayer today was clear and direct. "God of our fathers, please let me hear your voice so that I can know which of the two countries chosen will be the vessel that will contain your work tomorrow. Your voice will be my lottery."

For almost two hours, Nimer said and re-said this prayer. After each time, he would stop and listen for the voice of God. There was no voice.

The thought came to him that maybe God was displeased with him and would not answer his request. He could not think of anything he had done wrong, or anything to apologize for. So, he tried again: "God of our fathers, please tell me what to do." Again, there was no answer.

"God, I have knelt on my knees in prayer to you for the past two hours, and you do not answer me. God, my God, why have you not answered me?"

No answer yet.

Nimer thought it was time to stop trying so hard. Maybe just listen. So he sat down in a plain wooden chair to rest. As he began to doze from the exhaustion of the past few days, he wandered back to his young manhood when he was going to college and received a high number from the military draft lottery that would have placed him in a position to go to Vietnam.

Until this very moment, he had always thought that it was his own manipulation of the system in first registering for the National Guard that had kept him from serving in the war. He always felt that if he hadn't made the decision he did that he would have been chosen to go to fight, and that he might not have come to the point of being elected president. In fact, he would not have come to this momentous day. He knew now it was God's doing.

Just then, the answer came to him. Whether it was the clarity of the moment that found him between sleep and consciousness, or the purity of his quest, he did not know. But God was answering him. Not in the way he sought the answer, but an answer nevertheless.

"Lottery, my son. Lottery" came to him in a voice as clear as if Richard was in the room talking with him. A light shone down on the top of the right side of his head. It was like a laser beam of white light.

Sometimes, he thought, *God answers us in strange ways.*

He went down on his knees again. "Thank you, God, for showing me what I have to do. I ask you for one more favor. Guide my hand so that when I pick the country that is chosen in the lottery, it will be the country of your choice. Amen."

Nimer knew what he had to do, and immediately began to do it. He got out a piece of White House stationery that he had taken with him. He tore off the letterhead and threw it into the waste basket. He then took the leftover piece and tore it evenly in half, top to bottom, with the help of a ruler.

He took out a pen and wrote the words "Hanoi" on one piece, and "Ilulissat" on the other. As he did not wear hats, there was no receptacle except the garbage pail to put the papers in. He dumped the pieces of the last three days on the floor, then took each of the stationery pieces and rolled it carefully up into a ball. A nice, round ball.

He took each ball and rolled it against the wall to see if it was as perfectly round as he could get it. He picked them up and, one at a time, and gave each a final packing with his hand before dropping them both into the basket.

He picked up the basket and rolled it around in a circle, first right, then left. He put the basket on the floor. Before reaching in his hand to pick the one, he said, "Our Father, may your will be done."

Nimer chose one ball, opened it up and read the word "Hanoi."

25

Word went out to the world immediately that the communications room at the Pentagon had been over-run by two dozen highly trained Marines and explosives experts from the Navy.

Reporters had been cordoned off from the area by noon. It was about 12:30 when a loud eruption of the small room at Command Alert in the Pentagon was heard. Smoke could be seen rising from inside the huge courtyard.

A press conference, led by Secretary of Defense Jarvis and General Arena, was held quickly. Arena's natural leadership was now evident and pre-eminent. It was humbling to Jarvis to acknowledge this about the general.

"General, it is clear that you are the man of the hour. Your leadership at the meeting this morning was outstanding, as is the way you led the military earlier today in overcoming the men in the communications room.

"I am sorry for their loss. However, I think it is important for the nation to see this morning's raid as ordered by the elected civilian government. Many Americans have been a little edgy about what they call the abuse of their civil liberties, and they might get really spooked if they think this government is now being led by members of the military.

"I think it's important that I take the lead at the press conference and introduce you. You can be certain that I will give you all due credit today. I know that whatever the press first hears sticks with them, and is hard to change later."

In an uncharacteristically assertive way, he looked at Arena and said, "I hope you are okay with that."

"I am," Arena said curtly.

As they strode to the podium in the White House Press Room, everyone seemed to be breathing the air of triumph. The reporters even stood and applauded the two.

"Ladies and gentlemen, please sit," said Jarvis.

As they began to sit, he looked around the room at them and breathed a noticeable sigh of relief and smiled. This gesture broke the ice, and much of the tension that had been building for days left the room in a collective laughter of mutual support. They had had a rough few days together and they would always remember them in a bond that now had a chance to grow.

"We got lucky today," Jarvis said.

"As you know we have just stormed the communications room at the Pentagon where two lieutenants, experts in communications, were holed up to communicate President Nimer's orders to drop an atomic bomb on either Greenland or Vietnam.

"We all can breathe a sigh of relief now, as communications with the president have been cut off and he no longer has the capacity to order the bomb to be dropped. By that I mean he can no longer complete the transference of the order, which is subject to a complex sequencing of triggers that are coded.

"We still continue to try to reach President Nimer to ask about his most unusual actions. Unfortunately, we have not yet been able to reach him.

"I'd like now to introduce you to a man who is no stranger to us. You all know by now that General Arena, along with others of us, provided enormous leadership to this nation over the past few days. Without him, and I must say Vice President Rickert, we might not be breathing so easily this evening.

"It was General Arena's idea to blow down the heavy steel door of the communications room today so we could at least for now put on hold the imminent actions of the president. We have breathing room, and no harm has come to President Nimer. He is our president, and he has his reasons, I am sure. We just need to know what they are."

Arena was beginning to stew. As the one who led the move to stop the president, he would be on the spot with Nimer. And Nimer knew about his complicity in getting the bomb as well as the personnel ready for it to be dropped.

"I don't normally do this, but I'm asking you all to give General Arena a well deserved round of applause."

The reporters stood and did what they were asked, more in relief than in admiration for the general.

"Thank you," Arena said. "I'll give you a few specifics about the operation. Then the Secretary will answer your questions. I'm sorry but I cannot stay.

"At approximately 3:47 this afternoon, a specially trained group of Marines and Navy personnel attacked the Command Alert communications room at the Pentagon."

Strangely, Jarvis immediately jumped between Arena and the microphone to assure everyone, especially America and the foreign nations he dealt with every day, that he never would have agreed to authorize an atomic bomb drop. He just wanted to make that clear, and had already informed the governments of Vietnam, Greenland, Australia and Kenya of this, he said, before standing aside.

Arena continued. "The communications have effectively been stopped. I want everyone to know that we took this action not in opposition to the president, but as the result of a direct order from the Congress as it was convened by the vice president.

"Although it is a day of rejoicing, we have accompanying sadness. The two communications experts who controlled the technology are both dead. After the explosion, we immediately entered the area where the devices are, and found them both dead, their bodies apparently blown up in the explosion.

"Their names are Major Sherman Overstreet and Lt. Aaron Yucaneer. We do not know what their motives were in remaining in the room against my direct orders. I presume they were serving at the request of the president and, until further investigation reveals otherwise, I shall treat them both as heroes and wish that you would too in your accounts of today's actions.

"I have only a few minutes before I must get back to the Pentagon. Regarding the threat from North Korea, I would like the citizens of the United States to know that our forces are on twenty-four hour alert.

"We have planes from our bases in Okinawa on alert in that region. They are fully armed with weapons of the greatest magnitude, and in the configurations we have placed them they can reach North Korea in less than one hour.

"We will continue to make efforts to be in touch with President Nimer who, of course, has the first and last word in the chain of command to order these planes into action.

"As these are matters of national security and great sensitivity, I have said all I want to for now. With that, let me turn the meeting over to Secretary of Defense Jarvis."

When Arena left the room, he had a feeling that everything was going to work out fine, both for the nation as well as for his own career. He was being recognized as an international hero for his work in shutting down the Command Alert center for communications. In fact, it was his decisiveness in the face of an otherwise inert leadership that would be recognized as having prevented a disaster of cosmic proportions.

He was also lucky. The Hiroshima-yield atomic bomb he had prepared for Nimer's drop on North Korea was still in the air, along with two other aircraft, each holding sophisticated megaton A-bombs. The three planes had been in the air for the past three days, being re-fueled periodically by tankers in the air when necessary between sequenced landings for ordinary maintenance.

If it came to it that they could reach Nimer and he still wanted the bomb to be dropped on North Korea, everything might work out as they had originally planned.

Arena got back to the Pentagon as soon as he could in order to receive briefings about the state of the world.

There was rejoicing in the streets of Hanoi. By western standards, it was calm. The loudest show of happiness was the thousands of bicycle bells that everyone riding through the crowded streets of Hanoi began to ring when the good news got out, and continued to ring until evening in a crescendo of Buddhist happiness.

The first thing that Thanh did was to call Huong on his cell phone. He woke her out of sleep at the An Doh Hotel where she was staying in Hue.

"Please come back to Hanoi as fast as you can. Things will be different from now on. We will get to know each other, and I will put my rendezvous with Vietnam's destiny on hold.

"If you leave now, you can get here by early evening. I'll be at the McCain monument at West Lake at 6:00 tonight. I'll meet you there. We'll buy bowls of hot soup. We will sit on a bench and talk about us. Maybe about having children. And then we'll talk about how we will grow old together."

All Huong said was, "I'm on my way."

↘

Eirik received the news almost as fast as it was announced. The streets of Ilulissat were quite still. Most had left the city that morning and throughout the afternoon. He could, though, hear a few loud voices in the streets. Probably drunks who had slept through the evacuation. Or the less fortunate who didn't have any contacts with boats. Or those who, like him, didn't care much anymore whether they lived or died.

He was happy for everyone, yet sad that his dominant thought, as he lit a broken cigarette, was to wonder how much different it would be if his son were there.

When word spread that the communications room had been over-run at the Pentagon and the president's plan aborted, the ugliness in America turned to spontaneous joy. As civilians at war against their own government, many protesters had bonded with their fellows. When the good news came, they began to dance and drink with each other. Wine began to flow in the streets. Even the police joined in. Some of the younger ones were seen leaving arm in arm with the many college students who had attended the rallies.

The rally-parties went on well into the night. While many of the older folks were heading home to their families, the young reveled on.

Nimer, meanwhile, was beginning a conversation with Lt. Romero that would considerably dampen everyone's enthusiasm by the next morning.

26

"I can't tell you how grateful I am, Lt. Romero, for what you, Yucaneer and Overstreet, God rest their souls, have done to save the day.

"What you three have done is shown once again the difference between the citizens in totalitarian countries and ours. We train our people, from the schools on up, to think for themselves. Not to just respond when given an order."

Without notice, he shifted. "Now tell me how this works. I knew how to do it before today, but you've got to go over the new specifics with me now."

"As I've told you, Mr. President, when Major Overstreet, rest his soul, if you don't mind my repeating, sir . . . when he communicated to me how things were going in Washington, that he and Yucanner might be over-run, we both thought that a back-up plan for you would be in order.

"As you said, we're all taught to think on our feet, to have a Plan B when we can do it. What the major proposed to me and we did it, just in case, was something that we wouldn't even have told you about if we didn't have to."

Nimer interrupted. "Lieutenant, some day you will be rewarded in heaven for what you have done. But, it's almost midnight and we're going to have to start this thing about four hours from now. So, please, get on with the technical stuff."

"Yes, sir, I'm sorry. What we did was to work out something, mostly Yucaneer's work, to provide you with a system I have right here in these computers in front of us that allows you to direct the release of an atomic bomb, with all the codes and passwords necessary. We took the voice of the secretary of defense, which you had given to Yucaneer on tape, and have it ready to slip in at the right time.

"In effect, what we have done is to replicate the signals necessary for you in the morning to direct the dropping of the bomb. We have it all at our fingertips, literally, and don't really have to make contact with Command Alert at the Pentagon."

"Great work Romero, extraordinary."

"Before you say that, Mr. President, there is one thing you must know. The general, in his press conference today, as I've already told you, spoke about the three planes flying in the general region of North Korea. One of them has a small atomic bomb, the other two are loaded with really big ones, you know, the kind that can wipe out a big city like New York in a flash. None of us knows what his plan is for these planes. If he pulls them down, I'm afraid, Mr. President, your plan is Fubar."

"Fubar?"

"Yes, sir, it's an old WWII expression that means something like kerploop."

"Kerploop?"

"Sir, it's an obscene expression I don't feel free saying in front of the president, if you don't mind my saying, sir."

"I've got the general idea. Now tell me more about the possible problem with the planes."

"If General Arena thinks that the crisis with North Korea is over, or let's say he wants to restore some sense of sanity . . . I mean normalcy in the world for awhile, he might just order the planes down. If so, no bomb, sir."

"Son, you've heard the expression about crossing that bridge when we come to it. Well, here's a new one. If there's no bridge, we can't cross it. Meanwhile, we plan as if there is a bridge."

And then he asked, "How will we know, Lieutenant, if there is a bridge?"

"We rigged up the original replicated signals so that you could order the one plane carrying the small A-bomb to drop it where you tell it. General Arena had already provided Overstreet with the identification codes for the plane. The problem now is that there are three planes in the air, so we can't be certain if Arena has switched that code to one of the other two planes or not. At this late date, we didn't have enough information on all the planes to know the answer to that question.

"Here's the problem, Mr. President. Once we complete the first communication signals in the morning, the codes and all, we will get one plane only. And once the signal to that plane is established, for security reasons, all other signals cannot be received by the plane. In effect, it can receive signals from you only, no one else.

"According to established protocol, the only communication that the pilot of the plane is allowed are responses to my questions, as ordered by you. You can, if you want, talk directly to the pilot. But, as you might know, that is discouraged as it could lead to a discourse between you and the plane that you might not want. You know, stuff about people. Pilots of these planes are trained and directed to execute orders and not ask questions. Do you read me, sir?"

"Yes, Lieutenant, I read you."

Romero blushed as he realized that he had taken a wrong tone with the president, and began to apologize.

"No need to apologize, son. It felt good for a minute there to be a part of a great machine. You know, just a guy taking orders."

He paused for a minute while Romero waited.

"Yeah, it felt good to be really a part of this at the ground floor level. Like being a soldier in a war waiting to do his part.

"Let's get back to this issue of the plane. I guess where you're leading to here is that if we get one of the planes with a megaton bomb on it, I'll have to make a decision to drop it on the target, or to abort my plan. That's going to be a difficult decision. On the one hand, this opportunity to save the world from wars might never pass my way again. On the other, if I direct a drop, hundreds of thousands of people will die. Much more than I'd like. I mean more than I anticipated at first.

"If I'm right about my math, Lt. Romero, the chances of our getting the right plane are one in three, the wrong plane, two in three?"

"I think that's right, sir."

"Peter, I normally have lots of advisors around me to ask the kind of question I'm going to ask you now. I hope you don't mind. I'm not trying to put pressure on you, but I hope you understand that you're the only one I can ask right now."

By instinct Romero stood up before saying, "Yes, sir, I understand. Please ask me."

"If you were in my shoes, would you call it off?"

"Now, sir, that's a hard question to answer. I've thought from the beginning that what you are doing is the correct thing. You know, to make an honest attempt to try to end war. That is a noble goal, sir.

"I can only think that I, too, would like to see a perfect world. So, in that sense and in the sense that this chance might never happen again, I would go ahead, sir. If I were in your shoes, that is."

"Well said, young man. I would have done no less, no matter what you said.

"Get some sleep, Lieutenant. We'll start our day in a few hours, let's say zero three-thirty hours. I want to make sure of every last detail before I direct the plane to drop the bomb on Hanoi. I will give the order to the pilot of the plane at zero four-thirty hours. That will give him enough time to get over the drop zone by zero six hundred our time when I make the announcement to the world regarding what city it will be.

"It is critical that the bomb be dropped immediately after I make the announcement. Instructions are to be that the bomb is dropped at zero six hundred zero two E.D.T., which will be eighteen hundred zero two in Hanoi.

"I want no unnecessary panic and fear to happen to those people. Someday, the world will know that they are the real heroes. That they will not have died in vain. That their blood would be the blood that saved millions of others.

"I intend," he continued, "when this is over and the dust settles, to restore the city of Hanoi. We'll put an extraordinary monument to them in the center of the city. People will go there, just like they do to Hiroshima City now, to see the city of peace. Maybe even that will catch on with the media, Hanoi, the City of Peace."

Romero interrupted. "Mr. President, I am proud to serve you during these crucial days. I just wanted to let you know. One more thing, Mr. President, of a practical nature, the name of the ship carrying the Hiroshima-type bomb is the 'Pencader G.' I just thought you'd like to know."

He didn't have the heart right then to tell Nimer again that if the I.D. came up differently in a few hours, they wouldn't have the Pencader G. There was a two in three chance it would be the wrong plane.

27

Nimer could not sleep when he went to his room. He was disappointed in himself, as he wanted to tell the world later that he didn't lose a wink the night before making this historic decision.

He began to think of himself and how he would be seen by history. He thought that he had finally filled the shoes of the presidency, had finally signed his own signature on the history of America. Making this decision did not seem like a dream to him. He did not think it was someone else, as he sometimes did when he realized fully that he *was* the president of the United States.

He thought about Priscilla, Casandra and John, and wondered if they were okay. And Overstreet, that exceptional patriot. Someday, when the truth would come out, Sherman would truly be honored like the most well-known heroes. He had promised him that and he had to be certain to make it happen.

He spent the next few hours like a person who is tired but cannot fall asleep. When he was a child, his mother had referred to it as the "twinky zone."

A sudden and forceful knock on his door snapped him out of it.

"Mr. President, it's 3:30. I have some coffee for you. Please open the door. It's Lt. Romero. Pedro."

"Just come in."

He thanked Romero for the coffee, and asked him if he was ready.

"Yes, sir, I am. I have been going over the equipment and the routine of my training, along with the few specialties and wrinkles we've set up for you. Yes, sir, I am ready. The equipment is ready."

"Excellent. Let's drink our coffee, and get on with it."

It took about a half hour for Nimer to ask more questions about the technology of ordering the bomb drop. Romero was the best at what he did, as well as being an exceptional teacher. Ironically, no one had ever considered to brief the president about the smaller specifics of ordering an atomic drop.

At 4:25 the president stepped outside the door of the communications room so he could be alone for a few minutes.

"Well, God, this is it. I think I am doing the right thing here. Please bless my efforts, and be at my side. You know that I want to stop wars and killing. And I know that you do, too. Stay by our side, especially my family and those who are going to die today. I pray that they may die without pain, and that those who do suffer pain will be rewarded by the knowledge in heaven that what they do today will not have been in vain. I do this in the name of Jesus Christ, your Son. Amen."

He was now ready.

"Let's start the engine, Lt. Romero."

"Yes, sir, everything is ready to go. Machines, recorders, everything. Here is a mike for you to speak into. And, just like we rehearsed, wear this light headset. It will enable you to receive feedback from the pilot. His instructions have been to use his mike to confirm your order. Nothing more.

"Mr. President, do you have any more questions?"

"No, let's do it."

"Remember, sir, when I point to you, it's the cue that you're on. You have it all here in writing, just in case you forget the sequence.

"I'm activating the process now." He clicked the last switch in a sequence of seven switches.

The five-second wait to respond seemed like five hours to Nimer.

Like an old professional movie director, Romero swung about and gave the "Go" signal.

"This is President Fletcher A. Nimer, code Snappy, password Oreo. The sequence is as follows: ATQ dash 53197 dash RDM dash 82769. I repeat: the sequence is as follows: A as in Alpha, T as in Tango, Q as in Quebec, dash fiver three, one, niner, seven, dash R as in Romeo, D as in Delta, M as in Mother, dash eight, two, seven, sixer, niner."

There was a sudden click in Nimer's earphones when Romero gave him a "Go" sign.

"This is President Fletcher A. Nimer, code Snappy, password Oreo. . . ."

He repeated the entire sequence again, as Romero had indicated to him.

They immediately heard the response, " I am the secretary of defense, Norman Jarvis, code name Cobra, password Data. I am verifying and duplicating the specific command of the president of the United States." The recording worked.

"Okay, you're in, sir. You can talk to the pilot of the plane who will first identify himself, and then confirm your orders."

The president spoke with some hesitancy. "This is President Nimer. Please identify yourself, as well as the name of your plane."

"Mr. President, my name is Captain Robert Patterson, pilot of the Temple Bell."

The whole success of Nimer's plotting and scheming for months had been against the odds. He would not have bet against himself now. He was shocked, then, to hear it was not the Pencader G.

Yet, he was not surprised to hear himself give the order to drop the weapon on board. It was a decision driven by the goal to end wars.

"Captain Patterson, I am directing you to drop your weapon on the city of Hanoi, Vietnam, 21N-107.2E, at exactly zero eighteen hundred zero two, time at the target. Repeat the order.

"I am being directed by the president of the United States to drop the bomb housed in the Temple Bell on the city of Hanoi, Vietnam, coordinates 21N by 107.2E, at exactly zero eighteen hundred zero two time in Hanoi."

"You've got it right, Captain. Before I sign off, I have a question about your payload. What kind of bomb is it. Let me start again. I know it's nuclear, but how powerful is it?"

"Well, sir, it thermonuclear. Very powerful."

"Compared to the one dropped on Hiroshima, how powerful?"

"Mr. President, the bomb dropped on Hiroshima had fifteen kilotons of explosive power. This payload is fifteen megatons, a thousand times more powerful than the Hiroshima bomb. It has a kill zone radius of twenty-two miles."

In spite of the speed of his decision to drop the bomb, an involuntary gulp came out of Nimer's mouth.

"I'm signing off now, Captain Patterson. Good luck in your mission."

He said this almost indifferently, as his concerns for Patterson and his crew were less than about the aftermath of the bombing.

As soon as Romero sequenced the president off from communication with the Temple Bell, the plane would be on its own and out of communication with anyone until the bomb was released. This was a matter of procedure, a way to ensure that orders of this magnitude would be carried out without any interference from anyone except the president.

"Well, Lt. Romero, the package is on its way." He looked at his watch. "We've got more than an hour before we go on again."

⤸

That hour became a special kind of nightmare for what remained of the U.S. government, which by now was a curious mixture of civilians and military. Though Vice President Rickert was in nominal command, the real leader was General Arena, who, by 5:00 a.m. was beginning to realize that something was up.

He was awakened by a call from the Pentagon that the Temple Bell could not be reached on the exclusive channels. Arena ordered them to try all bands quickly and call him back.

They tried to no avail. In that faster than light way he had, Arena asked for the position of the Temple Bell when the last communication had been made at 4:28 a.m. EST.

"How many miles was it from North Korea?" he asked.

"700 miles, sir."

"And how many from Vietnam?"

"700 miles also, sir."

"How long would it take the Temple Bell from its last known position at 4:28 to reach Hanoi?"

"Give me a second, sir ... At maximum speed, one hour and twenty one minutes. However, the Temple Bell has been on a on northeast by southwest leg from Okinawa heading towards North Korea. Its instructions are to get no closer than 200 miles from the coast of Korea before resuming the southwest leg. The answer to your question depends on when the aircraft changes direction. Our present radar reading says the plane is now on a heading for Vietnam."

"What time would it be on arrival over Hanoi?" Arena asked.

"Give me a minute, sir ... 6:00 a.m. Hanoi time."

"Oh, my God!"

"Sir, is there a problem?"

Arena composed himself quickly. "No, Lieutenant. Stay right by your phone until further notice directly from me."

He was so stunned by the implications of the information that he needed a few minutes to re-open the synaptic impulses of his quick thinking. It would be about 5:55 a.m. before the Temple Bell began the sixty mile leg of its mission from Haiphong Harbor to the midpoint of Hanoi City.

He wondered how many Vietnamese along the route would see the bomber at that time of the morning, and for how many it might bring back memories from the American bombers of the past. It was consoling to know that most would be oblivious of the speck in the sky.

Arena looked at his watch. He had fifty three minutes to do something about the madness about to happen. His mind was like a fast calculating machine, the ones that spun twenty-two divided by seven out to eternity. Things both important and trivial were coming and going at rapid speeds.

The old question about how, if you had an hour left in your life, would you spend it, popped into his head. He could only remember that it was Sister Grace who had asked it in fifth grade. And then it popped out.

He could storm the Greenbrier. It would have to be a fast and incisive tactic. There was a strong chance, too, as the raid on the Pentagon had proved, that anyone inside a steel-walled shell might be killed. But, was killing the president an option?

Arena did not have any ideas that might resolve the dilemma. It was like trying to describe the sound of one hand clapping. And the hand belonged to Nimer. He picked up the phone and called the vice president, who was eating his breakfast.

"Jay, I think we have a real problem. I've just been informed that one of our super planes, the Temple Bell, has been out of contact and unreachable for about the past ten minutes. It is carrying a hydrogen bomb, and has the capacity to be over Hanoi at approximately 6:00 a.m., their time. As you know, the only time one of our situational planes goes incommunicado is when the president orders it. I have a bad feeling about this."

The silence of emptiness prevailed in these kinds of seconds that demanded being filled up with some kind of noise.

So it was that only noise filled them up.

"General, aside from waiting it out, or going in and possibly killing the president, I don't know what to do."

"What we can do is get on the phone to the Vietnamese ambassador to warn the people of Hanoi. I guess a half hour warning is better than no warning at all," Arena replied. "After that, let's place our own system on high alert and Code Red. We don't have a lot of experience with Code Red, so we'd better inform the emergency systems we have in place to kick in with the National Guard, local and state authorities, too. I'm mainly concerned with the possibility of panic in the streets. We must try whatever we can to avoid that. And then I guess we wait it out."

⤴

For some, the minute hand of the world's clock was speeded up. National Guardsmen were in a hurry to get to their posts. Local and state police were ordered into work early. Mothers who were accustomed to a certain morning pace, hearing the red alert on the morning news, began a flurry of phone calls to other mothers to see if they were going to send their children to school.

It was remarkable how fast the first early morning warning from the White House that placed the country on red alert spread quickly over the length and breadth of the country. Although no specifics were given about the raised alert, most people took it seriously, unlike when the Code Orange alert went out. Because no reasons were ever given for the Orange alerts, most Americans did not pay attention to them any more. The national joke was that the administration needed to keep the people scared and under control, and one way to do that was to raise the alert level.

This was different, simply because it was a first-time event as well as the highest level. Most people figured that something was up. And by the time they moved into full gear, President Nimer came on the air.

"Good morning. This is President Fletcher A. Nimer of the United States of America. I am here to fulfill the promise I made to the world two days ago that I would direct a small-yield atomic bomb dropped on a city and nation of my choice.

"I want to re-iterate that my intention is not to kill, but to do something so bold that men will sit up and take notice that wars and killing must cease from this day forward.

"May God bless the people of Vietnam."

Even with modern communications, a minute and thirty-three seconds was not enough time for a warning to be confirmed. That was the way Nimer wanted it.

It was just enough time, though, for Thanh and Huong, to be caught, along with three million other unaware citizens of Hanoi, in the periodic re-cooking of the great organic pie of America.

⤴

"I love you, Huong," he said.

As if tears were not enough, she responded, "And I you," before being sucked breathless, their love consumed in a magnificent ball of fire that rose as if in slow motion into the early evening air.

Within seconds, almost every living thing within a twenty-two mile radius was consumed like delicate paper torched. Hurricane winds helped the fires grow, while shock waves blasted bodies against steel. Knife-like chards of glass flew with the speed of bullets, cutting off limbs and heads.

Like a demented artist, the sudden heat emblazed shadows of some into concrete and steel fixtures. Among these were Huong and Thanh, the image of their last embrace stamped by sudden light on a tiny concrete peace monument erected at the lake many years ago.

Epilogue

Success is a word that tries to define achievement. It is flirtatious and can sometimes lead men to places not good for them. Failure, on the other hand, is a reality whose presence defines itself.

The failure of President Fletcher A. Nimer's perfectly motivated act was its success. As soon as the news of the hydrogen bomb drop on Hanoi flashed around the world, every country with nuclear capacity began to set into motion what was needed to protect itself against the madness of the man who had zealously anointed himself to fulfill the mission of his God to bring peace to the world.

If the pre-emptive war on Iraq had marked the beginning of corrosion in the relationship of many nations with the United States, the incursion into Iran spread the rot further. Yet Nimer's lottery was unquestioningly the one that destroyed it.

He had led a nation into war going it mostly alone, and now he had betrayed the people of that nation by going it alone against the world. Whatever trust he might once have had, even among friends, was now gone.

Although Nimer wanted peace in the world, he had forgotten that making peace was sometimes defined by what one did not do.

As no one was any longer certain of being immune to a U.S. attack, a mad rush to ready nuclear weapons took place immediately around the globe. Activity was first spotted early Wednesday morning in Siberia. The Russian missile launch pads were easy for American spy planes to detect against the winter snow and ice of the barren land.

The quick readiness of the Russians was not surprising. Even though they had reduced their atomic weapons in mutual agreements with the United States, their attack program had nuclear missiles aimed at America. They had talked the talk of peace, yet continued to walk the walk towards mutual destruction.

It seemed like only yesterday to middle aged Muscovites that they went to bed praying to get through a night of sleep made restless against the possibility of an American atomic attack. There had not been enough distance, though, between the years of those nights and the sudden bombing of Hanoi.

With a national memory that still bore the scars inflicted by the Japanese during the 1930's and 40's, and the massive losses on the Korean Peninsula during the 50's, the Chinese had grappled with American relations for half a century, especially regarding the question of Taiwan. The separating miles that had once kept the equation of war and peace balanced no longer prevailed. Until the previous day, they had been reluctant to pull the triggers that could launch their intercontinental atomic missiles on the United States. This day, though, things were different. Missiles in Mongolia were being armed and readied.

If the possibility of North Korea shooting nukes onto the west coast of America was only recently a manipulated prospect, it was now real. Perhaps Nimer was trying to prevent future wars, as he had said in his radio broadcasts, yet they considered him a madman who probably would come after them next. They did not have many atomic weapons and only a few missiles that could reach the United States, yet they felt they had no choice. The missile sites at Yongbyon were put on full and active alert, waiting for orders from Lee Joo-Chan.

Even Israel finally revealed its arsenal. After having spent years denying its nuclear strike capacity, it, too, began to arm its long-range missiles set near the Great Crater in the Negev Desert.

There was no fast or easy answer about why the Israelis were pointing their newly unveiled missiles at the U.S. Trying to hold the center together for years against the terrorist activities of the Palestinians had been difficult enough. Their own unwillingness to negotiate a peaceful settlement was leading them down a path that many Israelis felt was dishonorable. The deep paranoia that had been settling upon them for the past few years was beginning to darken so that even the United States, once it bombed Hanoi, fell under its shadow.

France, too, immediately armed its nuclear missiles, and aimed them at America. Whether or not they planned to use them was questionable. Their cunning, dismissive, and jealous attitude towards the U.S. in recent years was hard to assess. They seemed to enjoy being baffling to American diplomats, ready to take over the mantle of the old Soviets whom Winston Churchill painted as an enigma wrapped in a mystery. As with any mystery, it was hard to tell what their intentions were the morning after the Temple

Bell dropped the bomb. Who knew, then, when they would announce to the world that their nuclear sights were set on America?

For years, the Pakistanis and Indians rattled atomic-tipped sabers at each other in a kind of ritual ceremony of fear. Almost everyone knew that the ritual was more linguistic than real, a show of strength fearfully articulated.

Though Pakistan was more intertwined with U.S. politics in recent years because of its proximity as a safe haven for al Qaeda coming across the mountains from Afghanistan, both it and India trained their considerable nuclear weapons towards the west. If they could not reach America, they could certainly reach its allies, notably the British.

Missile launch pads around the world were being readied by early afternoon, American time, on Tuesday, and they were aimed at key cities and targets around the United States.

In trying to create a lasting peace, Fletcher A. Nimer had brought about a new era. The great organic pie of America was about to be re-cooked.

The End

Photo by Linda Napier

About the Author

Gerard Brooker has had over 300 articles and poems published, as well as two books of poetry. Among other awards for his efforts to encourage peace, he has received the Peace and International Understanding Award from the National Education Association, and the Jefferson Award from the American Institute for Public Service. He has received two honorary degrees, and holds a doctorate from St. John's University. Dr. Brooker lives with his wife in Bethel, Connecticut.

TATE PUBLISHING & *Enterprises*

Tate Publishing is committed to excellence in the publishing industry. Our staff of highly trained professionals, including editors, graphic designers, and marketing personnel, work together to produce the very finest books available. The company reflects the philosophy established by the founders, based on Psalms 68:11,

"THE LORD GAVE THE WORD AND GREAT WAS THE COMPANY OF THOSE WHO PUBLISHED IT."

If you would like further information, please call
1.888.361.9473
or visit our website
www.tatepublishing.com

TATE PUBLISHING & *Enterprises*, LLC
127 E. Trade Center Terrace
Mustang, Oklahoma 73064 USA